Penguin Bo...
A Coffin fo...

Gwendoline Butler was born in London: 'I come
from a family of *real* Londoners of which I am proud.
My family have lived in London south of the Thames
and many of them have been Freemen of the River
for the last two hundred years, perhaps longer.'
She read Modern History at Lady Margaret Hall,
Oxford, and then taught Modern History at two of the
women's colleges in Oxford, during the first eight
years of her married life. Moving to Scotland with her
husband, who was appointed Vice-President of
St Andrews University, she concentrated on writing
but now lives in the south, where her husband is
Principal of the Royal Holloway College at the
University of London.

Well-known for her crime novels, and particularly
for the creation of Inspector Coffin, she has published
nearly thirty books, several of which have been
serialized, one made into a play for the B.B.C. and
another bought by a French film company. Her novels
include *Receipt for Murder*, *Coffin in Oxford*,
A Coffin From the Past and *A Coffin for the Canary*,
published simultaneously in Penguins with this volume.

Gwendoline Butler has a daughter and her interests
include travel, and reading and writing books.

Gwendoline Butler

A Coffin for Pandora

Penguin Books

Penguin Books Ltd, Harmondsworth,
Middlesex, England
Penguin Books, 625 Madison Avenue,
New York, New York 10022, U.S.A.
Penguin Books Australia Ltd, Ringwood,
Victoria, Australia
Penguin Books Canada Ltd, 2801 John Street,
Markham, Ontario, Canada L3R 1B4
Penguin Books (N.Z.) Ltd, 182–190 Wairau Road
Auckland 10, New Zealand

First published by Macmillan 1973
Published in Penguin Books 1978
Copyright © Gwendoline Butler, 1973
All rights reserved

Made and printed in Great Britain by
C. Nicholls & Company Ltd
Set in Monotype Times

Those members of the 'surplus population' who – goaded by their misery – summon up courage enough to revolt openly against society become thieves and murderers.

> F. Engels, *The Condition of the Working Class in 1844*

If we compare the prostitute at thirty-five with her sister, who perhaps is the mother of a family, or has been the toiling slave for years, we shall seldom find that the constitutional ravages often thought to be a necessary consequence of prostitution exceed those attributable to the cares of a family and the struggles of virtuous labour.

> William Acton, *Prostitution considered in its Moral, Social and Sanitary Aspect, 1857*

Poor teaching, poor school books, much ignorance of the physical care of girls, these things were common in my school time.

> Mrs Humphrey Ward, *A Writer's Recollections, 1856–1904*

Chapter One

Oxford, like all great cities, is ruined once in every generation. My worldly-wise Uncle Lambton tells me that, delightful as London appears to me now, it is nothing to what it was in the seventies. He also says that there has never been a city lovelier than Venice when the Austrians had it and before the Risorgimento succeeded. And my darling friend Jessie tells me that her grandmother informs her that unless she had known New York before it grew beyond the Battery then she can never know what Old New York was like.

Be that as it may, my father says that the coming of women has ruined Oxford. Before we came, he says, what a pleasant bachelor world it was, with women kept safely beyond Folly Bridge. He's joking, of course, because in the first place he likes women's company, and there are always plenty of wives and daughters about, but what he means is that none were students of the University. We might attend the lectures on Art by Professor Ruskin (and indeed I did), but until the last year or two we were not found at the lectures on Greek, Latin or Mathematics held in the Colleges for the benefit of the young men undergraduates. We are a little tentative even now. Especially me. I had great ambitions. I was going to embark my ship on the sea of learning. I remember how happy I was.

I had no notion then that the approaching season would bring its own terrors, that I would learn how criminals live, and violence, kidnapping, murder would be all about me. Nor could I guess that it would deliver me a man's head on a charger like Salome. I left my victim alive and breathing which is perhaps the worse of me.

At first, when it was all newly over and I had survived, I felt like the victim of some natural disaster, an earthquake, say, or a shipwreck and that it had all happened by chance, the fall of the coin on the table. It is only now, looking back, that I see how much I, Mary Lamont, contributed, and that the climax sprang as much out of my own character as anything else. There was my spirit of pride and my impatience, together with a quick curiosity which made me always eager to know what was written on the next page. The gods keep a special fate for people like me. In short, I helped bring it on. To be an innovator you need a very sound social position. And no one could say I had that. The daughter of an artist, even though he did once win the Prix de Rome and is widely travelled, is not likely to move in the first circles in any society. Oxford society is more welcoming than some, and a lot of the ladies who go to learn draughtsmanship from my father at Professor Ruskin's School of Drawing have been kind to me and invited me to their At Homes and Soirées. Perhaps my father's gentle manners and sad good looks have something to do with the invitations. He does indeed look decorative in the drawing-room, and knows how to behave there, too.

He won the Prix de Rome when he was twenty-two, my age now. I was born in Florence and named Mary after my mother. My father brought me back to England as a baby, with a nurse called Elizabeth, who went back to Italy before I remembered her. My mother, he told me, died when I was very young. We settled in a little street in the shadow of Keble College, and my father never went abroad again until he won another award, the Sir Joshua Reynolds Prize for Portraiture. He won it two years ago, in the year Professor Ruskin suffered his first break-down.

I remember he came in his flowered brocade dressing-gown to where I was sitting in the drawing-room over my books. 'I'm off, Pussy,' he said, picking delicately at the cuff where the brocade was frayed. 'As soon as I can get away. To Paris.'

'Paris?'

'Yes.' He smiled gently. 'That's where one must go now, my love, for good painters. I wish you'd mend this gown for me, Pussy, my love.'

'I don't sew, father,' I said calmly. 'I housekeep for you, I cook

8

for you when I must, I even earn a little money, but sew, no. Ask Mrs Ely.'

'Mrs Ely, ah yes. She's coming with me to Paris. Shall you mind, Mary?' He came over and put his arm round me.

I dare say he was the only father in Oxford who would have asked me that, as I was the only daughter who would have replied, 'And shall you marry her, papa?'

I suppose he caught the sardonic note in my voice, because he got up and stood by the fire, stroking the silky damascene he was wearing.

'Well, not this time, Mary,' he said. 'And I'm not sure if she'd have me. She'll travel with her own maid and courier, you know.'

'Oh, yes.' I nodded. Mrs Ely would preserve all the conventions, except one, of course. I knew very well that my father's room and hers on the Rue de Rivoli would be conveniently close. But even this, in the circles in which she moved, was a convention in itself.

'She was doubtful at first whether she should come. They've had some notable jewel robberies in France lately. The Princess of Orléans lost a lot, and her maid was asphyxiated by the thieves. And Mrs Ely wondered if she ought to risk her parure of emeralds. But she's come to a decision: she'll bring her second-best jewels, and leave the best ones behind with Mr Train, to be cleaned and re-set.'

Mrs Ely had a collection of flashy jewellery, with which she was greatly preoccupied. I believe it was very valuable and represented a great part of her late husband's wealth. He had been a merchant banker. She must have been very fond of my father, to be willing to be parted from it.

'Shall you meet many painters in Mrs Ely's circle?' I said.

'I shall have a studio of my own, in the Rue St André des Arts,' he said briskly. 'Shan't spend all my time with Louise.'

I knew then, without him saying a word, that Mrs Ely would have rivals whom she might not know of in Paris, drawn from that other Paris into which my father would surely move just as he did in London and probably had done in Florence. My father's tastes had been catholic all his life and he liked the company of many types of people. He was unusual in that he let me know of them.

Perhaps something of my thoughts showed on my face, because he laughed, and patted me on the shoulder. 'What sharp eyes and ears you've got, Mary.'

I turned back to my books; I was studying Thucydides. 'And what about me? Shall I go on living here? In this house?'

The house was tiny, really just one comfortable room on each floor. It exactly fitted my father and me, we could live here with hardly any servants, only one daily maid. I *can* and do cook, but it doesn't do to rely on my efforts.

'You *could*, Mary,' said my father, thoughtfully, scratching his cheek. 'It would run away with the money a bit, though, keeping on the house. What about going up to Sarsen Place, eh? You have your room there. No? No, I dare say it wouldn't do to live there entirely.'

I looked out of the window into the dusk and, instead of the red brick gothic of Keble College, I was seeing a handsome stone-built house set in quiet shrubbery. Sarsen Place was only a comfortable gentleman's residence but it had something pleasing about it. You knew at once that life inside it was elegantly conducted. No frayed old dressing-gown cuffs or worn carpets there. My foot found the hole in the worn old Turkey red at my feet, and scuffed it.

My father had effected my introduction to Sarsen Place when I first began to feel my own powers. I had had a series of small teaching and coaching posts, but it was about the time I went to Sarsen Place as daily governess to the girl Alice Demarest that I realized that I must and would take myself seriously. If a woman doesn't value herself, no one else is going to do it for her. That's a lesson I learnt without words from my father. We are a society fundamentally hostile to women and children. We have fully earned our high infant death rate. There are various forms of infanticide, all more or less legal. My education, fortunately, had been good. I went to Miss Playfair's school in the Banbury Road and had excellent teachers. Miss Playfair herself has stood my greatest friend. Now there *is* an intellect. 'Mary,' she said, 'it has always been an ambition of mine that one of my pupils should be the first woman to read for an Oxford degree. It can hardly be expected,' and she sighed, 'that she should actually be allowed to take one and graduate, but that to read for a degree and take the final examination and perhaps be placed in the class list *will* come about, I am convinced. Events are moving that way. Too late for me, I'm afraid, but I should like to see Mary Lamont's name in the class list.' And she told me that a group of her friends were forming a little nucleus of Women Students and taking a house in Norham Gardens for them to live in. 'Mary Lamont,' she said, 'I should like to see you join them.'

I had earned a good salary at Sarsen Place and now had a little nest egg of savings. But, more than this, I had found sympathy and friends. Mrs Demarest had welcomed me at first as my father's daughter. She had been one of his earliest patrons, and his portrait of her hung on the wall of the drawing-room at Sarsen Place. It was a marvellous painting, but I have never been quite sure if she realized how good a picture it was, because as well as her patrician elegance and love of fine clothes it showed her pride and quick temper too. But it also showed her loving heart. And because she had a loving heart she worried over her withdrawn little grand-daughter Alice. Many times I saw her studying the small face with an anxious and puzzled expression. 'She is clever, Miss Lamont?' she asked.

'Very,' I replied briefly, for I had never known a clearer or more incisive little head.

'But not happy, Miss Lamont?'

'Not happy.'

Alice Demarest was a pretty, shy little creature, but for a girl of twelve she was too quiet and too detached. She was polite to me and even friendly in her aloof way, but she never let down her guard. I had been there two years and I had never even heard her giggle. All little girls giggle, it's a fact of nature. Heaven knows, I was a serious enough child, but I giggled. Alice rarely even laughed. But she went through her lessons with ease.

'She takes after her father,' said Mrs Demarest. 'My elder son is a very clever man.'

And also an unhappy one? I asked myself. I had not seen Mr Mark Demarest then. He was abroad, in the West Indies and then

Italy. He seemed rarely to come home. His house in Oxford was run entirely for his mother and his daughter. The old family home was in Dorset, but although the farms and the estate still existed, the manor house itself had been shut up for years. I had seen a drawing of the house, which was stone-built and very plain. 'That part of the country is behind the times,' said Mrs Demarest, 'and the society very small.' I knew from her conversation that she had been brought up in the great world, and that as a girl she had lived in St Petersburg and Berlin. 'And Vienna, my dear, where my father was "en poste". I was always used to living in that sort of atmosphere until I married. And then I married a country gentleman who liked to live at home.' She smiled, I thought the marriage must have been a happy one. Nevertheless, as soon as she was a widow, she had removed herself to Sarsen Place, which was a sort of dower-house of the estate. No one ever mentioned young Mrs Mark Demarest, what her name was or how she had died. Alice, her child, was very pretty and at first I expected Mrs Demarest to say of her 'She takes after her mother in looks', just as she had said of Alice's father and her cleverness; but she never did.

At first I lived at home, travelling up each day to Sarsen Place on foot or in the Demarest carriage, but often staying the night if the weather was bad, so that by degrees a small rose and white room near my charge's was made over to me, and became known as Mary's room. I still did not absolutely live there, but I found myself more and more at home at Sarsen Place.

And my father, of course, was never lonely without me. Even now, he was looking at me hopefully, glad I was declaring my independence and ready to help me achieve it – without too much cost to himself. But on this my father and I were perfectly agreed: if a woman is to be independent, then she must pay for it herself. That was lesson number two I had learnt from my father. In any case, he had all he could do to pay his own bills, poor papa. Perhaps I *would* mend his dressing-gown before he left for Paris, even though I was quite sure that before he returned the Rue St Honoré would have produced an even more elegant one for his delight.

'No, not Sarsen Place, father,' I said calmly. 'I have plans of my own. Oh, I shall continue at Sarsen Place if Mrs Demarest wishes, but I intend to become a woman student.'

'You've always been that, my love,' said father, playing with a pencil. 'Hard at it, as usual, I see.'

'I am going to join the group of ladies at Norham Gardens and follow a university course.'

'And afterwards, what will you do then?'

'I'm not sure,' I said calmly. 'Something to distinguish myself, I hope.'

'You won't go setting your cap at Mr Demarest?' he said. 'I've heard he's coming home.'

'Father!' He didn't usually make jokes of this sort; he had too much natural good taste.

'Behind that composed manner I know what a little gambler you are,' he said, half smiling. 'Still have that lucky dice, do you?'

I wouldn't answer. He had his secrets and I had mine. But my hand went to my pocket where the worn old ivory dice rested. I had found it in a gutter when I was three and treasured it ever since. When you find such an object, it is as well to take it seriously.

'You've got a good face you know, Mary,' said my father. 'And considering what little money you have, you're a well turned out girl. Don't you think you'll marry?'

'No, father. I have quite decided against marriage.'

Being my father, he didn't argue or look surprised, but merely drummed with his fingers on the table. Finally he said, 'You may be wise. It's rather hard on a man to have a distinguished wife.'

'I don't think most men would notice,' I said, preparing to return to my books.

'A little hard on us men, a little hard,' said my father. 'And when will this new arrangement of yours begin, Mary?'

'In October,' I said. 'When the university year starts.'

'And today is December 17. You have nearly a year to wait.'

'That suits me very well.'

'I'd like to be off in the early spring,' said my father. 'Sooner, if possible, but I have one or two commissions here to clear up before I go. They say Ruskin's mad, you know. Quite out of his mind.'

'I'll manage, father,' I said. 'Mrs Demarest is so kind.'

'She doesn't know about Mrs Ely, of course?' said my father hastily.

'Of course not,' I agreed. I had observed how there were two worlds, and the one really did not know how the other lived. At Sarsen Place my father was known as an artist, but they had no idea that he did not fall easily into the mould they had cast for him. Mrs Demarest would never meet Mrs Ely (although Mrs Ely had some surprisingly grand friends), but if she did it would never occur to her that between Mrs Ely and my father there could be any relationship. I knew better.

And I returned to my books. I was reading Thucydides. I am not a quick Greek reader: it comes slowly with me. But as I worked it seemed to me that two words, αἰ γυναικες, the women, constantly intruded and stood out on the paper. I was quite calm, quite happy, but so it was.

Could the words appear so often? Always I thought they could never appear in my *next* piece of translation, but surprisingly often they were; my eye would fall on them always just ahead. The women.

I had been several times to the plain brick villa which housed the first few students. Mr Ruskin was a supporter, and before he went mad had chosen several of the William Morris wallpapers which decorated the rooms. Dark and substantial as they were, I thought they would outlast many generations of pupils and still be there in fifty years' time. The students lived in rooms of varying size, furnished in a respectable but ordinary style. Living as I did between my father's home and the Demarests, I was used to some style and elegance. At home we were not rich, but everything we had was chosen for its visual quality. In the students' hall, except for the William Morris wallpaper, the furnishings were chosen for their durability and not their looks. But I liked the inhabitants and thought I would enjoy being one of this group of steady earnest girls. I could see I would have to hold myself in a little when I was with them. I didn't truly quite belong to their world of rectories and music societies and cycling clubs.

There was many a cold Oxford day to live through before I had a chance to start on my new ambitious life (which was, in truth, something I had been quietly determined on a long time), but I was prepared to be patient.

In the event I was a great deal up at Sarsen Place because it was about then that Alice started having her terrors.

The day they began (and I say 'they' because indeed the whole process seemed quite outside the child's control) her usual reasonable, calm little manner quite deserted her.

We were out walking in the Parks. I had been calling on my dear friend Mary Ward in her new house in Bradmore Road. One minute Alice was happy, talking, in quite a lively fashion for her, about the new hat she was making for her doll. I remember I was making a joke about her busy fingers when I felt her gripping my hand tightly.

'Alice,' I said in surprise. I stopped.

'No, don't stop, don't stop,' she said, in a choking little voice. 'Let's walk on.'

'Allie, what is it?' I looked round, but the Parks were deserted. It was a January afternoon, pale and cold.

'Walk on, walk on,' she said, her voice containing an uncanny imitation of her grandmother at her most commanding. Because she was trembling, I walked on.

By the time we were at home, having walked across Magdalen Bridge and up Headington Hill in silence, she had calmed herself. When we were in our sitting-room and I had turned to her and demanded, 'Well, Allie, what was all that?' she was enough herself to look at me blandly and say, 'What, Miss Lamont?'

'You know what I mean: in the Parks when you held my hand so tight.'

'Did I hold your hand tight? I am sorry, Miss Lamont.' She was busy getting out her books and setting them on the table before her. 'Shall we be reading *Lettres de mon moulin* this afternoon?'

'Don't turn me aside, Allie, something upset you. I want to know what it was.'

She clasped her hands in her lap. 'I had a pain, Miss Lamont. I was just being a silly girl.'

'Oh Allie, Allie!'

But I knew I should get no further, no one could be more reticent than Alice when she chose.

But that night she had the first of her nightmares. I heard her calling and screaming in the night.

I was sitting in my room, tidying my hair before the mirror. I had just eaten one of Mrs Ceffery's, the cook's, good dinners and was preparing to settle down to a good night's work on my Greek texts when I heard the first cry.

The noise came ripping out, one high-pitched scream after the other. I rushed down the corridor to Alice's room. She was sitting up in bed, staring in front of her. The screams had stopped and as I burst in she put her hands up to her face in an incredibly mature and adult gesture.

'Allie, oh, my dear,' I said, putting my arms round her. 'Whatever was it?'

'I think I was asleep,' she said, 'And I dreamed ...'

'What *did* you dream to make you scream like that?' I smoothed the hair away from her face.

'I dreamt ... I don't know what I dreamt. One always forgets what one has dreamed.'

I didn't probe. I hesitated to distress her further. But I had no doubt that she knew what she had dreamt and that she had remembered it. I got her a hot drink and sat by her while she went back to sleep. She didn't scream again, but once or twice she made a little soft moaning sound.

I left the lamp burning in her bedroom and went back to my own room. My books were spread out, the fire burning sweetly, it looked the picture of peace and tranquillity. It was my last day of real peace in Sarsen Place, however.

In the morning I went along to Alice's room. The lamp was off and the curtains drawn back. Alice was lying back against her pillows and laughing. At the fireplace a small figure in cap and print apron was kneeling by the newly lit fire. She too had been laughing, although she straightened her features hastily when she saw me.

'Good morning, Ellen,' I said. 'You're early this morning.'

'Oh yes, Miss Lamont, the mistress is coming back. We have to be beforehand.' She had a sweet rustic burr to her voice which I liked. I always imagined it must have been the way Shakespeare spoke.

'So she is. Allie and I are making ready too.' Mrs Demarest had been in London for two weeks, seeing her dentist, she said; but I suspected she was really seeing her dressmakers, and that very soon boxes of elegant new clothes would begin to arrive. She bought some things locally, a few hats and dresses, but ordered a great deal from the best London houses. Alice had been doing a piece of work to show her on her return. She hated to sew, but Ellen had taught her a very pretty new stitch and she had made a neat job of a little purse. I sympathized with her over her distaste for sewing, which I detested myself, but Mrs Demarest was old-fashioned enough to think a girl ought to always have a piece of fine needlework in the making. I felt sure Alice would emancipate herself from this within a few years.

'I'm glad you were laughing, Allie,' I said. 'Do you feel better now?'

'Better?' She raised her eyebrows in delicate inquiry.

'You had a nightmare.'

'Yes, it was silly of me. But I'm better now.' Nevertheless, she did not look at me directly, and I was uneasy. Alice wasn't a preternaturally truthful child, she had her little diplomacies and evasions as we all do. She never told lies, but she had a way of politely saying nothing if she thought it necessary. I thought she was doing it now.

But I didn't want to probe. I believed Alice had a right to her secrets. I think we assume too readily that the minds of children should be open to our questioning.

But I did put a discreet question to Ellen, the little schoolroom maid, because I knew that she and Alice had a quiet friendship.

'Oh yes, I'm sure I'd know if Miss Alice was out of sorts or had any worry. She couldn't keep it from me. I know her so well, you see. I'm to be her own maid when she's older, you know.

We've settled it between us. Oh no, she's been as bright as a bee all these months.'

'Yes, that's what I thought,' I said. 'She's been happier lately.'

'And, of course, she's always easier when her grandma's away,' said Ellen incautiously. 'The mistress does watch her so.' She stopped, obviously wishing she hadn't said so much.

But I didn't question her further. I am not above asking questions of the servants if I want. My father has certainly emancipated me from the conventional ideas of what a lady can or cannot do. If I want information, I know how to ask for it. But I had a strong feeling I must not harry Ellen. Apart from anything else, her mouth had an obstinate look to it. If I knew how to ask, she knew how to say no.

We spent a quiet morning. I thought my pupil a little less quick than of wont in her lessons, but otherwise she seemed as usual. At midday we heard a bustle outside and went to the window.

Outside was the Sarsen Place carriage with its beautifully matched hackneys. They were the laziest and most pampered horses I knew, as was the old coachman, Belcher. Like coachman, like horse, I always used to think. He drank too much and was a bad-tempered old thing. I never asked a favour of him if I could help it. I preferred to walk home down Headington Hill, even at night, rather than have him drive me.

Mrs Demarest was just getting out of the carriage. I could see the top of her close-fitting little hat trimmed with violets, and admire the curve of the dark soft fur round her neck.

'That's a new hat,' said Alice with satisfaction; she loved clothes. So did I (my father's daughter, when all was said and done), although I could see that hats and robes like Mrs Demarest's would never fall to my lot. Mrs Demarest looked up just then and saw us. She smiled and waved her hand. Then she pointed to a box which was just being handed out.

'She's brought me a present,' said Alice.

But it wasn't a present. At least it was, but not of the nature Alice had expected.

'Look,' said Mrs Demarest triumphantly from the sofa where she was seated in the drawing-room when we went to greet her.

On a round table before her was the box she had pointed to. Now I was closer I could see it to be a plain wooden box with the words Alice Demarest roughly chalked on it.

'Open it, dearest.' She seemed as interested as her granddaughter.

'Did you buy it for me?'

'No. See, it has a Paris postmark on the side. I think your father has sent it to you.'

'And it came to you in London?' Alice was a child who liked to get the facts straight. She was slowly working away at the knots in the string.

'He knew I should be at my hotel,' said Mrs Demarest. She was lying back now, watching her grand-daughter with amusement. 'What a careful child you are. Why not cut the string?'

'I like string,' said Alice. 'I like to keep it.' And to bear this out she was already smoothing out the string and folding it into a neat hank.

'I think you're more interested in the string than the present.'

'No, no, I'd like to see what my father has sent me.' She was opening the box as she spoke. I don't think her expectations were high; her father appeared to have forgotten his daughter's age and what her tastes were. Once he had sent her a jumping jack suitable for a child of six. On the other hand he had once sent a set of carved ivory balls from Peking that she would appreciate more when she was twenty.

She opened the box and put her hand in and I saw her eyes widen. 'It feels like fur,' she said. 'I believe it's an animal.'

She drew it out, a fluffy black and white toy cat. But instead of pleasure and amusement I could see she was swallowing. 'It's Fluffy,' she said, tears gathering. 'It's my Fluffy.' She pushed it away. 'It's too like my own Fluffy.'

Lunch was a strained meal at which little was eaten by Alice. After it was over and Alice was tidying herself for a walk, I said to Ellen, 'And who was Fluffy?'

'Fluffy was the nursery cat, Miss Lamont,' said Ellen, looking a little chastened herself. 'Alice was ever so fond of him. I was myself. He was a dear old thing. And a splendid mouser.'

'There aren't any mice here.'

'No, miss. He used to go out at night after them. I think that's what happened to him.'

'What happened to him?'

'He got lost. Went off and never came back. Cats will, won't they, miss?' She was looking at me sharply, her little face keen and intent.

'I never saw Fluffy,' I said.

'It was just before you came, Miss Lamont. About the time when Nurse left. Fluffy and Nurse Mackenzie went in the same week.'

'So Alice lost them both at once? I suppose that was why she was so upset. She must have been very attached to them both.'

'She certainly loved old Fluffy,' said Ellen.

I made up my mind that Alice should particularly enjoy her walk that day, and decided to let her choose it. But she was quite calm when she appeared and was wearing a new little muff that had just come from London; and when I asked her where she would like to go for her walk, she took my hand and said cheerfully: 'Anywhere you like, Miss Lamont, only not the Parks.'

It was not one of my usual functions to take Alice for a walk. I was that very special thing, a highly privileged and well paid governess. Not for me the hack side of teaching, such as taking a little girl for a walk. Usually Alice went with an elderly maid, who seemed to exist just for that purpose; but these last few weeks she had been ill, and I had given up my free time for Alice's exercise. In fact, we both secretly enjoyed our expeditions. But it occurred to me that I didn't really know where the pair usually went.

'Don't you like the Parks, Alice?' I said. 'Where do you usually go?'

'Oh, Christ Church meadow. By the river. Sometimes we just go to the Natural History Museum. I like that. Did you know they had some locusts there, eating away?'

I shook my head, amused. Alice had a great turn for science. I don't think she was really like her grandmother, in spite of her

20

love of clothes, but she was probably very like her father. Her father collected pictures and *objets d'art*: Alice collected facts. She was an observant little girl.

We went to see the pictures in the Ashmolean Gallery.

'Did you ever have a lover, Miss Lamont?' she said conversationally, as we stared at the picture of the Forest Fire.

We were standing in the room filled with early Italian paintings, which I love best in certain moods when I need reassurance and joy. This time, as I was gazing at them, I made up my mind I would go to Italy soon. Perhaps to Florence. The thought just flashed into my mind. Looking back, it is so strange that it should have done.

'Good gracious, no,' I said to Alice. It wasn't strictly true. Certainly I had never been in love, but my hand had once been asked for. By a middle-aged artist, a friend of my father's, who took my hand one day, gave it a hearty shake, and said, 'Mary, I have watched you closely, you will make an excellent wife. Will you marry me?'

I knew what he meant. The upbringing my father had given me had predisposed me to be a discreet and undemanding wife for a man of his temperament, which was in fact of an Athenian sort; he had the sort of feeling for young men that Socrates had. But I have secret thoughts and longings and he certainly did not fulfil them. Yet another man, a friend of my father's also, once asked me mildly if I wouldn't like a trip to Bruges with him to study the Flemish paintings there; and to him I must admit I did feel more kindly disposed. At least he had offered me pleasure, and I had an idea I wanted pleasure in any relationship of this sort I entered into; but it wouldn't do. The way society is arranged at the moment it is quite impossible for me to abandon its standards of morality. If I were a woman of independent fortune, now ... But I was not. These were very secret thoughts.

'I'm glad of that,' said Alice pensively. 'You didn't mind my asking?'

'No.' The funny little thing. I thought, and wondered what she had been reading. I knew she had the free run of her father's library. And there is the kitchen, too, I thought. I knew Alice frequented it more than her grandmother, Mrs Demarest, ever guessed; but I knew well enough that the servants had a secret life of their own which she never suspected. They turned one bland face to her and kept another to look at each other below stairs. 'Tell me what you think of this picture,' I said, to change the subject.

Alice smiled. 'It's a forest fire and the animals are running away. My father says it's primitive.'

'A primitive,' I corrected. 'That only means a painting in an early style, before the laws of perspective were thoroughly worked out. Over here is a painting where perspective has been used cleverly.' I led her to the picture by Uccello which we call the Hunt at Night and in which lines of horsemen tilt off at staggering angles. 'Some might say over-used,' I said thoughtfully.

'I like it, though,' said Alice. 'It's not about anything, is it? It doesn't say be good or be bad or be sad or be cheerful, it just *is*. I hate pictures that give you orders.'

I looked at her and was troubled. She was such a strange, sensitive, clever little creature.

She was so much alone, and I dare say she missed her old nurse, although she never mentioned her.

'Have you seen Nurse Mackenzie since she went?' I asked idly.

Then she said quietly, 'She hasn't gone.'

I stared.

'She's still here. Some of the time.'

'Are you sure, Alice?' I was startled into asking. I was quite sure Mrs Ceffery told me the nurse had left the district. Certainly I had never seen her.

'She comes back occasionally. I suppose she has friends,' said Alice.

'I expect I'll meet her then,' I said cheerfully.

'Yes,' said Alice in a polite voice.

'Let's go out into St Giles and buy chestnuts from the boy at the corner,' I said.

'I'm not supposed to.'

'I know.' I smiled. 'That's why.'

We went out into the windy street and bought a little poke

of hot nuts from the boy who kept the brazier. He was a short lad with the brightest blue eyes I had ever seen. I suppose he was about fifteen and had already built up a thriving business here in the winter. In the summer he appeared running errands for Madame Blanche, who made hats in an elegant house along St Giles, just where it turned into the newly built houses of the Woodstock Road.

We took the poke of chestnuts and walked sedately to the gardens of Worcester College, where, in a small arbour hidden from all viewers, we solemnly ate the nuts, dividing them fairly between us. They were charred and delicious. It was a ritual we knew well.

'Potatoes are good done this way, too,' said Alice.

'I know,' I said.

'I only said "I'm not supposed to eat them" because I love you to say it doesn't matter.'

'I know that, too.'

'The boy with the barrow always gives us a special smile, doesn't he?'

'Yes.' With surprise, I realized that he did. 'He likes us.'

'Yes,' said Alice, with satisfaction.

She had eaten her chestnuts so neatly and delicately that not a crumb lingered on her lap or round her lips. Without another word we rose and made our way through the college gates into Beaumont Street. The Demarest carriage, which had been sent to meet us, was waiting across the road. I didn't like Alice to take the long walk home, and we were usually met in this way. Old Belcher hated this afternoon chore, which did him out of his sleep by the fire, and there was a quiet war between us. He was a sour old thing, but he was fond of Alice. As he saw her, a wintry smile crept across his lips.

'Kept the horses waiting, you did,' he said.

'But not for long.' My voice was bright and cheerful. I knew those horses, cherished and lazy.

'I had to walk them up and down,' he said accusingly.

We got in and arranged ourselves on the comfortable grey plush seats. A large pink hat box tied with black ribbon rested on one seat.

'Don't sit on the 'at,' said Belcher from above, as I closed the door. 'And don't go playing no tricks with trying it on, Miss Alice.'

'Oh, I *wouldn't*,' said Alice.

'I have known such things,' said Belcher, giving his reins a pull. 'Get up, there.'

It was true that we had once taken the lid off a hat box from Madame Blanche's and gazed at a hat of white and mauve violets, and that Alice had for a moment set it on her delicately poised little head to make me realize what she might be in ten years' time, but this had been a hat already worn by Mrs Demarest, and being returned after a minor adjustment. We wouldn't do it with anything new.

I looked at Alice, waiting for her to laugh, but her frozen look was back. She had buttoned herself up in her reserve and was gone from me again.

I sat in thought as the horses laboured up Headington Hill. Belcher was a good driver. When he drank, it didn't show. In spite of his temper, I regarded him as one of the virtuous servants, because about his sexual misdemeanours, if he had any, I knew nothing. About some of the other servants I knew, for various reasons, only too much.

I looked again at Alice, and then, in one of those moments of illumination that come sometimes, I realized that she was frozen with fear.

Will Train was winding the big bracket clock in the hall when we arrived. He gave the bronze and ormolu a last polish, closed the case, and then made us a small bow. He did everything sedately and discreetly but I supposed he had more fire in him than might have been guessed. The clock was a handsome piece by Thomas Tompion, the great clock-maker of the last century, and I could see from the way Will handled it that he loved it. His father, a mean old man, so they said, was the owner of the principal jeweller's and silversmith's in Oxford. My father admired Will's work, and was teaching him drawing. I had taught him a little French. He said he needed it at Starlingford House where he looked after an early sixteenth-century clock in the old stables which must never be neglected. (Starlingford House, although now on a long lease to other tenants, belonged to the estates of the Bishop of Dorchester and had once housed an abbey of nuns.) He was a fine craftsman and if he had followed my father's advice would have taken his gifts to London, where they might have been better appreciated. But he stayed, designing jewellery he would never make if he remained in Oxford. It was strange to think of neat precise William Train and inside him these dreams of rubies set in clusters of diamonds, emeralds twined with pearls, and sapphires hiding themselves in swags of ornament on tasselled girdles. His designs were rich and flowing, very much in the modern style, with none of the delicacy of old-fashioned work. Sensuous was the word that crossed the mind, barbaric even. A woman wearing one of Will's great pieces would have no doubt what her main purpose in life was.

I returned Will's bow with one as polite as his own. We didn't speak. Alice took no notice of him.

Mrs Demarest stood in the drawing-room door and called to Alice. 'Splendid news, my dear. A telegram from your father to say he is returning home. He will be here by the end of the month.'

As far as I knew, Mark Demarest never wrote letters but communicated with his family entirely by cable or telegram. Once his man of business in London came down on a special errand, and there were long talks in the drawing-room and over dinner, from which Alice and I were banished to eat alone. (There were no schoolroom meals as a rule in Sarsen Place, for Mrs Demarest liked to have her grandchild with her.) What it was all about I never discovered, but there was another son, Charles, in the Household Brigade, and I knew he was often the subject of alarms. If the word 'shocking' was ever used in conversation in Sarsen Place, then its subject was likely to be Charles. I rather liked the sound of him myself.

'The end of the month,' said Alice, as we mounted the stairs. 'That's very nearly three weeks.'

'Yes.' Time for him to change his mind, I thought.

'Will he really come?'

'Yes,' I said firmly. Inside, I was doubtful. Alice studied my face. Apparently what she read there agreed with her own thoughts, for she sighed.

Now Mrs Demarest was back, I was in the habit of going home to work at my books each evening. Tonight I walked slowly home down the hill. It was a dark night, and the street lights seemed to flicker in the wind. I never minded walking home alone, any more than I minded sleeping alone in our little house in Museum Road. It made me feel independent. But on this evening I began to be uneasy. Behind me was a figure that kept its distance. I kept glancing over my shoulder, but although I could see the dark figure it never got closer.

As I came down into the town towards Magdalen Bridge, I approached a row of small shops. Deliberately I lingered in front of a display of china to allow the figure to catch up with me. Slowly it drew nearer.

I saw a woman dressed in dark sober clothes, very plain and neat. She had on a full cloak of some dark checked material, very commonplace and ordinary. I had worn one like it myself. She looked away as she drew near, but I had caught a glimpse of sallow skin and dark eyes. She was not old.

I walked on. Surely there could be no threat to my safety from so respectable a woman. And yet the feeling remained with me that she was interested in me and that she had been watching me.

My thoughts kept going back to her. In spite of her discreet appearance, I found myself wondering if she came from Tinker's. Tinker's was a dollar house on the road going towards Cowley, just outside the city boundaries proper, although well within driving distance. The University had power to control all ladies of easy virtue inside the city and to turn them away, but Tinker's was beyond their control. One or two of the young ladies from Tinker's had sat for my father when he was doing a large canvas with nudes, called *Afternoon*. You may suppose what sort of afternoon he had envisaged. My father had treated them with extreme good manners, and while he painted he always kept his hat on, I suppose as a mark of respect. I was only thirteen at the time but sharp and observant, and I took them in for what they were. All the young ladies were very affable and agreeable to me, and one or two became friends. One still is. Although nothing could have been outwardly more different than these girls, with their pretty opulent airs, and the tightly buttoned up dark lady I had seen, yet I detected a resemblance. In the glimpse I had caught of it, hers was a face that had not seen an ordinary life.

Perhaps my own face looked the same to someone truly sheltered like Alice. I knew of worlds that she could never dream of. Not just Tinker's, which, in its terrible way, was a scented pampered life for the darlings that lived there: while they did live there. But I knew that just as some of them could rise to an elegant house in Brompton, others could sink to a house of accommodation off the Haymarket, or even worse. I was very glad that my principal weapon in life would be my mind and not my body, and I thought that, although it is never easy for a woman, I would know how to fight my battles. Mary Ward had introduced me to her friend Mrs Fawcett, and she had opened my mind to what women could do for themselves. Whether we should stand on equal terms with men in political matters I was undecided. Whether we should lay claim to a vote, I had not yet settled for myself. But of one thing I was sure: in any relationship I had with a man, I would stand on equal terms. I would not be subservient, I would not be dependent, I would not be obedient. My father had, at least, emancipated me from all that. As a parent, he was something unusual, but as a teacher about life, he had been frank and explicit. His studio in St Aldate's was an education in itself. Rosemary Lane, in which it lay, was a world away from the sedate life of the colleges and the married couples in the new houses beyond the University Parks. In and out of it wandered the dolly mops, the macers and the lurkers, and all those other members of that sub-world the existence of which we did not admit. People like Mrs Demarest pretended it was not there at all, but I knew it was. Macer and lurker, these words were in a foreign language; but I knew the lingo. A macer was a cheat or sharper, and a lurker was a man with a story of hard luck to tell. As you can imagine, there were plenty of both in and out of Oxford. The superficial observer hardly knew these people were there. But I, by virtue of my youth and my father's privileged position, did know, and I heard their stories. Between the ages of eight and fourteen I moved in and out of their world, an innocent observer. To a certain extent I still was.

That evening I had an engagement with one of the ladies who would tutor me when I took my place in the ladies' college. It wasn't quite certain that they would admit me yet, but I hoped to discuss the matter this evening. I had just enough doubt to be nervous and full of self-appraisal. I dressed myself carefully, although I knew it didn't matter what I wore, as Miss Clough was famous for not noticing dress. She herself always wore the same, a dark blue merino dress with a white collar in winter and a dark blue cotton print in summer. They were all finely and delicately made, she simply didn't vary them. It was as if she had once made up her mind about clothes and that, for the rest of her life, would do.

To meet Miss Clough, I wore my best silk afternoon dress of sage green with front panels of green and white stripes. It was cuffed, and on the cuffs and around the hem were tiny green tassels. Inside was a label saying FROMONT AND LANDRY. It was a very fine dress indeed and was actually a cast off from darling Mrs Pat. I had seen her wear it once as she sat pensively smoking, with her delicate features silhouetted against the white panels of her elegant drawing-room in the Rector's Lodging at Lincoln College. Her formidable old husband, the Rector, Mark Pattison, was away at the time, in Berlin. When she offered me the dress I accepted with pleasure. I had altered it slightly, but I had no fear Miss Clough would recognize it.

I buttoned the neck and smoothed my hair. Outside my house was a gas lamp and as I stood at the window looking down on the street below I saw a figure standing under the lamp. It was the black-clad figure of the woman I had already seen.

Puzzled, I drew back from the window. But as I put on my tweed cloak I made up my mind to speak to her when I left the house. If she was in any trouble I might be able to help.

It was certainly possible that she had a connection with my father. Perhaps she was one of his models whom I did not know. He had used several girls from Mr Rossetti's circle and one of them, an unhappy moody girl, had quarrelled with him. But this woman somehow did not seem as if she had come to quarrel.

But when I opened the front door and stepped out the street was empty. The woman was gone.

I strode briskly through the streets to where Miss Clough lived across the University Parks in a newish house in Bradmore Road. The Parks themselves were closed and dark. I walked beneath the trees, enjoying the night air and glad to feel myself a person again. When I was at Sarsen Place, however much I admired Mrs Demarest and loved Alice, I was essentially a function and not a person to them. I was 'nice Miss Lamont' or even 'dear Mary who is so splendid with Alice'. Did either of them really think of me as existing outside this capacity?

I turned at a bend in the road and looked back. There beneath a tree I saw the dark figure. I stood still for a moment, debating what to do. But even as I looked the figure seemed to recede into the pool of darkness beyond the trees and was gone.

Inside Miss Clough's house all was warmth and light. The gleaming white paintwork and the blue and white delft plates on the walls were her own taste. She had newly decorated the drawing-room walls with a pretty flowered wallpaper. One of Mr Morris's, we were all mad for them.

'Oh, what pretty paper,' I said, looking at the deeply complex pattern of birds and flowers. 'With all the flowers and women's faces.'

'Women?' said Miss Clough smartly. 'There are no women.'

'No, of course not,' I said, confusedly. 'I meant birds.'

'Oh, there are birds.'

She began to pour out some tea. I drank it thirstily, glad to forget my stupidity. It had been a silly slip of the tongue. We discussed my work and then talked of friends we had in common, like Clara Pater and Mary Ward. Miss Clough had one of Clara Pater's little cats. The white kitten rubbed against her leg.

'Half deaf, poor little thing,' she reported in an amused voice. 'All her animals are like that, crippled or blind. She *prefers* them that way.'

'I admire her so much.'

'Yes, she's a good scholar.' Margaret Clough poured some

more tea. 'If you go to her you will find her a stimulating teacher.' Her plump face was serious.

'I'd rather stay with you.'

'Oh, on some subjects you will get much more from her,' said Miss Clough.

The little cat frisked around the room, carrying a piece of paper in her mouth. Suddenly she stopped dead, stared at the door, and gave a long cry. Then she trotted over to a chair and sat down.

'And yet you say she hears nothing. What *did* she hear?'

Miss Clough laughed and shook her head. 'Sounds *we* can't hear, obviously.'

'They say cats can see ghosts,' I said idly.

'There is no proof of that and never could be,' said Miss Clough briskly. 'A cat's perceptions are different from ours, I have no doubt, but ghosts ... And yet the study of apparitions and fantasies is very interesting. There certainly appears to be a very very strong emotional link between the apparition and the seer. Can minds really reach out and touch one another? One would give a good deal to know.'

'Or it might just be that the person who sees the apparition *imagines* it, because he, or she, is in an emotional state.'

'It very often *is* a woman,' said Miss Clough. 'And the apparition is more usually a woman in distress or an old man. Sometimes a child.'

'One never thinks of being a ghost oneself, only of *seeing* one. But I suppose one *might* be a ghost.'

'Without knowing it?' said Miss Clough, her eyes keen. 'What an interesting idea.' Her face was absorbed as she considered the matter.

'I suppose one could hardly know one was a ghost.'

'Oh yes, one might, indeed it might be part of being a ghost. On the other hand, it might very well be that one still considers oneself as real and thought the *seer* was the ghost. What *is* reality? It might be necessary to establish that first.' She seemed willing to throw up endless academic speculations.

'Yes, I suppose the scene in which a ghost is real would have to be described,' I said.

'Have you heard that a society is to be formed in the University to deal with matters of psychical research?' said Miss Clough. 'Some of the philosophers feel it is pertinent to their investigations into Mind, and Memory, and also to the Nature of the Universe.' She often spoke in capital letters when dealing with matters she felt to be truly important, underlining each crucial word with a quite unconscious little bow. It was impossible not to be fond of her.

'You mean they will investigate ghost stories?' I said.

'Yes. Every story will be subjected to the most rigorous examination.' I could believe that, having a fair idea of some of the learned gentlemen involved. 'Rigorous' was their word of the moment. 'Sources', that was a great word, too. 'Evidence' was another. On every side, or so it seemed to me, you could see the techniques of German textual criticism pervading the more intuitive literary English style of scholarship. We were all to be scientists of a sort. 'And they will have regular meetings during university term and read papers and so forth. It is all to be treated *seriously*.'

It did occur to me that a christian society might well have taken ghosts seriously before this, but I forbore to say so. In any case, one or two of the scholars concerned were convinced agnostics. Others were, in the current jargon, 'unsettled' in matters of religion.

'I'd like to go to a meeting. Will women be acceptable as members?'

'Oh I dare say, my dear. I think Mary Ward intends to go. And I shall go, of course. It would be nice to be quite sure of the immortality of the human soul.' She sounded wistful.

I wasn't quite so sure. Very often it seemed to me that oblivion might be a more comfortable fate.

'My brother has entered into an arrangement with one of his friends to communicate. Whichever one dies first will try to get in touch with the survivor.' Miss Clough was confidential.

'How will it be done? How will the one that survives be sure the message really came from his dead friend?'

'I believe they have come to some arrangement with certain key words. They will try to transmit these words through the writings of the survivor. I am not quite sure how this will be achieved, but I suppose he will find himself writing out certain sentences. His writings will be checked by a third person, to whom the special phrases will have been told beforehand. So, you see, this person will know what to look for.'

'Is that person you?' I asked bluntly.

Miss Clough shook her head. 'No, my dear.' She laughed. 'I'm afraid my brother doesn't think my mind clear enough.'

It was late when I left, and I went home in a cab, Miss Clough insisting on this. I was sleepy and cold and went straight to bed. The next day was a Sunday and I stayed at home. But on the morning of Monday Belcher came down for me in the carriage and I went round to Madame Blanche to collect the hat and mantle which were promised for this morning.

While I was waiting I idly picked up a newspaper which someone had left lying on the little gilt table. It was a copy of that morning's London *Times*. And I read that a woman's body had been found in the river at Iffley, just below Oxford. There was no drawing of her, but a clear description: she had been a young woman of less than thirty years and dressed in black.

I let the paper fall on the table and went to pick up the hat in its gay pink and gilt box which Madame Blanche was handing to me with a smile.

Madame Blanche was the chief dispenser of mysteries and arts in Oxford, far surpassing in her skills any of the tricks the learned doctors of the Middle Ages might have practised. She knew how to give soft curls to ladies with straight hair and blushing complexions to those whom nature had only given sallow cheeks. She made delightful hats and created dresses and mantles of a simple sort for select ladies. My own taste was more for the square-necked Liberty gowns with flowing lines worn by my friend Mary Ward, but I admitted that Madame Blanche's hats and gowns knew how to flatter. Only what they did to a woman I did not wish to offer to the world. There was a genuine link between Mrs Demarest and Madame Blanche, and that link was luxury. Mrs Demarest loved luxury, and Madame Blanche knew how to produce it. Mrs Demarest was, although I liked her very much, a vain woman. I knew that the smoothness of her complexion and the soft pink polish on her nails came in bottles and boxes from Madame Blanche. I didn't in the least blame her. I rather enjoyed knowing what few guessed: I was not my father's daughter for nothing, and had a keen eye for paint of any sort.

Madame Blanche sailed forward and deposited the box in my hands. Her usual delicate smile embroidered her lips. When I had never seen her but only heard of her, I had imagined her to be a plump and painted lady; but Madame Blanche was still young and very slender, her appearance simple and natural. Only the way in which her dress was cut about her, the snugness of its fit around her waist, and the soft folds over the breast showed that everything was deliberate and contrived. For the first time I understood what my father meant when he chuckled about the 'tricks of those Frenchwomen'.

'Can I show you something, Miss Lamont?' I was wearing one of Mrs Demarest's old London dresses and a flick of her eyes showed she knew it. 'In here, please.' She drew back a thick velvet curtain and showed me into a small alcove – a fitting room, I suppose it was. Naturally, I did not usually see inside these sanctums. A huge gilt mirror covered one wall and hanging against another was a black and white silk afternoon dress. The bodice was black velvet and the skirt ruffled white silk. 'A lovely thing, is it not?' said Madame Blanche in genuine admiration. 'Made by Janet in London. What style! But do you know, with all those fittings they didn't get the set of the waist right and Mrs Demarest has asked me to alter it.' She smiled at me, saying: 'Normally, of course, I wouldn't touch a dress made by another house, but I couldn't wait to get my hands on a dress by Janet. She has invented a new way of cutting the material *across* the weave which I long to see.' Her voice had dropped, her admiration was quite genuine. 'However, the cut is so *close* that in order to do what Madam wants I must cut into the bodice and that will make it quite décolleté.' Her eyes were bright and amused. *Of course, you know and I know that Mrs Demarest has put on weight but we won't say it.*

'I have invented a very pretty way of cutting the bodice,' she added.

33

'I am quite sure Mrs Demarest would admire it. But, of course, you cannot describe it to her without seeing it.' She smiled at me with her strong white teeth and snapped her fingers. 'Stella, please,' she called.

Presently, through the blue velvet curtains, Stella appeared. She was the tall sullen-faced assistant known to us as Miss Darley. Over her arms hung a blue and white silk dress with a low bodice, the intricate cut of which was demonstrated to me by Madame Blanche.

She claimed to have invented it. Unfortunately for her I had an excellent memory for dress, and was almost certain that I had seen such a bodice on a dress by Callot Soeurs already belonging to Mrs Demarest.

From behind the velvet curtains came a burst of giggles.

'Little cats,' said Madame Blanche, her easy good manners deserting her. She scowled at Stella, who pushed back through the curtains. Next I could hear voices raised angrily, then there was silence. Presently Stella emerged, followed by two young girls carrying between them a large doll, almost lifesize, dressed in an elegant velvet and fur walking dress. At least, so Madame Blanche described it, although I ironically reflected that the wearer of such a dress would probably not do much walking. The delicate boots worn by the model confirmed the thought. 'Oh yes, La Grande Pandore,' said Madame Blanche. Her French was excellent. She adjusted the velvet skirt over the doll's legs. 'Mrs Demarest wanted to see this model. I imported it myself from Paris.' The doll had a painted waxen face and an air of having aged without having matured. 'You will take it up with you in the carriage?'

The doll was lifted on to the padded seat by a long-faced Belcher, and I prepared to get in beside it.

'There's a note for you to deliver at Mr Champion's before we start back,' said Belcher, suddenly producing a white envelope from his pocket. After sitting there for half an hour or so, he smelt of tobacco smoke and horse.

'Pah, Belcher,' I said, holding the envelope delicately between my fingers. He grinned, he knew he smelt and didn't much care.

34

He had no objection to quietly giving offence to those who employed him.

The note, which was to Mrs Demarest's lawyer, required us to drive down St Aldate's towards the lower parts of the town. On a corner near the lawyer's office was my father's studio, at present kept clean but unoccupied. I handed Mrs Demarest's note to Mr Champion's clerk, who received it with a smile. Instead of getting back into the carriage, I rapped on the side to attract Belcher's attention.

'Will you walk the horses, please? I have one more errand to do.'

He nodded. 'The horses won't like it.'

'I won't be long. Fifteen minutes only. I'll look for you here.'

The studio, a large room with a north light and a sink in one corner, was the annexe to a small furniture warehouse. It was cold and dusty there, but my father, so careful of his comfort in all else, had never tried to move from it. I suppose in some mysterious way it suited him.

I unlocked the door and went in. The big room was orderly but smelt of stale cigar smoke. This is supposed to be a disagreeable smell, but, in fact, I enjoy it, especially when mixed with the smell of paint as this was. I moved round the room, feeling at once the familiar lightening of the spirits and the amusement that my father always brought. I suppose this was why ladies like Mrs Ely went with him to Paris.

Everything was neatly packed away. There was never any disorder in my father's work, everything connected with it was professionally done. I seemed to see his muscular brown hands moving tidily round the room. His easel was stacked against the wall. Also leaning against the wall were some half-finished canvases.

I went across to them and, kneeling on the floor, I studied them one after the other. One or two were not finished and I knew this meant that my father was disappointed in what he had achieved. Sometimes he went back; no disappointment was lasting with him, his hopes continually revived. He said this was what it was to be an artist.

The canvases slipped through my hands, a portrait or two, one landscape, one a picture I could hardly identify, more Turner-esque than Turner, a great swirling of colour which I could make nothing of.

'You stand too close,' my father had said. 'Try standing several feet away.'

'With Bellini or Titian you can see *every* detail,' I said.

'I agree,' said my father. 'But you see I'm not Bellini or Titian.' *That* was evident, I thought. 'Look at the background of a Raphael cartoon and you willl see what I mean.'

I suppose my scepticism was evident in my face, because he burst out laughing. '*How* you admire your father,' he had said.

All this was in the back of my mind as I worked through the pictures.

The large square face of one of his favourite models stared back at me from several canvases. Hers was not an appearance I was fond of myself, but it seemed to appeal to my father. Finally, when I was beginning to think I was mistaken, I found what I sought. On a completed canvas, but one which my father had started to paint over, I saw the face which had stared at me from under the gaslight.

Father had set her, against a background of trees, on a white garden bench, and she seemed to be wearing some type of gypsy costume: it was hard to be sure because my father's obliterating brush had already been at work. But there she was: younger, prettier, happier. She gazed at me from the canvas.

I replaced the canvases as I had found them. So I must have seen the woman before. Now it seemed almost certain that she had been trying to speak to me last night.

Behind my father's studio lay a crowded court. You entered through a narrow passage, painted dark green and running with water, and found yourself in a paved yard some twenty feet long and fifteen feet wide with doors opening into it from the crowded tenements. Here lived street vendors and poor labourers who could afford nothing better. They were respectable, but brushing shoulders with them were moochers and cadgers and petty thieves who stayed here and then moved on. Rosemary Court touched on the edge of the criminal world. I knew it, because I had lived near it as a bright-eyed child. But even I could not always be certain where the two worlds touched.

I had one friend, if you could call her that, who lived in Rosemary Court. She was a second-hand clothes dealer called Binny Agar. Although she was only about my own age or very little older she had already, to my certain knowledge, married and disposed of two husbands, retaining the name of Agar throughout.

She seemed pleased to see me but, of course, affability was a matter of business with her. Underneath was a tough astringent tone of mind.

'Hello, haven't seen you for a long time. Got any business for me?'

I shook my head with a slight smile. Although Mrs Demarest often gave me clothes that were rich and elegant, I never let them go to Binny, in spite of her offer of a good price. I had an idea that Binny's clothes found their way into some pretty odd places and it didn't seem right that Mrs Demarest's clothes should go there.

'Well, you're no help to me, then.'

'I want you to help me.'

'Ah, I thought you didn't come to see my pretty face.'

'Well, that too, Binny.' But it wasn't pretty, hadn't been pretty for years now. A sort of hardness was welling up from inside and gradually marking the regular features. 'But I wanted to ask you if you'd heard about that young woman drowned in the Thames at Iffley and if you knew her?'

'I did hear about it, yes. But know her? No, I don't know her. I never know dead people, dear, it's bad for business.'

'No joking, please, Binny.'

'Oh, you think I'm joking? It's no joke. You know too many dead people, and customers start to ask where you're getting all those clothes they're buying from you.' Her voice had a whiplash quality of bitter amusement.

'People have to die, Binny.'

'And I have to live.' It was the struggle to live which was marking her features. 'Now don't go meddling in things, Mary Lamont. Especially don't go asking about silly girls who drop themselves into the river. You'll only cause trouble. What's just an interest to you might be serious business for others.' She looked me in the face. 'I've annoyed you now.'

'Just a little bit, Binny.'

'You don't see things like me. I forget that.' Her voice was full of mockery that was directed at both of us. 'How's your father?'

'Very well, I think. He doesn't write.'

'Can't expect it, can you?' Her eyes were screwed up against the light. 'He was always talking to me when he painted me. I never used to listen. It's all in the picture, I expect.'

'I expect so.' What my father saw, he painted. 'About the woman, Binny . . .'

But she wasn't looking at me. A man had come into the court from a door on the opposite side. He was heavy and tall with a self-confident, cheerful air. He looked about him as if he was new here.

'Who's that?'

'Nice-looking, isn't he?' said Binny appraisingly. 'That's Christian Ableman, the kidsman.'

'Kidsman?' I said.

'You *know*: putting kids to crime, a sort of school for crime.' Her voice was replete with lazy amusement.

'Surely that's all done with now?' I was horrified. 'This isn't 1840, Binny, things have changed.'

She shrugged. 'Says he has a new twist.'

'Is Oxford the right place for him to look for recruits?' I said sceptically.

'He says there's good material to be found. Lots of University bastards here.' She laughed. She liked to say things like that to shock me.

I wasn't shocked. There are many worse things in the Greek myths, after all.

'Not much use for them in Oxford, I should think,' I said. Somehow I couldn't see a squad of little boy and girl thieves operating in Oxford.

'Oh, I don't say he'll speed them here. He'll speed them elsewhere.' She sighed admiringly. 'Yes, he's a marvellous kidsman, all right.'

As we had talked, Christian Ableman stood there sunning

himself, as if he knew and enjoyed the fact that we were talking about him. I dare say he did. Our eyes met. They were the coldest wildest eyes I had ever seen.

'Handsome figure, hasn't he?' said Binny. 'He was an actor once, I've heard say.'

I did not answer. I found his sheer physical presence disturbing.

'So you're off, then?' said Binny. 'What did you really come for?'

'I told you: I'm curious about the woman who was found drowned. Her name, who she was, and why she died.'

'Oh, you think she did it herself,' said Binny.

'I suppose it could have been an accident,' I said. I was reluctant to accept her death as accidental.

'I've heard she was smothered first,' said Binny; and she said it as casually and cheerfully as if she had said that the woman had treated herself to a cup of tea before going into the river.

I suppose I answered her. I remember walking away and thinking: thank God my father is in Paris. I had no notion then that there could be any close connection between me and the dead woman.

All the way up the hill, as the carriage trundled slowly, I was still thinking about the woman and Binny's dreadful suggestion. Murder. I didn't disbelieve her. I knew enough about the world in which Binny moved to know that death by violence happened in it easily. It was the modern world with gaslight and electricity and the electric telegraph, but people like Binny still lived at greater risk than someone like me. I knew it and Binny knew it.

We rolled sedately up the hill, the doll Pandora bumping against me as we went. She really didn't make a very pleasant travelling companion. Alice was standing sedately in the hall waiting for me. It was her pleasant custom always to meet me there when I was expected, just as she always walked with me to the door when I left. Her grandmother had trained her in charming manners.

'You're late,' she said forthrightly.

'I had some errands to do for your grandmother.' I gazed at

her with affectionate concern. Although she was cheerful, she looked pinched and white. 'Did you sleep well, Alice?'

'Of course.' She was indifferent and had already begun to turn away. But I caught her arm. 'No dreams?'

'I told you: I never dream. Or, if I do, I don't remember them.'

The footman came past, carrying a long box with Mrs Demarest's dress under one arm and La Grande Pandore under the other. Alice gave a little scream and clutched my arm.

'It's all right,' I said quickly. 'It's only a doll. She's called Pandora. I'll tell you the legend of Pandora in our Greek lesson today.'

'I know it,' said Alice, with a shudder. 'She had something hidden, and she let it out.'

'Well,' I hesitated. 'That's a very rough version of it, I suppose. But it means so much more than that, Alice. It's a very interesting story.'

'I'd rather do something else today, please. Let's go on talking about Homer. You know you're really much more interested in Homer yourself. I can tell by the way you talk about archaeology.'

'That's true.' She was a clever little thing. I was indeed much more interested in the historical background to Homer than in the legends and myths, however great the truths they symbolized. Trust Alice to have noticed. I had great hopes of Alice, if her mind could be put to use and not left to languish in a fashionable vacuum. Mrs Demarest, of course, knew that I would be leaving in the autumn, but Alice, so far, did not. I wanted her grandmother to send her away to school. There are so many good girls' schools now, but much would depend on Alice's father, whom I had never met. I found it hard to form a picture of him. From the servants I had gathered that he was not handsome like his younger brother Charles, nor so fond of dress as his mother. But from passing remarks I should have thought he was fully as worldly. I had long been silently puzzled that Mrs Demarest chose to bury herself in a quiet university town rather than spend her days in London, for the society of which she plainly had a taste and where she must certainly have the entrée. But that day Alice explained it all.

40

She was arranging her collection of stamps and gossiping as she did so. I was studying a Greek prose and putting in a word here and there.

'Grandmother had a quarrel with the Queen,' she said.

'Oh?' The strict law of etiquette which is supposed to rule the conduct of people like me enjoined me not to listen, but I am my father's daughter. We like to *know*. People's behaviour interests us. I let Alice go on. Indeed, I suppose you could say I encouraged her.

'At least, not Grandmother, truly, she never quarrels, you know.' After this adult observation she paused to move a stamp delicately with one finger, leaving me to speculate on the nature of the breach between Mrs Demarest and Her Majesty Queen Victoria. 'It was my grandfather. He did something and the Queen said he must never come and see her again.'

She leaned over her stamps, while I wondered what Henry Demarest had done that had got him forbidden the Court. Perhaps he hadn't minded too much. It was said to be far from gay. I looked at Alice's shining fair head and guessed that she had sat and listened to a conversation she was presumed not to have understood. Obviously she had understood enough to worry her and now she had told me.

She raised her head and her eyes met mine. I patted her hand. 'It is strange, I agree, Alice, but I don't suppose it was anything important, really.'

She seemed to accept this, but afterwards I admitted to myself that it must have been a social crime of some consequence if it resulted in Mrs Demarest's removing herself for ever from the scene.

One thing was apparent, however. It hadn't in any way interrupted the merry career of Charles Demarest, the younger son, around whom I suspected, from certain sighs and frowns of Mrs Demarest, yet another crisis was brewing. It must be a bad one this time if his elder brother was coming home. Or perhaps Alice's father wanted to see his daughter again. She didn't seem to weigh on him heavily as a responsibility. I had already formed the conclusion that the Demarest family did not value women greatly.

41

The day passed quietly for Alice and me. That night I stayed at Sarsen Place in my room with the rose damask walls. I worked late, reading the book of a new German scholar who wanted to prove that Homer had never existed. It was a humourless, but extremely thorough production, and I could see that it would need a steady application to the texts to answer it. Samuel Butler, the author of *Erewhon*, has decided that Homer was a woman, but although I am as convinced as anyone that women can achieve anything, nevertheless I do not think Homer was a woman. The Iliad and the Odyssey seem to me to display the male thesis at its most explicit. Women did not have a very elevated position in Homeric society, nor, indeed, in later classical Greek. On the whole, I was glad I was alive now. My thoughts drifted away to my future, the shape of which I was beginning to see so clearly. I would take my place in the autumn at the new women's college, I would read the degree course, I would write the papers in the Final Honours School, and thus I would achieve the nearest to a full degree that any woman could do in Oxford. I would be one of the first women to do so. I nearly said one of the first of my kind, as if women were a different species, and, indeed, sometimes I have felt they are regarded as such.

I went to the window and looked out. Inside all was warm and glowing, outside a light bitter snow was falling. I walked back to the fire and held out my hands; they were my father's hands, shapely but strong. I suppose they epitomized my character. I was not one of those women whom men felt a strong urge to cherish and protect. I knew well that the strength of purpose and decision that I felt inside myself must show in my manner, which probably lacked softness. But I had an idea it would serve me very well. I wasn't looking for or expecting an ordinary woman's life. I would carve out something different. In memory I could hear Mary Ward's voice.

'We are all on fire for women's education,' she had said one day, 'but hardly any of us are on fire about women's suffrage. I know we think that women should seek power through Local Government or perhaps through the creation of special machinery for bringing to bear the wishes and influence of women on Parliament. But is that enough?'

'You know I don't think so,' I had answered. I sat for a long time looking into the fire, seeing pictures in the crumbling coal and wondering how many of my dreams I should bring to birth.

Next day the snow had turned to rain and the air was soft. All the morning papers were on the breakfast table. In this respect Alice and I were liberally treated, as indeed we were over breakfast: fresh cream with our porridge, Mrs Ceffery's own sausages, freshly brewed coffee. It was impossible not to enjoy the good living at Sarsen Place. I was hungry and ate well.

After breakfast I picked up the Oxford paper. On the front page there was a short paragraph to say the inquiries about the woman found dead in the river were proceeding. Her identity, so it said, was still unknown.

Unknown. Unknown. Unknown. The word rang in my heart like a bell.

Chapter Two

I took a turn in the shrubbery, walking quietly on my own, in order to consider what I had read. The shrubbery was a gloomy place, not much frequented by anyone. In a small clearing of grass were several small stones with engraved inscriptions, clearly done by an amateur hand. 'For darling Trojan, the best dog a boy ever had,' this one said lovingly. Another simply said: 'Archibald'. I knew I was looking at the graveyard of the pets of the Demarest brothers. Judging by the overgrown state of everything here they had forgotten the tombs.

'I want to put up a stone to my puss,' Alice had said sombrely, 'but grandmother said no. Grandmother doesn't like graves.' I felt she was watching me, waiting, perhaps even hoping, for some comment from me. I had none to make. Afterwards, I remembered.

My father was a friend of one of the Oxford magistrates, a Mr Lark, and I knew a little about what would go on. A police surgeon would examine the dead woman's body, there would be an inquest, and the cause of her death would be settled. Sometimes if the body was badly mutilated or long decayed it was not possible to say what the cause of death was, but this could hardly be the case here. Then the police would decide if the death was accident, suicide or murder. The report in the newspaper was vague, clearly the reporter knew little, but if the dead woman *was* the one I had seen then I myself ruled out accident.

Perhaps she had killed herself, perhaps that lonely pacing of the streets had been the behaviour of one on the point of suicide. It could be so, I could imagine it, but the idea of murder had lodged itself in my mind. 'She was smothered,' Binny had said, speaking almost as if she knew more. Binny lived on the edge of a violent world. She was not herself a criminal, but she had dealings with those who were. The dead woman had looked respectable, like a servant. I knew that a disgraced or dismissed servant often took up with criminals, as the only way of surviving. Perhaps someone in the criminal world had talked to Binny.

Belcher passed me in the shrubberies as I turned back towards the house. He was carrying a bucket and a saddle and a strong whiff of horse came with him. I sneezed and the newspaper, which I was still carrying, fell to the ground. Belcher politely picked it up and handed it to me, rubbing the mud from it with his shirt sleeve.

'Reading about the young woman that's drowned, are you, then, Miss Lamont?'

'Yes, Belcher.' I was surprised. I wouldn't have expected it to interest him. But I knew the servants' hall took a great delight in crimes of violence and were constantly reading about them. Indeed, I could well imagine Mrs Ceffery attending a public hanging.

'Murder, of course, Miss Lamont.'

'Really, Belcher?'

'Yes.' He picked up the pail which he had set down to retrieve the newspaper. 'There's more known to the police than was told in the paper. The man that brings the milk from the dairy at Iffley says the spot where she was found was where no one ever does go in but those that are *put* in, it was where the miller from Wallingford was found after his son-in-law killed him. And the dairyman says the police know it as well as he does. And there's more besides.'

This was a long speech from Belcher; he must really want to tell me about it.

'She'd nothing on her to say who she was, no purse in her pocket, nothing. And she'd no cloak or shawl or anything round her on a cold night. You know, a person about to drown 'isself on a cold night will wrap a cloak around him to keep the cold out, that's strange, but true, ask anyone who knows. Human nature is strange,' he said meditatively.

'Yes, Belcher,' I said.

'Coachmen see most of the game, you know, miss, and there's plenty of time to think things over while you're waiting and walking the horses. Yes, one way and another, there's not much I haven't seen. Murder's nothing to it, nothing. Good morning, miss,' and he moved towards the stables.

'Good morning, Belcher.'

I returned to the house, and stood for a moment in the sunny hall, trying to assemble my thoughts about the dead woman.

A confused hullabaloo of voices from the kitchen regions roused me. In some houses you might hear a shindy coming from the kitchen any day of the week and think nothing of it, but not in sedately run Sarsen Place. I raised my head from the newspaper and listened. Someone appeared to be crying. I thought I could make out also the strong tones of Mrs Ceffery, the cook. In any crisis of the emotions she would certainly be involved. There was an old butler called Prince, but I had already noticed that in moments of stress he managed to be absent.

I went through the green baize doors into the other side of the house.

The first thing I noticed was a little group made up of Mrs Ceffery, Ellen Sweeting and another girl who was lying on the floor moaning.

'What's the matter here?' I said. Ellen and Mrs Ceffery turned towards me in surprise. The girl on the floor never stopped groaning. 'Poor girl,' I said; I knelt beside her. She was a tiny little creature still wrapped in her huge print overall. Her face was chalk white and covered in sweat.

'She's a proper little dolly mop,' said Mrs Ceffery. 'I reckon she knows all about the two-backed beast. Now look what's happening.' She didn't sound censorious, though, more regretful at woman's lot.

'It isn't so,' said Ellen. 'Fenny's not so.'

'You as well,' said Mrs Ceffery automatically, as if she too had said this more than once. Like many cooks, Mrs Ceffery was a woman of strong passions. I often wondered if Mrs Demarest didn't ask herself why it was that there was such a rapid turn-over among the young footmen at Sarsen Place. But if she thought about it at all I don't suppose she would have associated it with her cook, or realized that it had anything to do with Mrs Ceffery.

'We must fetch a doctor,' I said.

'One's on his way,' said Mrs Ceffery. 'Not that he'll do her any good.'

'Let me come.' A voice interrupted me and I looked up to see the doctor at my side. This was a young man with a premature white streak across his black hair. 'Dr Bean,' he said. 'Please allow me.' He pushed me gently aside.

I watched him quietly and neatly examining the girl. His hands moved very lightly over her body. All the same, I saw Fenny turn her head away as if embarrassed. The doctor spoke to her softly. Then he came over to me.

'She'll have to go into hospital.'

'What's the matter with her?'

He hesitated. 'I'm not completely sure . . . Can she be brought down to the hospital or shall I have her sent for? It would be better if there were no delay.'

'I expect Mrs Demarest will say the carriage should be used,' I said. 'I will go too.'

The great hospital, founded by Queen Anne's physician, John Radcliffe, was already over a century old and in sad need of new buildings. But the nurse who came forward to help with Fenny Lewis was a fresh-faced plump country girl with a soft voice.

No one took any notice of me, and I stood there observing the busy scene. I was in the entrance hall, beyond which lay the crowded wards.

Although full daylight outside, it was dark inside the eighteenth-century building and the room was lit with gas jets that made it very hot. I loosened the wrap around my shoulders and walked to the door to look out.

Belcher was standing there, holding the horses' heads. He had his back to me and was stamping his feet restlessly. Belcher was as fidgety as his horses. As he stood there I saw a man come up to him and pause to talk. I recognized him as William Train. I knew he was in charge of the clocks at the hospital.

'Miss Lamont?'

I turned round to see Dr Bean. 'How is she?' I asked at once.

'Not good. I'm afraid it may come to a surgical business. She seems very young. Who are her parents?'

'I believe there are none. She's been with Mrs Demarest for some years. You would have to ask her.'

'We won't operate unless we have to. There is some very severe internal inflammation,' he said. 'Beyond that at the moment we cannot go.'

'Then she's not ... ?' I stopped.

'She's not pregnant,' he said. 'She has a high fever and an internal obstruction, perhaps she may die, but it is a perfectly respectable illness such as even you might suffer, Miss Lamont, if you were unlucky enough. Is that what all you women were thinking? Poor child.'

'I'm sorry,' I said humbly. I should have been above the sort of speculation Mrs Ceffery indulged in. But I hadn't been. I was angry with myself. I suppose it will take generations of emancipated women before women cease to stab other women quietly in the back.

He walked with me to the carriage, and I got in.

'What did Mr Train want?' I said to Belcher, as he closed the door.

'Jus' talking.'

'I didn't keep you long after all, did I, Belcher?'

'No, miss.' He sounded gratified.

'Good. Because now I want you to wait again.'

He muttered something under his breath. He was only pretending he didn't want me to hear. He did want me to hear just enough to be shocked. But I wasn't shocked. Swearing was nothing new to me. The young ladies from Tinker's who had sat for my father's paintings could let out a string of profanity as soon as scratch their noses, and hardly notice they were saying anything. Of course, I didn't always understand what they meant, but I had heard the words.

Once again I left Belcher pacing his horses while I walked quickly through the narrow streets to my father's studio. I let myself in.

The room looked just as I had left it yesterday. Some day soon I would have to come in with a duster and do some cleaning. My father's painting smock hung on the door. So neat was he in everything concerned with his work, even this paint-stained article looked trim. It reminded me of him strongly and, for a moment, I wanted him there to talk to me with his usual lazy good sense. Selfish he might be, stupid never.

I walked over to the stack of his canvases, which still rested against the wall. Second from last, there it was where I had left it, the unfinished portrait of the dark woman.

I turned it over. My memory had not deceived me. The light was good in my father's studio, as you would expect.

In my father's scrawl, which I could hardly make out, I read: *L'Inconnue* – the Unknown Woman.

Alice had done the work I had set her, and then fallen asleep on her books. I found her lying there, her head resting, with its fair shining hair tumbled over her face. She slept quietly on. In repose, children are often said to look defenceless, perhaps we all do, but Alice looked secret, as if, even in her sleep, her thoughts and feelings were all her own.

I tidied my hair and got out some of my work: a Greek translation. I was halfway through and I hadn't touched it for several days. It was Herodotus recounting a myth he had picked up in Asia Minor about King Croesus consulting an oracle. Herodotus seemed to think that the King hadn't got such very good value from the favoured oracle, because he treated the matter with some irony. My eye fell on the phrase, 'But among the women all the secrets were known.' I hadn't remembered it, yet there it was in my own hand. I consulted the original. Yes, I had made a good enough translation. I had invented nothing. But how strange that once again 'the women' should appear in my translation.

I had made fair progress in my work before Alice woke. One moment she was asleep, the next she was watching me with wide eyes.

'I know you have to work at your Greek,' she said, propping herself on one elbow. 'Grandmother has told me of your plans for October.' As so often, she sounded older than her years.

'You don't mind, Allie?'

'That you will be leaving? I do mind *that*. I shall lose you. I shall miss you. But I'm happy for you.'

'I shall miss you too, Allie.' I had got very fond of the little thing. Before I knew her I would not have described myself as a child lover. Difficult exacting little creatures I have found them to be, often enough. But Alice was different. I found myself thinking of her as my friend. An alert-eyed and observant friend, too. Alice had powers of the mind that I was obliged to respect. I could only hope that her abilities would not be hobbled by the fashionable world into which her grandmother would despatch her. Perhaps the social misdemeanour of her grandfather would save her. A great deal would depend on Mark Demarest.

'We can meet often, though,' I went on to Alice. 'I shall be living so near.'

'But you will be busy. Grandmother said you will be very busy indeed.'

'Would you like to go away to school perhaps?' I questioned.

Alice sat up. 'Away from here? Away from Oxford?'

'Yes. Would you hate that?'

'No.' Alice considered. 'I might like it a great deal.'

I received the answer thoughtfully. I have to admit that I had asked the question on purpose, and Alice's answer confirmed what I suspected: Alice was not happy at Sarsen Place.

But where did the trouble lie? Not with me, nor with her grandmother, whose control of her was easy and humane. And yet for such a cherished and loved little girl Alice had sometimes a worn and harassed look.

'What was all the noise in the kitchen?' said Alice. 'I was listening.'

'I thought you might be. Then you know.'

'I couldn't hear everything,' said Alice. 'Fenny's ill. But I knew that. She's Ellen's friend, and Ellen told me.'

'I suppose you shouldn't listen too much to Ellen.'

'But Ellen doesn't tell everything,' said Alice with regret. 'Do I?'

'No,' said Alice, studying my face. 'No one does.'

You least of all, I thought.

'But I can often make it out,' she went on.

I had guessed as much, so I said nothing, but looked at Alice with a slight smile.

'I'll stay in the house tonight,' I said. 'I won't go home.' It was one of those lucky choices I occasionally make. Lucky for Alice, lucky, in the long run, for me.

Chance as much as reason had ruled my life, after all.

Alice's bedroom was hung with heavy silk damask curtains, and lit by gas, with an oil lamp which rested on a small table by the bed and was turned out by me when I said goodnight. I always suspected that when I was out of sight it was re-lit with matches Alice had hidden and she lay there quietly reading.

On this night there seemed a smell of gas as I left the room, so I checked the gas lamps on the wall. There were two, flanking the door. But they were safely turned off. There was a third gas bracket on the wall by the dressing table. This too was off. Satisfied, I departed.

I passed the door on my way down to my solitary dinner (for Mrs Demarest was out). As far as I could tell all seemed still and dark, but I doubted very much if Alice was asleep. She was waiting in her patient fashion for me to be well away downstairs.

I ate quietly, relishing the savoury dishes put before me, but at the back of my mind there was a feather of disquiet disturbing me. But what was it? What was worrying me? I ate the sweet, Riz au crème de la Turque, thoughtfully.

Then, as I was sipping my hot coffee, it came home to me: the smell of gas had surely been *stronger* as I paused outside Alice's room on the way down than it had before.

I pushed my chair back and ran upstairs. I was terrified that either Alice was even now drifting into poisoned sleep or that, any second now, she would incautiously light a match and all would explode.

There was no doubting the smell as I pushed open the door, but thank God, no fire, no explosion. I hesitated for a second, then I rushed in.

Alice was lying in bed, flopped back across her pillows, still wearing her dressing-jacket. Her cheeks looked flushed. I put my arms around her and lifted her. As I did so her eyes opened, then closed again.

I dragged her into the corridor and slapped gently at her cheek. Her eyes opened again.

'Alice,' I said urgently. 'Try to stay awake.'

She stared at me silently and drowsily. I slapped her cheek again. 'No!' she murmured. 'You're hurting me.'

'Keep your eyes open then,' I commanded. But already I could see she was more awake. She took a deep breath and then another.

'Stay where you are.' I prepared to go back into the room.

'Please don't.' she called softly after me.

But I was already in the room, pulling back the long heavy curtains, and let the moonlight stream in. The smell of gas was choking, but I threw open the windows and breathed deeply. My lungs full of fresh air, I turned round to look at the gas lamps on the wall. I put out my hand to press the tap, but as far as I could tell this one was as firmly down in the off position as it had been before. I put my hand over my mouth and nose and stumbled across the room to check the other lamps on either side of the door. They, too, were turned off.

Then my eyes fell on the curve of gas piping where it skirted the room. Where the piping disappeared into the skirting board was yet another tap and this tap was, for some reason, approached by a length of flexible metal tubing ending in a rubber lip pushed over the tap-fitting. It was this rubber which had been wrenched away, leaving gas pouring out of the unshielded pipe. I turned the tap off and the flow of gas stopped. Then I pushed the rubber lip of the tube back into place, went outside the room and took a long shuddering breath.

It was impossible to believe it had happened by accident.

Alice slept in my room that night. She lay quiet. I was awake, thinking. Mrs Demarest's opinion, expressed after Alice was in bed, was that one of the maids had pulled the gas tubing apart when cleaning and was now afraid to admit the responsibility. A maid had already been sent weeping to bed. Everyone accepted this because they could not accept the other possibility, that someone had wished Alice harm.

But I could accept it because *I* knew without being told that it was what Alice herself believed. I turned on my side and looked at the child sleeping there and I wondered what on earth to do.

On an impulse, I got up and took my ivory dice from my pocket and rolled it on the table. A six would mean: Go ahead, investigate, find out all you can. Any other number I would accept as a prohibition.

I rolled and there was my six. I gathered up the dice triumphantly and pocketed it. The answer was what I wanted really. I was as curious as Scheherazade. Satisfied, I went back to bed.

What a strange house Sarsen Place was proving to be. In the garden the animals' graves, in the house mysteries and terror. I no longer trusted anyone.

I suppose I slept, because I remember waking to the feeling that something was wrong.

I sat up and looked at Alice's bed. It was empty. But before I could jump up in alarm some slight noise made me look towards the window.

I saw her there standing motionless, the curtain in her hand, looking out for all the world as if she was waiting for someone, something, to appear in the garden below.

'Alice,' I said softly. 'What are you doing?'

I saw her body stiffen. I almost felt her disappointment that I had wakened.

'Nothing, Miss Lamont.'

'Come back to bed, Alice.' My voice was crisp.

'Yes, Miss Lamont,' she said, her voice calm. She turned her face towards me with a blank sweet smile. She would show me nothing. Nothing.

Sarsen Place, which had once been a friendly and hospitable home to me, now felt hostile. Even my pupil had removed herself from me.

Alice was calm and sweet in the morning, and said nothing at all about her midnight walk. I did not mention it either. But I was alert and watchful.

I was left so much to my own directions at Sarsen Place that occasionally I fell into errors of judgement just like any other young girl. Perhaps I did so now. I don't know, and yet so many consequences, both seen and unseen, flowed from the proceedings I now set on foot. Sometimes, in my sadder moments, I wonder if I did not indeed on that day open Pandora's box. But, no, it was really already opened by a woman's greed and ambition.

I ordered all the hangings and curtains in Alice's room to be stripped and taken away to be cleaned. I had a feeling that a room made bare reveals its secrets.

Without the blue silk the room was lighter and airier. If I had a criticism to make of Sarsen Place it was that its luxury was airless and over-heated. Alice complained of feeling tired and sat by the fire watching me. Mrs Ceffery, who knew more about the house than anyone else, produced a fresh supply of curtains and hangings from a resource of her own. They were cream and gold, very grand and rich, but Alice took a fancy to the articles and refused to part with them.

'They're almost royal, aren't they?' she said dreamily.

'Should she have them?' I asked in an undertone to Mrs Ceffery, who shrugged.

'I reckon she has a right to them. Belonged to her mother.'

I gave her a startled look.

'What you might call her nuptial curtains,' said Mrs Ceffery, with a hearty laugh. 'Come down, they did, when she was away.'

'Died, you mean?'

'Aye, that's it, dear, poor lady,' she answered sardonically. 'But not of sickness, more of heart trouble, I'd say.' And she laughed, tiresome perplexing woman that she could be. 'Mind you, you can't keep them for ever, Miss Allie, now. Only a loan.'

Allie nodded. But I knew she would cling to them with all her tenacious soul.

'What would we do without Mrs Ceffery?' I said as I surveyed the room. I now saw that on either side of the window and until now hidden behind the curtains, was an area of old panelled oak, perhaps belonging to an earlier stage of the house. From one of the panels protruded a small knob. I was looking at a cupboard. I pulled at the knob, but nothing moved; the cupboard was locked.

A kind of ruthlessness overcame me; indeed, I pleasured in it. I knew that downstairs in the kitchen hung many bunches of keys, some of considerable antiquity, as if they went back a century or two. I'm interested in keys. Well, locks *are* interesting aren't they, if you look at them properly? I felt sure I would find a key to open this cupboard. I left Alice by the fire and went to the kitchen to get the keys. Needless to say, I was observed, but as I have said, I had a privileged position in Sarsen Place and could do things others could not. I gave Mrs Ceffery a brilliant daunting smile and departed, jingling, with my chosen bunch of keys.

Alice *did* look up when I came in, but soon she turned her head back to her book with that particular air of intensity and concentration which was so unchildlike.

One key, two keys, three . . . I was working through all possible small, old keys. But I didn't despair for a moment. I was buoyed up by my inner conviction that today all locks would open to me. One should learn to distrust that feeling. I did, later.

At last a small blackened key turned in the lock and the door swung towards me with a creak. At first I thought the cupboard was empty, which was not what I was expecting, then I saw a collection of objects on the bottom shelf.

I saw a baby's rattle made of silver and coral, and a lock of hair, straight and pale, tied with blue ribbon in a silver locket. There was also a black-edged mourning card, but quite blank; it contained no inscription. Only when I turned it over I saw, scrawled in ink, the words, 'Darling, darling baby.'

I quietly re-locked the door and returned the keys to the kitchen. Alice had neither looked up nor said anything during all this. Only afterwards did I wonder at this silence from my sharp-eyed, observant little friend. And then I asked myself exactly what Alice *knew*.

I had had my revelation and somehow I had not found it a pleasing one. I wondered what I had found. Was it the relics of a Demarest child, a boy, I presumed from the blue ribbon, who had died? I looked at Alice. Perhaps she had had a brother younger than herself. If so, no one had told her or mentioned him to me. But this could well be, the Demarests were a secretive family. Even Mrs Ceffery could keep a still tongue when she wanted. But the more I thought about the objects in the cupboard, the more I became thoughtful. I am my father's daughter and know about craftsmanship. None of the articles was costly or beautiful, and one thing you could say about the Demarests was that they had good taste and used their money well.

The rest of the morning passed normally. I left my books in the hall, on the gilt and gesso table made by William Kent, when we went to lunch. The great door was open and through the inner glass door I could see out into the cold world outside. Where I was smelt of wax polish and Mrs Demarest's lilac scent; outside was fog and cold dead leaves.

Pandora was in the hall. Now I had a good look at her I could see she was above five feet tall with a preternaturally small waist and well developed bosom. Her legs were long, her hands and feet tiny. She was a blonde and pretty well life-size. She was sitting in the hall waiting to be taken home. They had taken off her fine clothes and draped her in a black mantle. Seen thus, she looked mean, seedy and indescribably furtive.

I saw Alice give her a nervous look. Children, even intelligent children, get strange fancies. 'She's only a *doll*,' I said.

'Oh, of course, I *know*,' said Alice, giving my hand a squeeze.

Mrs Demarest joined us after lunch. She took a small cigarette from a box and lit it. I had been surprised to see her smoke, but apparently in her circle it was quite all right to do this in private. Alice and I didn't count as an audience, although, in fact, we were one of her most appreciative and observant, and always knew if she had scented her cigarette with lilac or rose. Today was something new and rich, not flowery at all.

'That poor little wretch from the kitchen,' she said suddenly, taking a puff at her cigarette. 'A message has just come up from the hospital: she is to have an operation. One of us must go down and see to things. I myself ... Perhaps *you* would go, Mary?' She raised her eyebrows in a way I loved to watch.

'Can I take Ellen to the hospital with me?'

'Yes, of course.'

'You must both have a cab,' said Mrs Demarest. 'Then it can wait and bring Ellen back.'

A few minutes later I stood waiting in the hall for Ellen and the cab. I had picked up my books from their splendid resting place and pushed them into a little satchel I carried, on which

Alice herself had embroidered my initials, a labour of love from her, considering how she hated the work.

Ellen soon joined me and on the way down in the cab I could see that although she was genuinely concerned about her friend she was also excited and happy at the outing and the ride in the cab.

I looked inside my bag of books to make sure I had packed my Greek Grammar. It was then I noticed a piece of paper sticking out of it. I drew it out and saw that it was folded over to form a triangle. Curiously, I opened it. Inside was a pencilled message.

'Aren't we going fast, Miss Lamont?' said Ellen in delicious terror.

'Very fast,' I said.

I looked down at the message on my lap. All it said was:

If you say anything, then we will come and get you.

The message was printed in large, clearly written, flowing letters. It had, however, a certain air of bold self-confidence. The hand that had written it had not been well trained to use a pen, but it had what, for want of a better word, I called 'cheek'. Well, I had cheek of my own to put against it. I tore the message into small scraps and lowering the carriage window threw the pieces out into the road. Then I leaned against the cool satin lining of the carriage.

Ellen watched me, open-mouthed.

'Just rubbish, Ellen.'

'Yes, miss,' she said, her eyes amazed.

I did not know who had sent me the message, or how it had reached me. But once my father had received an anonymous letter and had straight away put it on the fire, rather to my regret, I must admit, because I would have liked to read it.

If people won't sign their letters to you, then you ignore them, he had said with his calm good sense.

When we reached the Infirmary, I let Ellen hurry on ahead and followed more slowly. If there was a chance for her to have a moment alone with her friend, then I wanted her to have it.

After ten minutes Ellen came out through the ward door. She

had Dr Bean with her. He seemed tired and a smell of chloroform hung around him.

'You've operated, then?' I said.

He nodded. 'I'm afraid she's not conscious yet. Just as well really, although these days we are able to do something about it. Ten years ago she would have had no chance with an internal blockage of this sort.'

'What was it, then?' Mrs Demarest would want a full report.

'An infection of the caecum.' He smiled at my look. 'It's part of the larger intestine. A fairly useless part. I've removed it.' He looked pleased. 'I may say that this is only the third operation of this type performed in this country.'

'I hope she will be all right,' I said doubtfully.

'She's a young, strong girl. She should survive, but she had no chance without my operation.'

'Can I see her?' asked Ellen.

'Better not. Come back tomorrow.'

The cab was still waiting in the courtyard outside the hospital when we came out, but the boy who sold the hot roast chestnuts was sitting up with the driver, talking to him seriously. As soon as he saw us he slid down from his perch.

'Saw you coming down St Giles,' he said in his hoarse voice. 'Followed. Wanted to talk.'

It was the longest sentence I had heard him say. He was usually speechless when Alice and I bought chestnuts.

'To me?'

'No, miss.' His eyes went towards Ellen, who was also speechless beside me. She continued to say not a word, but I was aware of a silent appeal coming out of her.

'You want to talk to Ellen?'

He nodded vigorously. Ellen watched me hopefully. She wasn't going to commit herself with a word until she saw what my attitude was. I looked at the cabby: his expression was neutral. 'All right,' I said. 'Five minutes.'

Five minutes thus granted is not to be interpreted literally and it was at least fifteen before they stopped their pacing up and down, heads together, and came back towards me. I watched them with sympathy and amusement. I supposed Alice and I would get even better chestnuts in future. No doubt Alice had known of their friendship all the time. And, equally, there was no doubt that by all the standards of worldly wisdom I ought not to encourage it. What could come of a friendship between a ragged barrow lad and a little maid-servant from the country? But something about their simple pleasure in each other tightened the muscles of my throat and silenced my prohibitions.

As Ellen departed, waving cheerfully from the cab window, I turned towards the boy. He was already walking away.

'Wait!'

He stopped and turned round, but didn't say anything. He knew all about waiting until he was spoken to.

'How long have you know Ellen?'

'All my life,' he said.

'She's not your sister?'

'Sister? *No*.' He was scornful. 'Her mother come from Deddington. I went to school with Ellen. But I left afore she did and set up on my own here. I was obliged, you see, being on me own.'

'I'm sorry,' I said.

'*No*.' Once again he was scornful. 'I'm well set up. Considering my age. Yes, I'm well set up, and shall be my own master.'

'You look as though you are your own master,' I said, amused.

'Well, yes. In a manner, so I am. But I have only the hire of the barrow and must pay a rent. I *could* buy the owner out, he's only a poor knacker, but chestnuts is only a seasonal business, and I doubt it's worth my while.'

'What about Ellen?' I asked.

'She's my sweetheart,' he said simply. 'Always has been, always will be. Ellen and I are settled to be wed. She's no dolly mop.'

'I know that. Mind you remember it, too.'

He gave me a long shrewd look. 'You mind your business, miss, and I'll mind mine.'

'I beg your pardon.' I accepted the rebuke.

'Then you'll do none.' He was magnanimous. 'And you wants to watch your own step, miss. No offence, you know, but I see more of the world than you think.'

He had given me back a swift blow.

'What do you mean?'

'I saw you talking to Christian Ableman.' He could weigh it up, too. 'He was studying you. He's best kept well away from, is, Christian Ableman.'

'I wouldn't dream of doing anything else.'

'If Christian Ableman takes a fancy to you, then your number's up.'

Honours were now even between us. I had accused him of sexual freedom and he had pointed out to me that I too was vulnerable.

'I don't think Christian Ableman is interested in me,' I said. 'I've heard he came here on other business. He's a kidsman and has come for recruits.'

'*No.*' He was scornful. 'There's nothing much done in that way nowadays.That's not his caper.'

'No?' I considered. So Binny didn't know everything. Or possibly she had been deliberately deceitful.

'No, he's on another lay.' He looked around at the crowded courtyard. Seeing no one he knew, and certainly not Christian Ableman, he went on: 'He's got a new bone, I've heard.'

'And what is it?'

'Not being in his pocket, I can't say, but trouble for someone.'

'Goodbye,' I said. 'I don't know your name, tell me what it is.'

'Jack,' he said.

'Goodbye, then, Jack.'

'Goodbye. And don't worry about Ellen. I'll never dab it up with her.'

He gave a leap, bounded forward and ran out of the courtyard of the Infirmary, weaving his way in and out of the crowd with great skill.

I followed more slowly, much more slowly, and deep in thought.

That afternoon I went for a walk in the grounds of Sarsen Place. These were small for the size of the house, and indeed, in order to be solitary it was necessary to take the path through the shrubberies of laurel and buddleia. By doing this you soon found yourself near the graves of the animals. This was a sombre place, much overhung with a dark yew tree and surrounded by banks of rhododendrons, but nevertheless I found myself responding to the melancholy charm which hung about it. My mood was suited by it.

I looked at the three animal graves, then crossed a flagged pathway, and so found myself looking at another small mound. Here was no headstone, but on the turf a small scattering of flowers, blue flowers, they were not so withered that I could not see the colour. Looking at the flowers it was not possible to be quite positive that they had been placed there deliberately. Perhaps they had fallen where they were by accident, perhaps this was no grave.

Deliberately I went back to the gardeners' tool shed and selected a sturdy cane of the type used for tying up climbing plants. This cane had a pointed end. I carried it back and pushed it through the soil of the mound as far as it would go.

The cane went down surprisingly easily for about a foot, and then I found resistance: it had come up against something hard.

I replaced the cane and with the soil still on my hands I went into the kitchen. Mrs Ceffery was stirring a pot.

'What is buried in the grave beyond the rhododendrons?' I said.

Her mouth went open in surprise. 'No one buried there that I know of, Miss Lamont. Unless you refer to the animals.'

'I think this is no animal.'

'Well, miss, I think you hardly understand what you're saying.' She turned back to her soup.

'I think it should be dug up.'

There was a pause. 'The gardeners would do it for you if you ask, Miss Lamont. I believe they are at their dinner now, but come tomorrow.'

'No.'

I left her, and with a controlled madness I took a spade and went myself to dig, throwing earth away from me in quick spadefuls.

I think I already knew what I was going to find, but all the same, it was hard when I saw the small wooden box. Not a coffin made in any professional workshop, but a box. Using the edge of the spade I prized at the lid which came away without resistance.

I closed my eyes and waited for the sickness to subside. Then I put out my right hand, which was gloved, and very delicately moved the shroud away. Beneath this piece of soiled, darkening blanket was a rough sacking bag, tightly sewn together. But imprinted on the canvas was the unmistakable stained impression of a human face. Eyes, nostrils, chin and brow had left their shadow.

I stumbled away.

Later the police came and the small body was taken away. I remember how quietly and smoothly the whole operation went, with the minimum of fuss, and this I put down to its being at Sarsen Place and not Rosemary Court. The word was put about that it was the child of some vagrant or gypsy. This I did not believe. Why bury it in unhallowed ground when any parish would have given it a Christian burial, however mean?

A great silence on the subject fell upon the household. Mrs Demarest, beyond one shocked exclamation, did not mention the subject to me again. Not at this time.

It was Mrs Ceffery who said: 'Dear knows, I don't think this is what I'd call a god-fearing household, but we don't go in for burying babies in the garden.'

I never believed in the gypsy. I could not forget the scattering of faded flowers, blue for a boy. I went home to my own house that night, sad and puzzled. I was beginning to realize that almost anything could happen in a house like Sarsen Place and be smothered by the weight of its prosperity and its knowledge of the world.

Yet events like this do not pass away and leave no hate. They dig themselves in, burrowing deep into the imagination like worms. The future is more shaped by such happenings than we know. Nor did I believe the police had forgotten it all. The servants were certainly questioned in the days that followed, even if few questions were put to me.

Two days later, when I walked into Sarsen Place, I walked into confusion and excitement. There was a great pile of trunks in the hall and a short dark manservant whom I had never seen before was superintending their passage up the stairs. From behind the closed doors of the drawing-room I heard the deep tones of a man's voice.

Alice came hurrying down the stairs. 'Guess,' she said. 'Guess what's happened.'

'Your father's here,' I said, without surprise. 'Your father's arrived home.'

'Yes,' said Alice ecstatically. 'Early this morning.'

Doors banged. I could smell the scent of rich Turkish tobacco, and above and beyond it all, the deep even flow of masculine conversation. Mark Demarest was back.

'And we're to go in and see him,' said Alice, taking my hand. Eagerly she pulled me forward and threw open the drawing-room door.

Mark Demarest was sitting in the big bow window. A silver tray of coffee, served in the best, dark red Crown Derby china, was beside him, and he was half turned away so that I could not see his face.

He rose politely as we came in and turned towards us. My first feeling was one of disappointment; he was not handsome, and was very quietly dressed. But he came forward with a pleasant smile and took my hand.

'I am grateful to you for the care you have taken of Alice and I want you to know it.'

It was nicely said and even meant, but it had the effect of setting me in my place as his daughter's governess. And now he was close I saw that his clothes, although sober, had a care and richness about them that was not ordinary. His voice was quiet, but I had the feeling that quietness had been imposed on it and that it knew very well how to be peremptory.

I stood there, feeling I had nothing to say for myself – not a sensation very usual with me. I could commonly speak up, even when it was better I should have kept quiet. So I was doubtful and confused about my reaction to Mark Demarest. But about the gentleman who was standing reading a newspaper by the fire and ignoring my existence there could be no doubt whatever. He obviously represented the gilded apogee of a sophisticated society. There was no mistaking his assurance, and air of elegant self-esteem. So must the men of the age of Pericles have looked, and the courtiers of Louis-Quinze. He knew what to wear and how to wear it, whom to talk to and whom to ignore. I wish I could have thought him stupid, but he didn't look stupid, only young and handsome and spoilt. It was I who felt stupid. No one introduced us, but I knew he was Charles Demarest.

Then, to my fury, he put down his newspaper and walked towards me with an engaging smile. 'Mary Lamont? I know your father well.' And, as I looked amazed, 'He painted me and my brother officers – a very fine group portrait, and very handsome fellows we all look, too.'

Then I remembered the painting; it had fed us and housed us for a whole year. 'A lot of oafs, my dear,' I remembered my father saying. 'But, by jove, I made young gods of them all.'

'Oh yes, I remember the picture,' I said. 'At least, I remember hearing about it. I never saw it. My father travelled up to London to paint you. I believe it was exhibited in the Academy?'

'Yes, it was the picture of the year for '76,' said Charles. 'You couldn't get near it for the crush. I went three times myself, just to look. Where is your father now? Abroad, I hear?'

'In Paris.'

'Lucky fellow.' He gave a deep sigh, and I remembered my idea that a crisis of some sort was hovering around his head. He looked at his brother. 'Paris now, eh, Mark?' he said hopefully.

'No, Charles, *not* Paris,' said Mark Demarest. 'Not for you.' He sounded firm. I imagined he had to be firm with Charles.

'Six months' leave from m' regiment?' he said. 'Or seconded to our Paris Embassy. Do me a lot of good. Solve a lot of problems.'

His brother did not answer, but occupied himself with settling Alice in a chair by the window.

'No?' said Charles. 'Pity. Like to get away.'

'That I can understand,' said his brother, and there was a note in his voice that I should not have welcomed.

It was strange to spend the day, as I did, in the background, just watching them all. The whole house was alive and full of laughter and light. It was what I had never expected. Much of it, of course, came from Charles Demarest, who was out to please, but some came from his mother's eager response to both her sons. Surprisingly, a lot came from Alice, who was gay and talkative as I had never known her before.

The food that day was superb. Mrs Ceffery had risen to the occasion magnificently, as, with her temperament, she was bound to do. I could imagine the glitter in her eyes as she responded to this male invasion with a suprême of chicken and spun sugar baskets of ice cream. The new young footman spinning between her clutches in the kitchen and his duties in the dining-room looked harassed, and I didn't wonder. I sat at the dinner table with shining damask cloth stretching out on either side of me and admired the heavy silver bonbon dishes, the red roses, and the deep gleam of the wine in the glasses. I felt quite apart from them all, while at the same time deeply involved. I knew so many things that they, in this protected world, did not. I had friends in circles they would never know. Except professionally, I reflected cynically, thinking of my friends at Tinker's and their possible conjunction with Captain Charles Demarest. But as I sat there I doubted if people like Binny and the world of Rosemary Court could ever touch their lives.

'Blinkered,' I thought, as I looked at them. 'Rich and sheltered and blind.' Mark Demarest looked up at me and caught my eye. I might have wondered then, seeing his quiet perceptive gaze, if he didn't know more of the world than I guessed. I thought I was the expert then in the seamy side of things.

I went home at what was for me a late hour, Belcher driving. He was as tipsy as could be for once and I was glad to get out of his care and leave him to drive off home.

I took out my key and prepared to let myself into my dark and shuttered house. The quiet little street seemed empty. Then a figure came out of the shadowy basement at my feet.

'Been waiting for you,' said Jack's hoarse voice. 'Glad you didn't scream. Thought you might.'

'I nearly did.'

'I wanted to talk to you. Got something to tell you. 'Bout Christian Ableman.'

'Come in and talk. We can't talk here on the step.' I unlocked the door, lit the gas and let him into my little sitting-room. He stood by the door, holding his cap in his hand. He didn't twist it or look abashed or awkward. He wanted to talk to me, so he had called.

'Well, what about Christian Ableman, then? Is it to do with him getting children to become criminals?'

'No, he's off that lark. Not so easy these days. The youngsters are more watched over: there's the School Board, for a start, asking questions if a boy goes missin', and they'll send round the attendance man. And then the lads themselves don't seem to take to it like they did. It's all the educating that goes on.' He nodded his head wisely. 'Not that Christian don't try for a recruit now and again, just to keep his hand in.'

'How do you know so much?'

'Tried me, didn't he? Offered me a place. Wouldn't take no for an answer. Told me I was likely stuff. But it's not my lay.'

'Well, what's he after, then?'

He took a deep breath. 'He's come here to properly lift a child.'

'What do you mean?' I was slowly taking in what he said.

'Take away. Steal. Kidnap. He's come to kidnap a girl child.' He was staring seriously into my face.

'Why are you telling me?' I gripped his arm hard.

'You know a valuable little girl. Alice Demarest.'

I drew back, and let my hands fall into my lap. When I looked down I could see they were trembling as if they had a separate life of their own.

'Be very honest with me. Do you *know* or are you inventing or guessing? Why should you think of Alice?'

'A bit of both,' he said. 'Her name has been mentioned.'

'By whom? Tell me.'

'By Christian Ableman,' he said reluctantly. 'Saw her out walking with you this morning. Asked me who you were.'

'And the kidnapping?'

'I guessed that. But he's getting a room ready with bars on it.'

'And how do you know?'

'Carried the bars on my barrow!'

'Where to?'

'Back o' Binny's place. And I saw he had a knife in his pocket.'

When he had gone, disappearing silently into the night, I went back to my sitting-room and sat huddled there in the cold. He had given me a lot to think about, to work out.

To begin with I wasn't sure if I believed him. I understood he was telling me the truth as he saw it, but I also saw how wrong he could be in what he made of Christian Ableman's plan. Why kidnapping? Why Alice?

And yet, there had been a stronger note in Binny's voice when she spoke of Christian Ableman, as if she admired and feared his audacity. She had had an air about her of seeing some joke that I could not see. This was hardly a fact, but what was a fact was that Christian Ableman had seen me with Alice, and found out who we were.

I tried to be reasonable and sensible, and yet I felt fear for Alice Demarest.

Then I remembered she had a father and an uncle and a grand-mother, all of whom nature had provided for her protection. She didn't have to rely on Mary Lamont. Tomorrow morning, early, I would see Mark Demarest.

So I went to bed. My hands had relaxed and no longer kept up their nervous dance. But I had a strange feeling in them, cold and dry as if the wind was blowing through my fingers.

The next morning when I arrived at Sarsen Place it was to find the whole house quiet, with all three Demarests closeted behind the drawing-room doors with Mr Champion the lawyer and a gentleman from London.

The old butler pulled a long face when I asked for my employer and shook his head.

'Be at it for hours in there,' he said.

'At *what*?'

'Counsel's opinion going on in there. The lawyers are at it. Captain Demarest, it will be. A very unsteady young man.'

'I'll speak to Mr Demarest at lunch, then,' I said, preparing to go to Alice. For once she wasn't waiting for me in the hall. I found her upstairs, talking with Ellen. The two girls drew apart as I came in. I took off my coat and settled my hair. I noticed that this time it was Ellen who looked upset and Alice who was calming her.

'Wait a minute,' I said, as she prepared to hurry away. 'What's wrong? Is it Fenny? Is she worse?'

'No, no, she's a little better. Holding her own, anyway, they said.'

'What then?' Her face was flustered.

'Ellen says she believes someone followed her when she went out to post a letter, and it frightened her.'

'You shouldn't have been out posting a letter, should you, Ellen, so it was probably your guilty conscience making you think you were being followed.'

'Yes, Miss Lamont,' said Ellen. Her face had an obstinate, unconvinced expression.

But her story reinforced my desire to talk to Mark Demarest. I waited as patiently as I could. At luncheon I was greeted with the news that all three Demarests, together with Mr Champion and their visitor, had ordered the carriage half an hour ago and taken the fast train to London. There was no mention of when they would return.

There was nothing for it but to go to the police on my own.

Looking back, I can see that only someone with immense self-confidence and rather less worldliness than I thought myself to possess would have set out on such a business. I did have enough sense not to start talking of a little girl being kidnapped.

The police station in St Aldate's was bleak and new. It was the first time I had been in this raw and unpleasing building. I dressed myself carefully in a blue velvet day dress which made me look older than my years and someone to be taken seriously. The dress had been a gift from Mrs Pat, and a little of her personality still clung to it. However, I was nervous, which showed, and robbed me of some self-possession. Moreover, I was angry with myself for being nervous when confronted by this very ordinary man seated behind a plain wooden desk. I didn't even think him particularly intelligent, although it turned out that he had a certain skill in asking questions.

He got my name and address written down and extracted the information that I was governess at Sarsen Place. I could see the name meant something to him and I thought of the baby's grave.

'Ah yes,' he said thoughtfully. 'Had a little trouble up there, haven't they.' He looked at me keenly. 'Is it about that you wish to see me?'

'About the gypsy's baby? Oh, no.'

The expression which crossed his face at that moment convinced me that the police knew better than to think the baby the child of a wanderer and vagrant.

'But I see you don't believe it to be the child of a gypsy,' I said. 'It's more closely associated with Sarsen Place than that, isn't it?'

He looked at me and I thought he seemed troubled. 'I should think it's very likely, Miss Lamont. Are you sure you don't have anything to tell me? You *are* the young lady responsible for the finding of the body?'

I shook my head. 'I don't even know what sex it was or how it died.' I am thankful that my genuine innocence prevented me guessing what was in his mind at that moment, although I thought of it afterwards. He wondered if it might be my own child.

'A baby boy of some three months, Miss Lamont,' he said briefly. 'He seems to have died naturally. Probably not a very strong hold on his life, poor little fellow.' He paused, then said: 'So, it's something else you want to see me about.'

'I think I have something to tell you about the woman who was found drowned at Iffley,' I began. 'I read of her in the newspaper. You don't know who she is?'

'Not yet, miss, no. We will do so in time, I dare say. Unless you're going to tell me *you* know.'

'No.' I had to be careful how I phrased it. 'I believe I may have seen her. I think she followed me: she may have wanted to speak to me.'

'Had you seen her before?'

'I don't remember. I may have done. I can't remember where.' I had to be very careful here; I did not wish to involve my father. And it was true, I did *not* remember seeing her in his studio. But her portrait was there. 'I think she knew me.'

As he asked questions, I responded with the tale of how I had seen this woman in the street. At the end, having got what he could from me, he said: 'Perhaps it was just as well she never did speak to you. In her pocket she had a sharpened knife. She may have been going to use it.'

It was hard for me to absorb the fact that she might have wanted to attack me. Even when I had understood what he was saying, I found it hard to believe, and I sat in silence.

'Well, we'd better make sure it's the same lady we're both talking about, hadn't we?' he said briskly, getting up. 'You'd better have a look at her. Would you be willing to come down to the morgue?'

Now I sat very still, frozen into reluctance. My very feet felt heavy, and stuck to the floor with my repugnance. 'Yes,' I whispered. I found it hard to speak. 'Yes.' I forced myself to say the word.

'Her appearance will have changed. Will you prepare yourself for that?'

'Yes.'

How much does our identity depend on our physical appearance? The face of the woman before me on the slab had been rendered unrecognizable by the water and the manner of her dying, and yet something about her reached out to me and was acknowledged. Perhaps identity depends on the essential proportions of the body, and these she had retained, although prolonged immersion would have destroyed even this in time. I suppose everyone is impersonal in the end.

'Yes, I know her,' I said.

'Well, that's something established, then, even if not very much.' He covered her face. 'And you only saw her on these occasions you named?'

'Oh yes.'

'We're a little further forward, then.'

'And she *was* drowned?'

He was silent. Then he said: 'We are not quite certain yet how she died. There are some unusual signs.' Then, as if regretting he had said too much, he opened the door to show me out. I remembered Christian Ableman, whom Binny had heard called 'The Executioner'. This seemed my moment to speak.

'There is a man come into the city who is a dangerous criminal.'

He heard me out.

'So you say this well-known criminal is in the city, miss? Who did you say he was again?'

'Christian Ableman.'

He rubbed his chin, not giving away whether he had heard of Ableman or not. It was his job to have heard. But I suppose it was equally his job not to show when he was ignorant.

'And who says he's such an important man, miss?'

I was silent. I was reluctant to name Binny or Jack, even if either would have been regarded by him as a good witness. 'I've heard it,' I said. He gave me a long look. 'Have you seen this man yourself, miss, or is it all just hearsay?'

'I have seen him,' I said promptly, and, I now see, innocently.

'What sort of man is he, now?'

'Dangerous,' I said.

'I see.' Again he rubbed his chin. It seemed to be a habit of his when thinking. 'Perhaps you were deceived by appearances, miss. A bad-looking customer isn't always the most dangerous, you know. Can't go by looks. Just because he looks ugly and deformed don't mean he's depraved.'

'He's handsome and strong,' I said.

'Is he now?'

I felt myself flush, but I kept my temper. A woman has no chance in a masculine world unless she remains cool.

'You don't think, miss, that you've been upset by this business of the baby and allowed your feelings to get the better of you?'

'No,' I said, holding myself steady. I could see he had me written down as an imaginative woman.

However, he wrote down what I had to say, and, I thought, at the end of it all he took me more seriously than at the beginning.

'Children, you say? Yes, the old kidsman stuff is over and

done with. But there's lots of other uses children can be put to. Especially girls.' For the moment he looked grim.

'Thank you, miss. I promise you it shall be looked into and if this Ableman is what you say then he shall be dealt with.'

He rose and saw me to the door. 'Goodbye, Miss Lamont. We'll look after you.' He shook my hand politely.

As I walked away, I thought that I had not managed too badly. I had drawn the police's attention to Christian Ableman without mentioning Alice. To be laughed at, however, politely, as an imaginative woman was a small price to pay.

And, indeed, he had taken what I said and amplified it in a professional way. I thought I knew now the particular 'new twist' that Christian Ableman might have in mind for the children he recruited.

And yet I was logical enough to see that Alice Demarest could not be fitted into the pattern. She was a rich and cherished child, whereas Ableman must surely be looking for the nameless and unwanted children. Perhaps I was wrong to fear for Alice. But my mind was full of apprehension, vague and formless. That day in Alice's sitting-room I found something strange. I saw the edge of something white protruding from behind the small gilt mirror fixed to the wall above the mantelpiece. I pulled it out and saw that it was a photograph. I knew exactly what had happened: the photograph had been propped against the wall and had slipped between the mirror and the wall and not been missed. Or missed and not found. Or hidden on purpose.

As I stared down at the picture, I was looking down at Charles Demarest's face. He was standing there erect and soldierly, looking extremely handsome. Another person had once stood by his side but this part of the photograph had been cut away and only an arm and what seemed to be a woman's foot remained.

And on the back, in a round clear hand, was written, Mrs Charles Demarest, and then, again, Mrs C. Demarest.

I didn't believe it for a minute, of course. I had seen that sort of thing before. Mrs Charles Demarest, but no wedding ring. I had a strange feeling as I looked at the writing, as though some inward ear heard an echo. I could not disassociate myself, draw away entirely. Mary Lamont, I thought, there but for much education and some sophistication go you. I had a notion that this photograph could be the key to a great deal. I tucked it back behind the mirror in as secret a fashion as I had found it.

But it troubled me.

It was still early evening when I got home. I lit the fire, which my little servant had laid ready, and made myself some tea. Then I put a light to the gas lamp and got out my books.

I was in a strange state, my mind alert as if listening for some message it would presently receive. I drank my favourite Lapsang Souchong tea, leaning back in my armchair.

I thought about my studies, about the nature of Greek society. It seemed to be all about women. When I had translated Herodotus, the story had been about the women who knew all the secrets of the oracles. Now I found myself reading 'the position of women in law was extremely unprotected'.

So, I thought to myself, women know all the secrets and the law does not protect them, an interesting conjunction of thought. When I next saw Miss Clough, I must tell her this.

It seemed an apposite and an alarming thought as well, at the time.

Chapter Three

Next day a white mist rolled up from the river and covered the city. Oxford lay beneath a cold, damp blanket which muffled even the sound of the bells. I hesitated at the door for a moment, wondering whether I could face the journey up to Sarsen Place. But today, of all days, I didn't want to leave Alice alone. Alone except for a houseful of servants, of course, none of whom I regarded as wholly trustworthy. I had to go, but walking would not be possible. I turned myself towards the cab rank in St Giles.

At the end of the road where I lived ran a narrow passage which debouched into the wide cobbled thoroughfare of St Giles. This passage had on one side a huge old chestnut tree and on the other a yard belonging to a public house called *The Lamb and Flag*. I usually avoided this little passage because the smell of ale was stronger than the scent of the tree, even in high summer.

As I passed through, avoiding a deep puddle by the tree, a young woman brushed against me as she hurried past. She seemed a respectable enough young woman, who made a muttered apology as she pushed by. I could still see her figure just ahead of me as I turned into St Giles. I hurried but I never seemed to gain on her.

The great stone walls of St John's College hung above me in the mist on my left hand side. I could hear traffic passing on the road to my right, but there seemed no one else on the pavement except us two. Yet as I walked I began to imagine I could hear footsteps behind me. I turned to look, but I could see nothing. Only, as I walked on, I seemed to hear the feet padding softly behind.

In front of me was the hurrying woman, behind me this quiet tread. I was between the two.

There was one cab waiting. The cabby looked cold and miserable. Even his horse looked more cheerful than he did. 'Jump in, miss. Where to?'

'Sarsen Place, please.'

'I daresn't take my old horse up that hill in this fog for all the tea in China,' he said at once, cheering up, although he knew and I knew that no tea except strong sweet Indian ever touched his lips.

'Oh, drop me at the foot of the hill,' I said irritably. 'I'll walk the rest.' The woman walking in the fog had gone from my view, but as we drove off I put my head out of the window, and it seemed to me I could still hear footsteps.

I leaned back on the grimy leather seat and the sound of the footsteps was with me still.

Do people really walk so loudly in the fog that other folk hear them? Had there really been someone walking softly behind me or had I imagined it? Or had it been what is not quite imagination and not quite real, the calling up by my mind of feet that had once walked and now walked no longer. For I believe we do not see or hear ghosts, but make them.

Had I made a ghost in my mind from my memories of the woman who had waited outside my house and then been drowned? Had I created figures to walk the streets both before and behind me?

The mist was thinning as I walked up the last of the hill and turned into Sarsen Place. Of course, there were no ghosts here.

There were no Demarests either, except Alice. The train bringing them back from London was not running because of heavy fog beyond Reading. Even this was only speculation passed on from the stables to the kitchen and from the kitchen to Ellen and through Ellen to Alice and me seated at the tea table.

Mrs Ceffery appeared and drew me aside for a murmured conference.

'Fish in cream sauce do for the little lady's dinner tonight? Proper off her food, she is. You staying?'

I shook my head. I was disturbed by what she said about Alice, and made up my mind that when Mrs Demarest got back I would ask her to let Alice see Dr Bean. 'I'm going home tonight.'

'Pity.'

'Why is it a pity?'

'She's better with you here.' Mrs Ceffery was fussing with her stiff white cuffs. 'Feels safer, we reckon.' She was taking care not to meet my eyes.

'Safer? What do you mean?'

'Well, she's frightened, isn't she? Scared someone's going to do her in. Or take her away. Terrible nightmares, she has.'

'Yes, I know that. Do you have an idea of the cause?' Annoying and sinful as Mrs Ceffery certainly was, I respected her judgement, and I had every reason to believe in her acute observation.

'No, nothing has come my way that I can lay hands on,' she said with regret. 'And that's strange in itself, if you think; for I'm here all the time and see most things. No, it must be something outside the house. Something nasty's happened to her outside the house.'

'She's frightened *inside* the house,' I said.

'And how are *you*?' said Mrs Ceffery. 'You aren't looking yourself.'

'I'm worried,' I said.

'Aren't we all?'

'Ellen's going down to see Fenny this evening,' called out Alice, her eyes bent on the piece of bread she was spreading with honey. 'She says Fenny's getting better.'

'I know.'

'I thought she'd die.'

'I thought so, too,' I admitted.

'She's going to tell me all about it when she gets back. I'm looking forward to that.' Now she had her big blue eyes fixed on mine. 'Are you?'

'It's nice to be private with Ellen.' I turned away, not willing that she should see how her casual cruelty had hurt me. So Alice, like all the Demarests, could be arrogant and careless. Then, because she had said what she had and I was hurt, I went home that evening.

As I walked down the hill, I thought I saw the figure of Ellen flitting in front of me. But I supposed I was mistaken.

*

76

When I got home I went up the three steps to my front door and opened it with my key. Then I paused.

Just for a moment I thought I could smell tobacco smoke.

I closed the door carefully and took two steps into the narrow hall. I wasn't mistaken. It was tobacco.

At the fragrance I felt a rush of unexpected pleasure and relief. My father was back. Never would I have guessed how pleased I would be to have his casual reassuring presence.

I ran up the stairs to the little back sitting-room. I could see the light. The door was open. I rushed in.

'Father –' I stopped.

A tall figure arose from the armchair and faced me. 'Hello, my dear. I heard you were asking after me.'

'Christian Ableman!'

'It does me good to see you breathing fast like that.'

'How did you get in here?'

He laughed. 'Your locks wouldn't keep out an old betty boy like me.' He put his pipe on the arm of the chair. 'Come to think of it, you'd better have 'em changed or you'll have who knows what gonophs or trassenos in here.'

'Go away!'

'Haven't you heard about that old king who sat on the beach and told the sea to go out? You're like *him* and *I'm* like the sea. I'm in and I'm not going out. Not yet, anyway.'

Although his accent was not that of an educated man, it was not uncouth either, and he knew how to use the English language.

'You haven't screamed,' he said, eyeing me.

'There's nothing to scream about.'

'Not yet. There might come to be.'

'I suppose that's a threat,' I said.

'That's a stout heart beats beneath those pretty little breasts of yours.' He reached out a hand lazily to me. I drew back. 'You're more frightened than you let on: I can see you pant.'

I tried to remember my father's advice about what to do in case of rape. So far as I could remember, it resolved itself into shouting and having a container of pepper handy about one. I had no pepper and I was determined not to shout. It was true there was a box of snuff on the bookcase, but even if I could reach it I wasn't

77

quite sure what I should do with Christian Ableman when I had blinded him. He would still be in the same room with me, enraged and very strong. It seemed to me that my father's advice was more suited to an attack in the open air and that, like much of his counsel, it wouldn't *quite* do.

'I'm not frightened,' I said. (It wasn't true.) 'But I'm very angry.'

'You shouldn't have gone to the police. Why did you? I'd like to know. Speak to me home, mince not the general tongue.'

'I suppose it was you that sent me the note warning me not to speak,' I said contemptuously. I had an idea that words were my weapons and that with words he might be worsted. More than ever I found his speech puzzling.

'Didn't give you much of a welcome, did they? I know all about it.' He gave me a slow smile. 'A dangerous man, am I? And what put it into your head that I'm so dangerous?'

I didn't answer.

'Or perhaps I should say who?' he went on. 'Was it Binny?'

'No, not Binny.' I didn't want to bring his anger down on Binny's head.

'I didn't think so. Binny's an admirer,' he laughed. 'We know each other well, Binny and me. She knows how I'm dangerous and what for. As for you, you know nothing.'

'I know you're after children,' I said. 'You collect them. To use.'

'A lie,' he said, not discomposed.

'I know you're preparing a strong room like a prison.'

'Find it,' he challenged.

'A woman has been murdered. I dare say you knew her. I'm sure Binny did.'

'I've never killed a woman yet. Now that I can swear to. Everything else to them, but not kill.'

'I thought they called you the Executioner,' I said rashly.

He looked at me without speaking. Seen close to, his eyes had a strange kind of quality, at once cold and yet compelling. They were as clear and bright as grey glass and as hard.

'Don't touch me,' I said, moving back again.

'That's what you don't like,' he said, making it somehow half a question and half a statement in a strange unnerving way. 'There's nothing in that, one way or another. It don't mean you aren't willing.'

I had a very strong feeling that I would have to hit his face hard but I knew I must not be the first to use violence.

'It's very quiet in this little back room, don't you find? And if we close all the windows and doors we'll be as private as could be. I *like* to be private. I'm a private man and don't wish to be talked about.'

The door behind me was wide open and I had no intention of closing it. I took a tiny step backwards. 'Rubbish !' I said.

'Going to deny it at first, weren't you? But you couldn't. You were there all right. I have my sources of information. Not all policemen are above a touch, I don't mind telling you. Why, the word was round to me before you were home.' He smiled lazily. 'And I was round here before you had time to expect me.'

I took another small backward step. He reached out and took my wrist. He hardly seemed to move, but suddenly he was close to me.

At such close range I could almost feel the muscular tension in him, just as one can feel the heavy strength coming from a Giotto figure. The solid stance, the broad shoulders were formidable. I was frightened by him, but it was a deep, faraway fear, as if I couldn't quite bring it to the surface of my mind. He put a hand, firm and compelling on my arm, and I felt a strange ripple of emotion begin remotely inside me. It began deep down and rolled triumphantly through me until I trembled.

'Well now,' he said. 'So you're not a dimmick, after all.'

I didn't understand the word, but there was no mistaking what he meant. I had already observed in myself a tendency to certain inadmissable emotions to which I had no desire to put a name.

His grasp tightened and he seized my other wrist. I tried not to move: I knew we were poised together on the knife-edge of violence. I saw a bulge in a breast pocket and the gleam of metal. I knew a pistol when I saw one. He saw my look.

Holding both my wrists in one hand, he ran a hand over me. 'Not armed, are you, my dear? No, not except in the usual way. Flash in your eye, colour up in your cheek. I like that.' Once again

I was impelled to notice that, although not a gentleman, he was not rough. He could be coarse, though. 'We mustn't go off at half-cock, must we?'

When it came to the point I found I did not need my father's advice. Without thinking, just acting, I sank my teeth in his wrist.

He took a deep breath and dropped my wrist. I stared at him in triumph mixed with alarm.

At the same moment there was a voice from the stair.

'Mary? Mary Lamont? It's Amy Clough. Shall I come up? I came in, as the door was unlocked.'

I kept my head. 'Go,' I said to him. 'Go down the stairs and out. And be polite to Miss Clough as you go.'

'I came here to teach you a lesson, but I think you've taught me one. And I shan't forget it.' He threw me away from him.

My stairs are narrow and it is impossible for two people to pass each other on them without going very close. From the head of the staircase I watched him draw aside, bow slightly to Miss Clough, flash me a look, and go down, and out through the front door.

'What a very strange man!' said Miss Clough.

Strange things do happen, I thought. 'He came to see me because I called on the police,' I said.

'Oh, a policeman,' said Amy Clough doubtfully. Obviously he didn't look like any policeman she had ever seen in Oxford.

'He's from London.'

'Oh, London! Oh well, one knows London policemen . . .' Her voice trailed away. She still wasn't quite happy.

'I had a small piece of information about a woman who was found drowned. You may have seen about it in the newspapers.'

'Not I, my dear. How did you come to leave your door unlocked? That you should never do.' She was mildly reproving. 'Close it carefully as we leave.' She had double locks on her own doors, for all her non-interest in the police news.

'I will.'

But as I closed the door behind me I found that the lock was broken. I tried to hide the fact from my companion, but it was useless. She saw everything.

'My dear, the lock is broken. Did you tell your visitor?'

'Oh, he knows.'

She watched me wedge the door without comment. She herself had double locks and a maid who slept in. I walked to the lecture and sat through it, knowing that my house was wide open to Christian Ableman.

When we said goodbye I came home and sat through the night, sleepless, in a turmoil of emotions I dare not name, in case Christian Ableman came back.

Chapter Four

The next morning I packed my things together and put myself into a cab for Sarsen Place.

On the way I called on my dear American friend, Jessie, a constant pleasure in my life, even though I rarely mention her. I talked to her urgently.

'Hold on. Just hold on,' she said. 'There's nothing wrong in your feelings. It's natural enough. But concentrate. Work hard for the next few days. Work will be your salvation. The turbulence of your emotions will die down.'

She saw I was disconsolate. 'You aren't alone, you know. It happens to other women too.'

'Does it? Would it to you?'

'To me? No, not to me. I'm exceptional. I have no fire in me, you see.'

Sarsen Place was in a state of suspended excitement when I got back, much as the palace of the Sleeping Princess had been. All the adult Demarests had arrived back late the night before and were still asleep. From the hints and nods of the senior servants I learned that there was indeed a crisis. For the first time I heard the word 'divorce'.

Alice wore her pale alert look and had probably slept poorly again. She said little and was almost unfriendly.

'You didn't come back last night.'

'No.'

'I thought you might not.'

'Why did you think that?'

'You had your funny look. You've got it now.'

I looked at myself in the big mirror: face thin, eyes big, mouth tense. Yes, a strange look had settled on my features.

'That's the look. Take it off.'

All the arrogance I sensed in her father was in her childish voice.

'Alice!'

'It's a horrid look. You look as if something dreadful had happened.'

'I've had a lesson about myself,' I said. 'That always takes some enjoying.' Then I saw that she was trembling, not with arrogance but desperation. My mouth softened. 'Alice.' I put out a hand.

'That's better. You look nice again, now.'

'What is it, Alice? You're frightened.'

'No, not really. But people change don't they? You think "Oh, that's all right, I'm safe with that one", and then you look up, and their face is quite different, and you're not safe at all.'

It was the classic terror of childhood: the unreliability of the adult world which tells you loving lies and lets you down, or turns protectors into ogres. It is the root of almost all folklore and many fairy stories.

Who had terrified Alice? Who had turned from a friend into an enemy in front of her eyes?

'I don't change *very* much, do I, Alice?'

'No.' She was watching me carefully. 'But a bit. You all do. Grandmother not so much.'

'Yes, your grandmother is always consistent.'

'Only because she sees so little.' Alice's smile was jarringly adult.

'Let's open our books.' I wasn't anxious to embark on an examination of my employer with my pupil. I was beginning to see that Alice could be a clear-sighted critic. Nor was I sure that Mrs Demarest saw so little. In some ways, I thought, she saw quite a lot. In fact, I was puzzled by her grand-daughter's comment. I didn't dispute it, though, even in my own mind, because I was coming to see that Alice always had a reason for what she said. I thought I would observe Mrs Demarest for myself.

Alice was willing enough to set to work, and I could see that the task calmed her. She would always be a person who found her salvation in the intellect.

But, as she worked, I thought about her and wondered what

was wrong, and how far I contributed to it, and why she was like a child lost in a fairy-tale nightmare.

I kept guard by Alice carefully all that day. Perhaps I was wrong, perhaps there was no threat in the world to her, but I wanted to be sure. As soon as the older Demarests awoke and were ready to be seen I would talk to either her father or her grandmother.

Ellen appeared with their cloaks later in the morning, when it was time for Alice's walk in the garden. Mrs Demarest had instituted this habit of a walk before luncheon at Dr Bean's suggestion some weeks ago. Sometimes I went with the two girls, sometimes I took the opportunity to be on my own. I watched Ellen tuck them both into their heavy tweeds. What she wore was, I suspected, an old garment of Alice's. Probably one Alice had disliked, because it was by no means worn out. Seen together they were much of a height and size, with Ellen's sturdy plumpness hidden in the enveloping brown folds. I saw that her eyes were puffed and red as if she had been crying.

'Is anything wrong with you, Ellen?'

'I was late back last night, Miss,' she said. 'So Mr Prince had to punish me.'

'What did he do?'

'Said I couldn't go out for the next month or longer.' She sounded despairing.

'And that made you cry?'

'I shan't see my friends.' She meant Jacky, of course, but it wouldn't do to say so. Mr Prince would incarcerate her for longer than a month if he knew about Jacky, Nothing was more forbidden to a young servant like Ellen than a Jacky in her life.

'I see,' I said noncommittally, making up my mind to help her when I could. 'And how is Fenny?'

'Better.' But even this didn't make Ellen look cheerful. In fact, both girls looked wretched. I saw this and felt powerless.

'Go into the garden, then,' I said, turning away. 'I'll follow you in a few minutes.'

I was in my room for a few minutes and then went down the stairs towards the back door of the garden. In the little back lobby

I met Mrs Ceffery; she had her sleeves rolled up and was inspecting the game larder. 'That's ripe for eating,' she prodded a fat pheasant, 'and that and that.' Judging by the smells, it seemed to me that one or two of the occupants might be over-ripe for eating. 'What's that smell?' I said. 'That's a nice bit of venison,' she said. 'Nice and high, isn't it? The Captain shot it. Not the only thing he's brought down, hum, hum,' she gave her rumble of a laugh. 'Oh, he's a lovely man.'

She gave me a sharp look.

'Oh yes, handsome, indeed,' I said coolly. 'The handsomer of the two.'

'Yes, he has the master beat. And for manners, as well.'

'No,' I said, still coolly. 'There I think Mr Demarest has the better of him.'

She retired from the battle, having been unable to worst me. 'Well, I'm fond of them both,' she said. 'And so will you be when you get to know them better.'

'You like all men,' I said, over my shoulder.

'So do you, miss,' she called after me. 'Don't think I haven't noticed how you look at them. And why not? You've got two legs and a waist like me. So has the Queen, and Mrs Gladstone.'

I ought to have been angry with her, or abashed, or mortified, anything but amused, but in spite of myself I laughed, and within myself I admitted the truth; she and I (and possibly Mrs Gladstone) did have something in common. It was strange how the knowledge about myself which had distressed me this morning was converted, by Mrs Ceffery's joking appraisal of it, to something real and human. She had done more for my self-respect by being her Hogarthian self than had my friend Jessie. 'Women are human beings,' Mrs Ceffery was saying. 'You're a woman.'

As I put my hand forward to open the garden door I heard a piercing scream, then another and then another. Then silence.

I dragged open the door and stood there listening. The echoes of the screams still hung there in the calm air and it seemed to me the cries had come from the right. There was a short path leading through the shrubberies to an old aviary, long since disused. Alice kept a pet rabbit there and I thought it was where they had gone that morning. I ran out.

Mrs Ceffery was following me up the path, panting as she went. A gardener appeared up another path hurrying towards me with alarm on his face. I heard a window thrown up in the house behind and Mark Demarest's voice.

Outside the aviary, Ellen, her face bloodstained, was lying on the ground, her cloak flung about her, face up to the sky. There were trampled footsteps on the muddy ground. Alice was gone.

'Alice, Alice. Where is Alice?' I heard myself babbling.

Mrs Ceffery took a grip of my arm. 'Miss Lamont, come to your senses, it's Alice lying there.' She pointed. 'And Ellen that's gone.'

I put my hand to my forehead. 'I'm sorry,' I said. 'I was confused. For the moment it looked like Ellen.'

'They have the same face. Have you never noticed?' said Mrs Ceffery grimly. 'Come along, Fletcher, pick the child up and bring her into the house. Take her shoulders, Miss Lamont.'

'Ellen! What about Ellen?'

'We'll look for her later.'

Mark Demarest met us at the garden door. 'What's this? Miss Lamont, what has happened?'

'You heard the screams? We heard them too and rushed out. We found Alice . . .' I turned round, her eyes had come open and she was staring at me. 'Alice?' My voice rose.

She seemed to mutter something. I leaned towards her.

'Man.' This was what I thought she said. 'Man.'

'Who was it?' I asked urgently. 'Where is Ellen? Has she been carried off? How, Alice?' I was talking wildly. Alice looked at me vacantly, her eyelids began to close.

'Don't question her any more.' Mrs Ceffery was firm. 'With a blow like that she'll be out of her mind for a bit, poor child. Mop the blood off her brow, Miss, it's trickling all down.'

Mrs Ceffery was keeping her head much better than I was, and better indeed than Mark Demarest. He was paper-white and looked as if he might faint.

'Take the master inside,' commanded Mrs Ceffery, 'and I'll see Alice is put on her bed and the doctor sent for. Go to the master now,' she said, her voice urgent. 'He's going to faint.'

But Mark Demarest did not faint. He let me lead him into the library and pour some water from the silver jug on the big round table. When he had drunk it and sat with his eyes closed for a moment, he apologized.

'I don't think she's badly hurt,' I said. 'You saw for yourself she was conscious.' And, indeed, into Alice's eyes had come a look of recognition and I did not at all accept Mrs Ceffery's judgement that she did not know where she was.

'I must go to her.' But he still sat where he was. 'You don't think she is badly hurt?'

'No. But we shall have a better idea when the doctor has been. You stay here.' I started to move towards the door. 'Come in a few minutes when we have Alice tidied up and the blood removed. I know that for some people blood is . . .'

'No, it's not that.' He got up slowly. 'I'm ready now.'

In Alice's room were her grandmother, her grandmother's own maid, Mrs Ceffery (still in charge, although battling for position with Mrs Demarest), and the gardener, whom everyone had overlooked and who was standing by the door looking interested.

'You can go now, Fletcher, thank you.' Mark Demarest was in control again. He walked over to the bed, where his mother hovered anxiously. 'What happened, Alice? Can you tell us?' Alice stared at him silently. 'Have the police been sent for?' He looked round.

'No,' said Mrs Demarest.

'And where is the girl Ellen?'

'Gone,' said Alice in a husky voice.

'Where? How? Can you tell us?' He laid his hand gently on his daughter's.

'Ellen's gone,' said Alice again.

'We must know what's happened?'

'She can't tell you.'

'I'm worried about the other girl.'

'I know. So am I. But it won't do to badger Alice now.'

He walked away and stood by the window. 'What about the doctor?'

'On the way,' said his mother. She had somehow got rid of Mrs Ceffery, who was somewhat inclined to regard herself as the heroine of the moment (which to an extent she was), and we were alone in the room. 'Miss Lamont's right, we mustn't worry Alice. There's been an accident, clearly, and we must find out what has happened, but it must be done slowly.'

But Mark Demarest would not stop.

'Alice, was it you that screamed?'

She shook her head slightly, frowning as if it pained her. 'No.'

'Ellen, then?'

'Yes, Ellen.' She sounded doubtful.

'I don't think she really remembers,' I said. Alice looked at me gratefully. She let me take her hand and hold it in mine. I could feel her pulse, which was steady and strong. She had been stunned and shocked, but not, I thought, seriously hurt, although the doctor would have to tell us about this. But she was frightened. I got the impression that her sleeping nightmare had wakened now into life.

When the doctor arrived I went to my own room.

Mrs Ceffery tapped on the door and entered with a tray bearing a wine-glass and decanter.

'A little madeira. In case of shock.' I guessed that she had already tried a little of her own medicine. She watched me sip mine. 'The doctor's still here.'

'And the police?'

'Haven't come yet.' She took back the empty glass. 'I dare say you feel the better for that. I know I did. I was all shook up. Quite a scene, wasn't it?'

'Yes.' I didn't want to talk to her, but I knew I had to be polite.

'Funny thing about the little girls, isn't it?' Her eyes were bright and confidential. 'Them being so alike, I mean. Funny you'd never guessed about Ellen.'

'Guessed what?'

'She's Mr Demarest's natural daughter, you know. We think she's the child of one of the country girls down at his place in Dorset.'

'Does everyone know about Ellen? Does Ellen herself know?'

'Oh, no, only we upper servants,' said Mrs Ceffery. 'As for Ellen, not a thought of it, take my word.'

'I can hardly believe it, all the same.'

'Oh, it's true, depend on it. He's fond of her, too. I've sometimes thought him to be fonder of her than the other one.' She lowered her voice. 'And who's to say if he wouldn't prefer her to be his heiress?'

'Oh, Mrs Ceffery!'

'Well, a funny thing happened here today, didn't it? How do we know what's at the bottom of it?'

'You read too much police news, Mrs Ceffery.'

But she was not to be silenced. 'And then there's the Captain. Wouldn't *he* rather be his brother's lawful heir?'

'Oh rubbish, Mrs Ceffery.'

'Money's never rubbish, Miss Lamont.' She wagged her head. 'It's usually at the bottom of everything. Money and the other thing.' She smiled at me in triumph, conscious of having scored.

'Oh, but to make her the servant of his legitimate child! How cruel.'

'The gentry are cruel, my dear. Haven't you noticed?'

'But Mr Demarest . . .' I stopped.

'Don't make a God out of him. He's only a plain little man when all's said and done.'

Suddenly I was as irritated by Mrs Ceffery as I had been amused before. I was glad when she took the tray with the glass and departed from the room. Her broad back had no sooner retreated than there was a knock on the door.

'Will you go to Mrs Demarest, please miss?' It was Mrs Demarest's own maid who was speaking, a straightfaced woman who barely mixed with the other servants. She had lived a lot of her life in France and the other servants said she despised them. She certainly never had time for me. Even now she was polite but curt.

I wrapped a shawl round me, for I was conscious of feeling chilled, even in this warm house, and hurried after her. She took me to Alice's room. Mrs Demarest was still there and also the doctor.

'Mary!' Mrs Demarest seemed relieved to see me. Whether I was Mary or Miss Lamont depended on her mood. She was never unkind or rude but just sometimes she seemed unable to place me, as if she wasn't quite sure of my status in her world. 'You are to stay with Alice. A policeman has just arrived and will want to question her. You are to remain with her while he does.'

'And keep her calm, Miss Lamont.' Dr Bean smiled. 'I depend on you for that.'

Alice was lying flat in bed, looking at once composed and desperate. My recognition of the desperation in her was spontaneous and immediate. I perceived this quality even though I had never seen it in a child. 'That child is desperate,' I said to myself, just as if I had said 'She has measles'. I wondered her grandmother did not see it herself as she stood there so composed and elegant.

'She must tell us what has happened,' said Mrs Demarest.

She won't say anything, I thought. Nothing. Perhaps she can't.

I sat myself down by Alice as Dr Bean and Mrs Demarest left. For a minute or two I was silent. She sighed.

'Don't worry about the policeman.' I took her hand. 'I'll look after you.' She smiled, very very faintly. There was something chilling in the sight. 'Alice, what is it? Did you truly not see what happened?' Her eyes were big and dark. 'Or not recall?' I had heard that a blow shattered the memory. 'Is it about Ellen? What *did* happen to Ellen? Where is she?'

'Grandmother,' began Alice.

'Yes, yes, your grandmother. Do you want her? Shall I call her?'

'No, not grandmother. *La Jolie*,' began Alice, then she stopped.

'Jolly?' I said. It didn't sound right. I listened again.

'*La Jolie*.' She nodded.

'*La Jolie?*' I repeated, trying to make sense of it. The pretty lady?

From outside a hearty, masculine voice boomed into the room. I couldn't hear all that it said, but a little came through to me. Alice heard only too clearly.

'The little girl . . . come to get her . . .' I think he finished with the words 'get her story'. I heard this, but Alice did not. When I turned round to her she was lying back across her pillows unconscious.

She had fainted from terror at the words.

Chapter Five

It was an uneasy wretched time. I knew that several policemen were searching the shrubberies and outhouses. From an upstairs window I saw that they were working in pairs, and at intervals each pair would report to a central point where a senior police-man stood. From the shaken heads and the depressed looks I guessed they were finding nothing to help them.

I was told by Mrs Ceffery, although I saw nothing of it myself, that the police were also searching the immediate neighbourhood for signs of how and in which direction Ellen could have been spirited away. Certainly weary and mudstained constables were seen at intervals going into her kitchen to restore themselves with hot tea and possibly with something stronger. I went down to the kitchen on the pretext of needing some tea myself, and watched and listened.

'I'll take some tea by the fire if you please, Mrs Ceffery,' I said politely. 'Just a cup from the kitchen pot.'

She allowed this graciously: no orthodox housekeeper would have permitted it for a minute. I took the cup and stood by the fire, staring into its red heart and listening to the two constables sitting at the table.

They were talking quietly to each other, and throwing in an odd word to Mrs Ceffery at intervals.

'The stableman at the livery stables across the way says there was a covered wagonette by the gates just about the time the girl was attacked,' I heard one say.

'Might be an innocent tradesman's van,' responded the other.

''Tisn't one the lad knew, so I've heard. And if the lass was taken off, then this could be the means.'

'She didn't fly off, that's sure,' agreed the other.

'And the horse stood a few minutes – there's droppings.' The speaker finished his tea and made ready to leave. 'Thanks, ma'am,' he said to Mrs Ceffery.

I continued to stand quietly by the fire. Then I, too, left and went away unnoticed.

William Train was in the hall, attending to one of his clocks. Time seemed to be running fast these days at Sarsen Place. I had a terrible feeling of things hastening forward to a conclusion I could not grasp, as I stood there by his side. He looked up from the clock and nodded.

'I don't know what's the matter with the clock,' he said, confirming my suspicion that time was awry.

'I thought it wasn't the day of the month when you usually come to check.'

'No.' He closed the clock. 'I came up today especially.'

He walked with me to the foot of the stairs. 'And how's Miss Alice?'

'Asleep.'

Dr Bean had returned in haste and given Alice some chloral; she was now quietly sleeping. I suppose the doctor was right to put her to sleep, but from what I had seen of my charge lately her sleep was no refuge. She might prefer not to be thrust into the heart of dreams she could not escape from. But I have noticed that doctors, even humane doctors like Henry Bean, never heed considerations of this sort. The body to them is everything. Control the body, they seem to say, and we shall sway the direction of the mind.

Looking down on Alice's sleeping face on her pillow, I hadn't thought her slumbers particularly tranquil. Her eyelids fluttered, and she moved restlessly.

'You seem to know all about it,' I said to William Train.

'Oh, I do. Of course. What else do you think the servants are talking about? And then, of course, one of the policemen, Sergeant Ing, is a friend of mine. He thinks it's a professional crime, abduction, motives as yet unknown.'

'I see.'

'Yes. But the servants speculate that Alice was the intended victim and that her uncle is responsible. For the sake of the inheritance.'

'What monsters they must think the Demarests are.'

'No, just creatures of another race.' His tone was dry. 'And the Demarests reciprocate the opinion.'

It was true: the Demarests, although the kindest and most humane of employers, believed a gulf existed between them and their servants. This was why they found me difficult; sometimes I was in one world with them, and sometimes I was on an island all my own. They did the same with Will Train. When he and Mrs Demarest discussed the craftsmanship of Fabergé or the jewellery of Boucheron, then Will was an equal; when he wound the clocks he was not. It was quite simple and workable, really. I didn't mind. I liked having a foot in both worlds. Will Train's reaction was more ambiguous. Perhaps he did mind.

'Will, that rigmarole of the servants can't be true.'

'No, we are not living in the times of melodrama.' His voice was still dry.

'The policeman badly upset Alice.'

'How did he do that?'

'I'm not exactly sure,' I said. 'But somehow he said the wrong thing.'

'Did he talk to the child at all?' He gave me a keen look. One forgot how bright and perceptive Will's eyes were, because he hardly ever let one see them. He was always looking at something on the wall, like a clock or a picture. 'It seemed to me he came out pretty sharp.'

'So he did.' In less serious circumstances I would have been amused; the man had shot backwards out of the room like a character in a Feydeau farce. 'Perhaps it was just his voice.'

'Silly man,' said Will, irritably.

'Thoughtless and unlucky, perhaps.'

'She might have told him everything.'

'If she knows much. Perhaps she doesn't. But she'll probably tell me eventually, sooner than anyone else.'

'You must be careful, Mary,' he said urgently. 'Take great care. It may be dangerous to you if she pours out a story to you, and you are involved. She has been close to danger.'

'I'm not sure how much she herself is really involved, and how far I am truly outside it all. I have been close to someone violent myself.'

He looked at me in surprise. For a second I thought of telling all my worries and suspicions to Will, but the moment passed.

Later that day I had to go down into the town to do some shopping. I walked, enjoying the exercise and the unexpectedly fine day.

My errands were trivial. I suspected Mrs Demarest of having invented them to get me out of the house. She knew how much my spirits depended upon fresh air and exercise, and she was capable of little kindnesses of this sort.

She may also have had another motive. I had not missed the low angry rumble of masculine voices from behind the closed library door. I recognized the tones of Mark Demarest and the lighter voice of his brother. The Demarest family were angry with each other. I might have listened at the door, in a polite kind of way, of course, but even as I crossed the hall Charles Demarest came storming out and nearly knocked me over. He steadied me against him for a second, said: 'My apologies, Miss Lamont,' and hurried on. His brother watched him from the door; then he turned back into the room, giving the door the tiny bang of the controlled but angry man.

So, although it was kind of Mrs Demarest to see that I took a walk in the afternoon sun, she was also mindful of herself. She had smiled at me and told me to enjoy the air. What she didn't know was that I wanted to see my American friend Jessie again.

Mrs Demarest had sent me to a chocolate shop in St Giles to pick up a box of French bonbons, and Jessie lived above the shop. When I say lived, she was hardly there at all, but she kept three rooms, one for herself to sleep in, another to work in, and a third for visitors. Jessie's visitors could range from Marie-Louise Boulanger, the noted French socialist, to Lady Agatha Spencer Haddon, who was organizing a welfare centre in the east end of London and was famous for her flaming hatred of drink, drugs and almost any pleasure except hard work. This she adored. Jessie said life was a trial when Lady Agatha came to stay, but it was worth it because Agatha was an organizational genius and knew how to set up a machine and then retain control of it. Jessie intended to learn from her. Jessie's own work took her from the Haddon Settlement to meetings with Mrs Fawcett about Women's Emancipation and back to the book on ancient philosophy she was writing in the Bodleian Library. This book was not strictly speaking her own work. Jessie's true work was more subversive. I liked and admired her but I had to admit that, at heart, she was a wrecker.

'I'm an *agent provocateur* for women's emancipation,' she said to me once. Jessie didn't talk about herself much, but to me, now and then, she did. 'I stir things up.'

'But you wouldn't betray them, would you, Jessie? That's what *agents provocateurs* do in the end.'

'Oh yes, I would, if the silly creatures didn't benefit from what I taught them,' she said coolly.

'Don't you like women, Jessie?'

'Not if they won't help themselves.'

Yet she wasn't hard, and she took in Rose Blanc, who was the daughter of Louise Blanc, and had fought in the Paris Commune, and Vera Zasulich, a silly woman if there ever was one.

Mrs Pat and Mary Ward were Jessie's sworn enemies. I suppose in a way I was quite frightened of Jessie myself.

But before I called on Jessie or at the shop I had an errand to do for myself. Walking quickly, I made my way to my father's studio. The little road was quiet and empty, except for one woman cleaning her windows till they shone in the sun. A sad labour of love, because it would surely be rainy or foggy before morning. I looked around carefully but there was no sign of Christian Ableman. He could be watching from a door or a window, but to me he was invisible.

I got out the keys to the studio. Once again I was on edge and sharply observant. There was no sign that anyone had tried to break open the big front door, but on either side of the lock were scratches, as if someone had tried to force the lock. The attempt had been unsuccessful. I smiled. My father, negligent in so many things, was careful in matters of this sort. The lock was new, strong and of an advanced type. I let myself into the peaceful interior. For a second I stood on the threshold but was soon convinced that no one had set foot inside the studio since I had been here last.

I went over to the picture I had studied before. Drawing it out once again, I set it on an easel. Then I drew up a drawing table, laid out paper and crayons, and sat myself down to make a copy of the face of the lost lady, *L'Inconnue*.

I have no real talent, but I have been taught to draw, and some of my father's skills and tricks have descended to me. I knew I could make a reasonable job of this. I suppose the work took me about twenty minutes, and at the end of it I had not only an adequate copy of the face in the picture, but also a clear likeness to the woman I had seen. My own pencil had perhaps been more creative than I knew.

I put the picture back, carefully hiding it behind several canvases as I had found it. Then I dusted my hands and sat down for a moment to admire my work. The couch was soft and I realized that I was tired. I sat there, mindlessly enjoying its velvet comfort. I never understood why father kept this Turkish divan in his workroom, but I supposed he rested on it sometimes like me now. As I got up reluctantly, my gaze fell on the long bolster pillow which formed one end. Across the green velvet was a shallow indentation. The indentation of my father's head after so many weeks? Perhaps it was. It was, however, something to consider.

In the distance I heard Great Tom, the clock of Christ Church, strike four o'clock and I knew I was late. I got my things together and hurried on.

I collected Mrs Demarest's box of bonbons from the chocolate shop and then ran up the narrow stairs to Jessie's door above. I hoped she was at home. I rapped smartly, using the little brass knocker in the shape of a dolphin. Presently I heard Jessie herself slopping along the passage in her flat slippers which she imported specially from Turkey to wear with her Liberty dresses. She looked at me dreamily for a moment, far away in thoughts of anarchy and rebellion. Jessie, I should explain, is not poor. In fact, she is a living example of my thesis that to be an advocate of radicalism you need a certain income. In spite of her opinions Jessie is received everywhere and is welcomed indulgently in many celebrated houses because she has a large income in dollars and her father was American Minister in Rome. So Jessie can dare many things I cannot, and I know it.

'Oh, hello,' she said. 'Come in. I've been very busy. This evening I am having a meeting.'

She might just as well have said 'I'm having a coven', she sounded so rapt about it. I often thought that Jessie, two hundred years before, would have been a New England witch.

'Can I have a cup of tea?'

'If you're quick.' She had her eye on the clock. 'We begin soon.'

When she had poured the tea and I had drunk a little, I produced my drawing.

'When you visited Tinker's, did you ever see this face? You went there several times, didn't you? And met most of the girls?'

'Yes, a hopeless lot. Not one of them listened to a word I said. Couldn't seem to take it in. Didn't listen, didn't care. You'd think women with that sort of life would see the point of women's emancipation, wouldn't you? But they seemed happy as they were.'

'No, not happy exactly,' I said. I knew them better than Jessie did. 'But they think they are doing the best for themselves they can. And some of them *will* end up with smart little houses in Brompton.'

'And others in an accommodation house in Covent Garden,' said Jessie sharply.

I nodded. I knew they thought the risk worth taking. For women there were few professions which offered a chance of riches. Perhaps the stage was the only other.

She picked up the picture and studied it. 'A poor drawing,' she said absently. 'Bad style. The line is weak. Who did it?'

'I did. I'm not asking for an artistic judgement. Do you know her?'

'Yes, I seem to know the face. I did see her once or twice. A French girl I think.' She laid the picture down. 'Why? What's the matter with her?'

'She's dead.'

'Oh.' She raised the picture and looked at it again. 'How?'

'She was drowned.'

'Oh, poor thing. Did she drown herself? It happens with girls like that?'

'She was killed.'

Jessie looked startled. For all her anarchy she was not in touch with violence.

'Well, poor thing.' Jessie's mind always worked well, you could rely on her for that. 'She called herself Louise de la Vallière, I think. I don't suppose it was her real name.'

'The police say they have no idea of her identity.'

'I shouldn't think that's true for a moment.'

'No, I don't think it is. They must know all those girls up at Tinker's. But they must have some reason for denying it.' So the dead woman was important to the police. One of my father's worldly aphorisms is that we only suppress things that are deeply important to us, an observation that makes me wonder sometimes about *him*. Apparently very open, my father contrives to let you know very little. For instance, although he had written to me several times from Paris and each letter had two or three pages, his big sprawling handwriting filled the pages with a few words and less information. He was painting, he was happy, the weather was fine; that was the tally of it.

'Yes. I think they are very interested in Tinker's and keep a sharp eye on it, although they pretend the place isn't there at all. They certainly knew I had been there those two occasions, because the Chief Constable, whose daughter plays tennis with me, managed to say he didn't think it was a suitable place for me to go to.'

No one would carry tales about me, I thought. Unless it was Christian Ableman. No doubt he was known there.

'What did you wear when you went there?' I asked. Suddenly it seemed important.

'My newest dress and my great-aunt's pearls,' said Jessie promptly. 'You won't get in there if you look as if you're carrying a bible.'

I laughed.

The sunlight had faded when I got out into the street, and it was beginning to be night. The street lamps were being lit, and as I walked along St Giles I was following the lamplighter. Precisely and neatly he hooked at each lamp with his long pole and the gas jets flared into life. He did the job with the economy of effort that came from long practice. Behind him he left a little flower of gas blooming on its metal foliage. The effect, to one in my heightened mood, was strangely pretty. The lamplighter was an elderly man whose face was known to me. As I passed I saw he had a magazine sticking out of his hip pocket. It was far enough out for me see what it said. TALES OF CRIME, I read, THE TORTURE CHAMBER. I had a moment to reflect on the powerful and deep-rooted taste in the common people for tales of crime and horror and to wonder from what lives of frustration and boredom it sprang. The lamplighter turned and looked at me. We were close enough to speak and I saw he wanted to.

'Good evening.' His voice was unexpectedly gruff, as if some accident had injured his vocal cords. His eyes were pale blue and red-veined, not particularly kind, not particularly friendly. 'I was told to look out for you. We all was. He says to be careful and not to use your tongue too freely.'

'*He* says?'

'You know who.' An unpleasing little smile flowed across his lips and disappeared. He hadn't touched me, hadn't even come very near to me, so it was odd how I had the feeling of a physical encounter. I didn't look back to see him moving along the street behind me.

A policeman moved out from the edge of the road and said: 'Was that man offensive to you, miss?'

'No, oh no.' I licked my lips. 'He only asked me the time.'

The policeman looked sceptical as if he knew a tale worth two of that. 'All right, miss.' He walked on.

I don't know why I didn't tell him and yet I do know. Christian Ableman. Christian Ableman. Christian Ableman. I hated to say the name, but it was always there at the back of all my calculations.

I was well on my way home to Sarsen Place, almost there, when it occurred to me to wonder why the policeman had been so observant of me.

It came to me then, in one of those uncomfortable moments of illumination, that I was an object of interest to both the police and the criminal world.

*

The evening was no time to go to Tinker's. Business was done then, when the pink lamps were lit and the velvet curtains drawn. Afternoon was the time to pay social calls, when the ladies had risen to their late breakfasts and were drowsing through their time of leisure. To some of them, of course, it all looked like leisure. 'The work's not hard at Tinker's dear,' said one of them to my father, in my hearing, 'for we have our regular days and our regular callers, too, some of us. And we're very well treated in the matter of clothes and food.' I saw her smooth her satin skirt. She was called Amabel by some, but mostly Mabel. 'I don't know where else I'd get a silk like this to wear, *and* made to fit me. And they're all my own, you know. Oh yes, I can keep my clothes if I ever leave.' I remember my father handing her to the door with especial gentleness and politeness that day; he had moments of great humanity, my father.

I settled in my mind that I would go to Tinker's on the afternoon following to see what I could find out about Louise de la Vallière, whose picture in my father's studio had the words 'the unknown' written on it in French. I do not believe in coincidence and the violence which had struck her and at Ellen and Alice must have a connection. I had other good reasons for meditating a visit to Tinker's. It was not only Louise. When I had first picked up the photograph hidden behind the gilt mirror in Alice's room, I had at once noticed a particular smell of patchouli and cigar smoke which I associated with one place and one place only: Tinker's. I have always been particularly sensitive to smells and I could swear this photograph had, at some time, been at Tinker's.

I put my hand into my pocket and took out my gaming piece, my ivory dice.

I spun it round and threw, carefully, slowly. A six would take me to Tinker's.

I got a six straight away.

Then I cheated a little. *Two* sixes it had to be, I said to myself. So once again I spun and threw. The ivory cube fell on the table, hesitated on one edge and then fell lazily over.

My second six: the devil's throw. But there was an evening and a morning to be lived through first.

I was glad to be back in Sarsen Place. Alice was awake and

ready to be amused. I read to her while she had her supper, talked to her cheerfully, and asked no questions.

I could see from her face that no answers would be forthcoming.

Mrs Demarest met me outside Alice's room when I had said goodnight.

'Is a nightlight burning by her bed?'

I nodded.

'And *still* she says she remembers nothing?' said Alice's grandmother.

'It could be true.'

'It must be if she says so. Alice is so truthful.' Her grandmother sounded distressed.

'She is.'

'The doctor says there has been no concussion. It must be shock. And yet we must find Ellen. I have had them searching for her all day.'

Alice didn't want to talk. I didn't blame her, but it was absolutely clear that she was in a state of terror. She was on her guard with me, her family, even the doctor. I had seen the truth in her watchful eyes.

'You're very fond of Ellen,' I ventured to say to Mrs Demarest.

'Yes, of course,' she replied absently. 'She's a good child. And she's my responsibility.'

'And I suppose you've known her family a long time.'

She didn't answer.

Every story has so many sides as it has people in it. If I am telling this story as my own voyage towards love and self-discovery it is also a story of crime. All the time the police were at work. I kept my eyes and ears open and learned that there were two detective officers at work, young men, from the newly created Detective Office in Oxford. They worked on the new system of careful interviews and minute checking of statements. There was nothing slapdash about their work and nothing was to be taken for granted; they were trained men of a new type. I have an idea they were not over-popular with all the local constabulary, some of whom were of the old slacker sort.

Everyone in the household was interviewed. My own interview was very quiet and formal. I felt that I was protected by being so close to the Demarests. All the same, I was aware I was being quietly assessed and I knew that if I failed to tell the truth or to speak precisely, it would be noted and remembered. I would not go so far as to say they suspected me of anything criminal, but they were watching me and wondering.

They were silent men. Discretion was their watchword. Even Will Train's friend in the Oxford police, who was one of the old sort, could get nothing out of them, although I know he tried.

In the privacy of my room that night, with the fire burning brightly and my lamp on my writing table, I considered my position. I had spoken to no one except Alice and Mrs Demarest, and that briefly, and had seen hardly anyone else since my arrival back at Sarsen Place. The Demarest brothers were still shut up together. Even my dinner had been served in my room by a silent servant. The parcels I had brought back from the town that afternoon still rested, untouched, on the library table, which confirmed my suspicions that Mrs Demarest hadn't really wanted them and had only wanted me out of the house.

It was inconceivable that any harm could come to me here in Sarsen Place or at Tinker's the next afternoon. In an underhand kind of way I was persona grata at Tinker's, where I think they still thought of me as the child I had been in my father's studio, without grasping how adult I had now become.

After a little thought, I sat down and wrote a letter to my father.

The first page was full of domestic detail, such as the need to refurbish the sitting-room curtains, how the hard frost had killed a little shrub in the garden, and so on. Then I went on to more disturbing matters . . .

'I think it began before I ever came to notice anything amiss. It must have started, as trouble, in the days before the French girl was found dead in the river. *She* knew about it and possibly wished to tell me. Or she may have been watching me at the request of others. I *am* watched now. But even as early as this autumn I was troubled about Alice. She is unhappy, Father, as no little girl should be, and she fears something. Now she and Ellen, her maid, have been attacked and Ellen has disappeared.

'Has Ellen been kidnapped instead of Alice, and by mistake?

You see, the two girls were dressed alike. The servants even say that there is a family resemblance. They hint that Ellen is Mark Demarest's natural daughter.

'Now, it may be that I am involved because I am Alice's governess, or because I am your daughter and thus was known to Louise de la Vallière, who may have wanted to confide in me. Or possibly I am independently involved, on my own account, for a reason I do not know.

'I called on Binny in Rosemary Court and I think she resented my questioning her about Louise de la Vallière. Or, more likely, she resented it on behalf of some friends. What it seems to be, Father, is a plot to kidnap Alice Demarest. But Alice has an enemy and this enemy is sometimes very close to her at Sarsen Place. Her own behaviour is perplexing. She knows more than she tells me. There is a lot of the picture I do not see, I believe.

'If this is so, Father, then very probably I should not go to Tinker's; and yet I am convinced that I am physically, mentally and morally stronger than those girls there, so how can they possibly harm me? So I *will* go.'

There spoke, I reflected, the girl of the late nineteenth century, advanced and adventurous by her grandmother's standards, perhaps a shade obstinate and self-assertive.

I sealed my letter, and posted it that evening.

In the night Alice moaned and screamed. I went to her at once. Her room was cold and dark; the nightlight had burnt out. She stopped screaming when I shook her awake, but started to shiver.

No one came to us, in spite of the noise she had made, and I think it was then that I realized how cut off this wing of the house was. Alice's bedroom window was open and I walked across to shut it. I looked down and saw that a descent could be made from her room to the ground by means of a monkey puzzle tree which stood outside. No other room was similarly gifted. Perhaps it meant nothing.

I didn't say anything to her about her screaming. I didn't know what to say. I was beginning to think she had plenty to scream about. Instead, I said, brutally and quite deliberately: 'Have you been thinking about Ellen and wondering what has become of her?'

Alice's eyes looked huge and blank, but I saw understanding flash into them. 'I don't know what's happened to Ellen.'

'But you've got a good idea.'

'No. I don't know where she is.'

'But you know who attacked you both? Go on, Alice, tell the truth, you do know.'

She was absolutely mute.

'What about Ellen?' I said. 'Don't you care about Ellen?'

'Yes.' She started to cry. 'She's my firm friend.'

'But you won't help by telling what happened? I'm sure you know. You know something. You can't deceive me as easily as the policeman. I'm sure your grandmother wonders about you, too.'

Alice gave me a startled look. She didn't like what I'd said about Mrs Demarest.

'Grandmother never notices anything,' she said.

'She's noticed this.' I put her shawl firmly round her shoulders. 'I despair of you, Alice. Here you are, a very clever girl, who certainly understands a good deal of what goes on in the world around you, and yet you won't be sensible about this. You won't tell someone adult what trouble you and Ellen are in.'

If I had thought to frighten her into a confession I was out of luck. Alice was made of tougher metal.

She shook her head. 'I don't understand what you mean.' She had her imperious Demarest face on. 'Leave me now and I will go back to sleep.'

I felt like slapping her. But she looked small and cold and white and I was, in a way, very fond of her. I took a deep breath. 'You're cold. I'll get you a drink.'

I made my way quietly down to the big kitchen. The huge kitchen range had still a heart of red fire burning in it. I fetched some milk and heated a little in a copper pan. The kitchen clock struck three as I stood there waiting. It was the lowest ebb of the night. I yawned.

By the strict rules of protocol that prevailed in the household I knew that I should not be in the kitchen at all. What I should have done was to have awakened the housemaid who would have aroused the under-cook who would, no doubt in a fury, have heated me a little milk. All this sort of thing was Ellen's work; she was the one who bridged the gap between nursery and kitchen.

The milk rose up to a foaming mass like a white pudding while I thought about this. Ellen came and went between the two worlds. As sharp and observant as Alice, she had an excellent chance to see almost everything that went on. Ellen was not the innocent bystander just caught up in trouble. Whatever was happening in Sarsen Place, she was as deep in it as Alice.

I looked about me. Ellen did not have a room of her own. She slept with the other maids in a bleak room upstairs. I had never seen it, but I knew enough of life in the servants' quarters to know that anything Ellen wanted to keep private she did not keep up there. Indeed, she would be hard put to it to have any private hiding-place of her own. But across the room from where I stood was a small cupboard with open shelves above, covered with the dishes and china which we used upstairs in the schoolroom when we were there. This cupboard would be in Ellen's charge.

I put the cup of milk on a tray and walked across. The cupboard door opened easily and inside I saw the neat stacks of rose-sprigged china. It was simple stuff compared with the rich blue and gold Worcester porcelain used in the dining room, but I liked it best of all. I knew from the marks on the back that it had come from France. Here were several chipped and cracked pieces. Ellen must have quite a heavy hand with the china. I bent down and swiftly searched inside the cupboard. Tucked away at the back, behind a serving dish with a broken lid, was a cardboard box carefully tied up with string. The box was small, about the length of a hand. I hesitated for just a second before stretching out my hand and taking the box out. I put it on the table and untied the string. Inside the box were a small blue notebook and some sheets of paper with writing on them. I looked at the notebook, and saw that it was closely written in Ellen's hand and was a sort of diary.

I was reluctant to invade Ellen's privacy too readily, and put the book aside: for the moment anyway. The papers I felt less scruple about. I took them out; in fact, there were three, and on each was written the same:

Say nothing and cause no trouble
or we will come and get you.

The handwriting was, as in the message I had received, simple and yet clearly formed. Without a direct comparison it was impossible to be sure that it was by the same hand, but I thought so.

Without conscious thought, I replaced the box and its contents in the cupboard. One way and another, I couldn't see Ellen examining the box in the near future.

I carried the tray upstairs to Alice, who must have wondered why I had taken so long, although she did not say so. She received her hot milk without a word. I sat and watched her drink it.

'Friends?' she said, hopefully, as I tucked her up again.

'Friends, of course, never anything else.'

'I hope not,' she said soberly.

'Don't open the window again and get cold,' I said.

She turned and looked at the window. 'I didn't open the window, Miss Lamont,' she said. Then, without another word, she put her hand under her cheek and closed her eyes. I was dismissed.

One way of getting out of Alice's room was through a little ante-chamber, formerly a dressing-room, in which Ellen occasionally slept. I went through here and I saw that one or two of Ellen's possessions were about, as if by these simple means she had tried to impress her character on the room and claim it as hers. It was a harmless enough thing to do. On a table was a drawing of a cat with the legend underneath 'Ellen's cat Tibby drawn by her when she was six'. Ellen at six hadn't made a bad job of it. And by the little white bed was a blue shawl which I knew to be hers because I had seen her wear it. Underneath the bed was a pair of slippers with 'Ellen' embroidered on them.

It was hard to believe that the owner of these girlish treasures could have penned the missives I had found below. But it did occur to me that the girl who could plant about the place such conspicuous evidence of her identity might not be so ignorant of the servants' hall gossip about her as I had supposed.

Back in my room I found I could not sleep. In any case it was now nearly morning; I could dress and begin the day's studies. The luxurious ways of Sarsen House kept all the rooms warm with hot-water pipes, and I did not find it hard to betake myself to my work table. But once there it was hard to keep my thoughts on Greek history, to think about the Bronze Age and Homer rather than the problems of me, Mary Lamont, in the last quarter of the nineteenth century. And I began to consider whether perhaps I had let the dramatic events of the last few days obscure my judgement. How much of what I thought I saw of plots and intrigues was due to my own imagination and how much was real? The letters were real, the disappearance of Ellen was real, the drowned woman was real, but the rest might be a cloud of romance thrown up by my mind, fevered by its contact with a new and stimulating force. How much had I made up because I didn't know what to make of Christian Ableman? Was I moving in an invented dream? A woman in my position had to handle her dreams with circumspection. I did not know what might become of me in the future, but I knew it would be determined by the flames that burnt inside me. They could create a future for me, or burn me up. This is what happens to women. I knew the history of Mary Wollstonecraft, dying in childbirth, creating Mary Shelley, to whom Frankenstein in turn was born. 'Women are great fools,' she said, 'but nature made them so.' I think what we are acquiring in our generation is the power to outwit nature. Which is, after all, what civilization aims at, the control of dangerous forces. But nature, I knew, has a power of popping up like a jack-in-the-box. Pushed down at one point, it will come bursting forth elsewhere. Sexual respectability, is alas, essential. For me even to think of Christian Ableman (how dare I, how could I?) was madness.

Now the thought was out of my head and walking round the room. I almost groaned aloud. I did like the man. I had had days and nights to think about these things, and this is what they had resolved into.

But was I creating an artificial adventure to escape from the real one?

In this dead secret hour before the dawn, my thoughts were low and bitter. I had intended to solve Alice Demarest's problems, but I was face to face with my own.

The clock struck six in gentle melodious tones. All the clocks in Sarsen House were a pleasure both to see and hear. But in spite of the efforts of William Train, few of them were accurate time-pieces. This one was no exception. A glance at my watch pinned on a velvet stand before me showed me it still lacked twenty minutes to the hour. Very soon now the first stirring in the house would begin, and the little between-maid, the lowest in the social scale in the household, would creep out to sweep the grates and rebuild the fires. I felt sorry for her, a girl not much older than Alice and younger than me, obliged to get up at this hour for such a dirty job. Our paths were so far apart that I had never seen her and only knew of her existence by the fires that were flowering into light and warmth every day as I came down. However, side by side with these fine feelings, came the thought that if she *was* lighting fires she might as well light mine first.

I went in search of her down the back stairs. I could see a light burning and smell that peculiar smell that freshly lit paper and sticks make. I turned into the kitchen, once again feeling sympathy for the hands that had built the fire.

I ought to have known the comfortable ways of Sarsen Place better. It is true that a small figure in a large print overall was in the kitchen, but the fire there was already burning brightly, and there was a pleasing smell of hot tea floating from a large brown pot on the table.

The maidservant looked at me, surprised. 'Good morning, miss.'

'Good morning.'

'I'm just taking up Mrs Ceffery's cup before I has my own.' She looked at the tea-pot. 'Would you like one, miss?'

'Yes, I would.' I suddenly realized that there was nothing in the world I would like more than a fragrant, hot cup of tea.

'It's very strong, miss. Mrs Ceffery likes it strong.'

'I like it strong, too.' I accepted the dark brown liquid and cooled and weakened it with plenty of milk. I sipped it with pleasure; it was very good. For Mrs Ceffery, of course, it would be good. Who eats and drinks better than the cook in a large household?

Then I became aware that the girl was looking at me in a worried way. 'Are you all right, Miss Lamont? I mean, you're up and dressed . . .'

I looked down at my dark serge. 'Oh, there's nothing wrong. I was working.'

'Oh yes, miss.' She looked slightly surprised. 'There's not usually anyone up at this time but me and the kitchen cat.' The latter, a huge black neutered tom, was sitting by the fire, staring at me in a bored way. I put out a hand to pat him and he simply looked past me. The girl seemed to be in his confidence, however, because she said in a soft voice: 'He does miss his friend, Miss Alice's cat. That was a sad business.'

'It was before I was here.'

She shook her head. 'He just disappeared.'

'Cats do.'

'Oh, not that one, miss. Always around he was, you could fall over him any time of the day, you could. He was always either stretched out on the stairs or on the rug before the fire or sitting on Miss Alice's bed. He did what he liked. A real little king, he was.'

'And he just went away?' I sipped my tea.

'Or was took.' She sounded gloomy. 'I kept my eye on this fellow afterwards, I can tell you.' The cat gave me a knowledge-able stare. 'Take more than you know to catch me,' he seemed to be saying. 'Mrs Demarest had the grounds and the stables searched, but there was never no trace, not a whisker. Mrs Ceffery says Miss Alice has never been the same child since.'

'Oh?' I pricked up my ears.

'Of course. Nurse Mackenzie left at the same time. She'd been here a long time.'

'Did she disappear, too?' I said, half jokingly.

'Not her. Left to go to London and better herself. So she said.' She screwed up her face and looked knowledgeable.

'But you don't think so,' I thought. I looked inquiringly.

'She was going to get married to a gentleman in the grocery business that lived in Brixton, which is north of the river, so she said, although Mrs Ceffery said she didn't believe it. But we have heard since she's been seen in Greenwich, which is south of the river, as everyone knows.'

I reflected that it was very difficult to escape the vigilance of those who kept Sarsen Place running. And doubtless if they didn't know a piece of news they made it up.

'Or a woman very like her at all events,' said the girl, confirming my thoughts. 'Mrs Ceffery's brother's wife's sister who's married to a policeman told us. And if it was her that was seen she was a good deal thinner than when she left.' She gave a meaning laugh. I knew what she meant, that Teresa Mackenzie had been with child. Pregnancy is the common hazard of all women, I reflected ruefully, from the Queen to the girls like Mabel and Teresa. I knew there were methods of guarding against it. Conception could be controlled by the method jovially called 'La Chamade'. I wondered if my friend Jessie would not be best employed as a propagandist for this delicate subject? Surely the control of unwelcome pregnancies was their best method of liberation for women?

She seemed willing to go on talking. 'Won't Mrs Ceffery want her tea?' I said, sipping my own.

'Oh no, bless you, she's never in a hurry in the morning. And I never puts the tray *inside*, just knocks and leaves it on the table *outside*.' She gave a giggle.

Not so young and innocent as she looks, I thought, or Mrs Ceffery's even more indiscreet than I gave her credit for.

'Still, I ought to be getting on.' She picked up a tray, and I saw with interest that Mrs Ceffery allowed herself a very nice choice in china indeed. Not French from the Sèvres factory or Worcester but a pretty Wedgwood in blue and white.

She set off up the stairs, leaving me alone in the room. I finished my tea and got up. The black cat got up, too, stretched leggily and asked in a hoarse voice to be let out. I was willing to co-operate, and I went to open the door. This door opened on to a small lobby with the big back door to the garden at the end. The outer door was bolted and locked. 'Sorry, puss,' I said. He gave me a sour look and leapt lightly to a window. I moved the catch, pushed the window open and he jumped through in one single bounding movement, and without a thank you, either. I closed the window.

The back lobby had two doors on the right hand side which

obviously opened on to pantries and closets. On a wooden board hung a set of household keys with labels bearing words like 'garden shed' and 'china pantry' and 'lower hall back'. On the wall opposite were pegs for coats and cloaks. One of the top cloaks was a dark plaid that I connected with William Train. Probably he had left it here absentmindedly, on one of his calls. But at the end of the row was a black woollen mantle that made me feel cold.

It was so like the cloak I had seen Louise de la Vallière wear the night she had stared at me through the river mists. One black cloak so much resembles another, how can you be sure? I put out a hand to touch it. My hand came away with a sour ammonia smell to it. The cloth was damp with a lingering residual moisture as if it had dried slowly.

I walked upstairs slowly, my heart sick. I had made enough discoveries for one night. I did not want to believe that this cloak had gone into the river with Louise de la Vallière and then, mysteriously, returned here.

Because, apart from anything else, the really alarming thing was that it was my cloak.

Chapter Six

Upstairs again in my room I fumbled myself into my proper day clothes, deliberately choosing my richest and best. Try as I would, my fingers were cold and would shake so.

There was no mystery about where the cloak had gone, only where it had now come from. It had formed one of a parcel of clothes I had passed on to Binny in Rosemary Court, not to sell, although she did insist on giving me a few coins, but because I had thought they might be useful for someone in need. The cloak was not worn out; but I had, strangely at my age, gained an inch in height in the last year and it had grown short. So I gave it to Binny. Perhaps Binny had an answer to why my cloak had now appeared back in Sarsen Place or perhaps she had not. In any case, Binny would only tell me the truth if she thought it in her own best interests. And I knew from experience that truth, when it did emerge from Rosemary Court, often had a strangely dishevelled air, as if the struggle had been intense. A short sojourn in Rosemary Court would have disabused any philosopher of the idea that truth was absolute. Truth is not absolute, it is relative; and in Rosemary Court more than anywhere else the truth varied according to the narrator. I could ask questions in Rosemary Court and so could the police, and I would get one answer and they would get another, yet both answers might be true, in a manner of speaking. My father said that life there was a constant reminder to the artist that truth, like beauty, was in the eye of the beholder.

There was an air of strain abroad that day in Sarsen Place. Even the ease and gloss of this prosperous household could not withstand the shock of having a child of the house attacked in the grounds and a servant apparently abducted. In addition, the police had returned in force and their appearance all about the house and grounds was a strange feature of the day. The servants were nervous and silent. Even Mrs Ceffery seemed a little daunted and didn't emerge from the kitchen all the morning.

In the event, it was easy for me to escape that afternoon. Alice went back to her bed to rest and read, Mrs Demarest retired to perform whatever mysteries she did perform in her white and blue sitting-room, and no one asked me where I was going.

I went to Tinker's.

Tinker's had another name. It was called Starlingford House, and I believe this was the address the tradesmen used on their bills; but those who visited it called it Tinker's. There wasn't a Mrs Tinker or a Lady Tinker or a Duchesse de Tinker, and the origin of the name was a mystery to me. The presiding genius was a Mrs Sanctuary, a plump lady whom I had seen at a distance. I think my father did not like her very much, for he said of her only that she was a good businesswoman and not paintable. I had noticed that he could always paint the people he liked. But that she *was* a businesswoman was borne out by the impression Tinker's made! Behind the ease and luxury she so cleverly imitated there was no mistaking that it was a commercial establishment; the most unsophisticated could not have been deceived. And when you come to think about it a double impression like that is both clever and desirable; it makes the position clear from the very start.

It may seem surprising that I was so open-eyed about Tinker's, when many girls of my age would have pretended to understand nothing and then whispered about it in private; but I have always found it difficult to profess an hypocrisy I do not possess. And then, too, my father was so apt to speak the absent-minded truth to any of my questions.

So arriving at Tinker's presented certain problems to me. It wasn't just a question of turning up and offering a visiting card. In any case, as an unmarried girl I didn't have any cards. However, there were many ways into Tinker's, and one of the best was a side door through a conservatory. It was locked, of course; one of the characteristics of Tinker's was that its doors were always locked, but someone always came, day or night, if you rang the bell. But to get in by any door it was essential to be well dressed and, as Jessie had realized, not to look like a visiting evangelist. They had had one or two of those at Tinker's, come down from London specially on purpose, but I believe they cut no ice with the inhabitants and went away abashed. I wore my green moiré silk and matching hat. It wasn't my own taste in clothes and, like so many of my more expensive clothes, had been the gift of Frances Pattison, who bought many fashionable garments and then capriciously discarded them. This set, dress, hat and mantle, had been made by Madame Blanche. They were new this season, but Frances Pattison said they gave her a migraine every time she wore them, though in fact I believe she disliked them because the green cast a sallow reflection on her pale skin. I dare say they did the same to me, but I had a healthier, rosier look and could stand it.

I pulled the bell and waited. After a minute I heard a dog bark. One of the pleasures of home provided by Tinker's, together with down pillows and embroidered counterpanes, was a pack of little dogs. They were white, with flat faces and a keen bark. I believe the progenitors of the group had been smuggled out of the Summer Palace in Peking.

The barks came nearer and nearer and eventually, to a fusillade of light yaps, the door was opened for me by a thin servant in a black dress, looking like an unfrocked nanny.

'Good afternoon,' I said. 'I want to see Nancy.'

'Not at home.'

'Mabel, then.' Nancy was the cleverest and most observant of the girls, but Mabel really suited me best. I had wanted Mabel all along, Mabel would talk more, but I knew better than to ask for her first, you had to use diplomacy at Tinker's. This may sound as if I was a constant visitor but, in fact, I had only been there twice before, when I had seen straight away that deviousness was the key.

'Mabel's having a little rest.' My smart dress was being eyed and appraised. I smiled, hoping I looked like a friend of Mabel's who had made good, or bad, depending on the point of view.

'Tell her it's her friend Mary Lamont.'

'I could ask,' she agreed, eyeing the cut of my jacket. The

little dog had stopped barking, because he was chewing the frill on my skirt. Then he stopped that and stared up at me with black eyes, bright and unfriendly.

'Not fond of strangers,' said the woman.

'How difficult of him.'

'No, not really. We give him an introduction to every gentleman that comes more than once, and then he's all right.'

No flicker of a smile on her face. He'd met *me* more than once, but no matter, no introduction would ever be effected between us, or desired.

'Well, can I come in?' However, I was in, and the fact that she had let me slide through the door unimpeded meant that no hostile message had been sent back about me. They had *some* method in Tinker's of checking on visitors, but I had never discovered how it was worked. Probably a peep-hole high in the wall.

'She's just having a little lie-down, but I dare say she would come along. What name did you say?'

'Tell her it's Mary Lamont.'

'That's a nice name,' she said appreciatively. 'Not fancy, but got class. Well chosen.'

'I like it.'

'You don't want to overdo it with names. Some girls are so silly.' She sighed.

Like Louise de la Vallière, I thought, choosing the name of a king's mistress. Much good that had done her.

'To my mind you can't beat a real good English name with a sort of tone to it. Here you are, sit you down here and wait.'

She had shown me into a small room with a moss-green carpet and deep green velours chairs. A gilt clock stood on the shelf over the fire, which was well alight. All the same there was an atmosphere about the room of windows that were never opened. A small urn of bronze stood in front of the fire and within it some oil burned with a pungent yet pleasant smoke.

'You look as though you could do with a rest yourself.' She gave me a look up and down. 'Been overdoing it, have you?'

'A little.'

'Well, I dare say Mabel won't keep you long.' She nodded kindly as she closed the door quietly behind her.

I sat down in the opulently soft seat and found that I was giggling. A multitude of emotions welled up inside me and found expression in this simple feminine way.

Mabel did keep me waiting, of course, long enough for the hand on the clock to move round fifteen minutes. Then she came rushing in with a little flurry of merino and swansdown, pretty and silly and shrewd all at once, as usual.

'Guess what,' she said, making a little moue of anger and impatience. 'I think I'm knapped.'

I didn't pretend not to understand her. The word had filtered through to my child's comprehension years ago.

'What will you do?' I was disconcerted and saddened.

'Well –'

She gave me a sideways look. 'That's telling.'

'Oh, Mabel.' I was deeply shocked, for I knew what she meant.

'Lord, don't take on so, my dear. Anyway, it may all be a mistake.' She sat herself down comfortably. 'I shouldn't have talked to you about it, I suppose.'

'Oh, what rubbish.'

'Well, it is rubbish, and to tell you the truth I mentioned it because I thought you might help me. Oh no, not with *that*,' she gave a titter, 'but I'm thinking of taking a short holiday and Mrs Sanctuary agrees with me, all in all, that a break would be good for me.'

'Where will you go?'

'Well, that's just it, I'm thinking of going to Paris, and that's where your dad is.' She gave a jolly laugh. (How did she know?) 'I thought you might know of the address of a nice set of rooms or a pretty little hotel' (she said 'purty') 'and I'll be off. It's providential, you coming. I was *praying* for some advice.' I was not in the least surprised to hear about Mabel praying. She did it all the time: for a new hat, to get the set of her hair right, to have someone give her a present. And all to a simple-minded, open-handed deity with a strong interest in women's fashion. The strange thing was how often she got an answer. As now.

116

Difficult as it was to equate it with modern theology, it looked as though Mabel was a child of grace.

'I do know the name of a *pension* where I stayed myself. It's very plain and even austere.' I was doubtful. 'Would it do for you, Mabel?' And would you do for it, I was thinking.

'Oh, I can make myself comfortable,' she laughed again. 'And remember I'll be on holiday. Not working,' she hinted delicately. 'I might take some French lessons. It always does a girl good to know some French.'

'You won't learn much French in a few weeks, Mabel.'

'Oh, just a few words, dear. I don't actually want to learn the whole language. Just a little bit here and a little bit there, *you* know. I can bring it out later with good effect.'

I nodded.

'There you are, you see, it's all worked out. Write the address down for me before you go, won't you, Mary. I'll look your dad up, of course.'

'He's a difficult man to contact if he doesn't wish to be found, Mabel.'

'Oh, gone off on a lark, has he, then? I always thought it of him.'

'He's painting,' I said coldly. I hoped he was.

'He might paint me. That time he painted me was the best time of my life,' said Mabel wistfully. 'Perhaps it'll all come again. It *was* lucky you dropped in.'

She seemed absolutely convinced I had come in the answer to prayer. Perhaps I had, who could say? Perhaps the whole perplexity in which I found myself had really been confected by some master-magician in order to get me here for Mabel.

'And so you're staying at Sarsen Place? Now that's a respectable house. I shouldn't mind an establishment of that sort myself. Who knows? Girls have been luckier.' She gave her delicious giggle.

'Yes.' But I remembered the baby's grave and thought that Sarsen Place had its shadier side too. 'Did you ever hear of a gipsy girl burying her baby in someone's garden, Mabel?'

'I don't know any gipsies.' She bridled slightly. 'But it don't sound likely. I should look closer to home.'

'So I think. It's Sarsen Place, Mabel. Any guesses?'

'Sarsen Place?' She looked startled. 'My lord, that's news, that is. Be a poor servant girl, I should spec'.'

'Yes. Perhaps. But it takes two to make a baby.'

She tittered. 'We all know that, dear.' She looked at me shrewdly. 'And you're wondering *who*, I suppose. They keep a good staff of menservants, don't they?'

I nodded. But I thought I could understand the impudent defiance of placing the grave where it was if the father bore the name Demarest.

'Or it could be one of the gentlemen,' speculated Mabel. 'The younger one is one of the lads. Known here, he is. Yes, I'd say so.' And she rolled her eyes. 'You'd never guess his particular thing. He leaves a photograph. If he's well pleased he hands out a picture of himself. Some of us girls have had ever so many,' and again she giggled.

'I had something else I wanted to ask you, Mabel.'

She smoothed the fluttering swansdown on the blue merino morning gown. A little frown puckered her pink forehead, but soon she had that smoothed away, too. 'I hope I can answer it for you, Mary,' she said. 'I'm not very good at answering questions. I try. I try to answer as I should, but it doesn't always come out right. I can remember my mum saying to me, Mabel, she said, you don't seem to know what the truth is.' She reflected sadly for a moment on her lack of honesty, and then she said earnestly, 'But I tell you something I've learnt, Mary, truth isn't always what people want. They say it is, but it's not the case. That's something I *have* noticed.'

'As a matter of fact, you always tell the truth,' I said.

'I do? How?'

'You let it out, Mabel. It comes out with every movement you make and every breath you take.'

She looked at me for a moment and then said, in a tone different from any she had used before, 'You know, Mary, I usedn't to think you were like your father, he's a gentleman with such a nice way to him, a girl could never feel ill at ease with him; but now I see you are. I see a likeness. You speak the same way.'

'Do you know Louise de la Vallière?' And I produced my drawing.

Mabel picked it up and looked at me. 'Lord,' she said. 'I should say so. I should just say I do know her.'

From outside there started up the noise of a small orchestra, violin, cello, piano, and horn. Four instruments only, I judged by the sound. All the same it was making quite a noise. It was one of the features of Tinker's that there was music and dancing. I had forgotten this fact, and obviously I had strayed into rehearsal time. Mabel got up and ran to the door.

'They're beginning a polka. I do love a polka, don't you? I must watch.'

'Oh, Mabel.' I followed her along a short corridor to where two rooms had been opened up to make one big space. 'Oh, Mabel,' I sighed.

Mabel watched the orchestra and the dancers, a pair as wild as gypsies, her own foot tapping. She was like a child.

'About Louise,' I began again.

'Oh yes, Louise.' Her eyes were following the swirling dance. 'You know her? Know about her?'

'Do I?' The two girl dancers were prancing round like game young ponies, banging loudly with their feet. Even I could see they had a bizarre sophistication, a wildness that was marvellously well poised. 'Don't you just love their shoes?' They were wearing high-heeled red slippers with black velvet ribbon, and not a lot else.

'Oh Mabel, whatever can I do with you?' I had the words out before I realized what I had said. Until that very minute I had never understood I *meant* to do anything with Mabel. But I saw now that I had been nurturing a plan by which Mabel was to be emancipated from Tinker's and set up as an honest working woman somewhere. 'Saved', in short. I was as bad as Jessie. But what could you do with a creature as feckless and pleasure-loving as Mabel? I saw now that if I *had* ventured to suggest one plan or another she would have turned me aside with an incredulous laugh. 'I *prefer* this to slaving in an old shop. I'm saving money. *Quids* of it.' What could I do for a girl like Mabel? How stupid I was. Mabel had the odds weighed up better than I had. I was a messenger bringing glad tidings to a land already converted to a different religion.

The music had come to a peak and Mabel's blue merino and swansdown wrapper was swinging round her ankles as she tapped in time to the rapid beat.

'I came to ask you about Louise because she is dead,' I said.

'Oh, oh?' Her eyes opened wide. I could see the pale blue irises and the dark pupils, contracted in the light.

'She used to work here, didn't she? Answer me, please, Mabel.'

'Work? Oh, yes.' I still didn't have her full attention. The dancers were repeating a portion of their dance which had apparently not pleased them. 'She wasn't really up in things, though, dear.'

'What do you mean?'

We were not the only people watching the dancers. Across the room were two other girls, both wearing loose gowns and with their hair on their shoulders. With them was Mrs Sanctuary, looking as sleepy as usual. She glanced across, and saw me.

'What do you mean about Louise?' I repeated.

'She wasn't one of us; she looked after our clothes.'

'A sort of ladies' maid?'

'That's it.' She saw the humour and gave a giggle. 'But what her past had been, Miss Mary, I do not know.'

'Was she indeed French?'

'I don't know; perhaps she was, she spoke in a foreign kind of way. It was pretty. She came from Soho, but it's very foreign there, isn't it?'

The music had stopped again and the dancers were taking a rest. All about me I could see evidence of lavish expenditure, which, even if not to my taste, showed the hand and eye of someone remarkable. There was a barbaric force and splendour about the jagged splash of colour. It was exciting and new. I could see that it was in style different from anything I had ever seen before. One wall was draped in deep purple, a scarlet divan heaped with golden cushions stretched against another. There was a good deal of black about and somewhere a touch of emerald green. The ceiling was hung with brocade, like a tent, and from the apex of this tent a silver moon swung, like a decoration from a book of Persian miniatures. It was slender, elongated, more elegant than any moon that ever shone in the sky. The whole effect of the room was jewelled, startling and very original. It was as if a camp follower of Genghis Khan had swept in to do the decorating. I had never seen anything like it in my life before.

'Oh, I do love a dance, don't you?' said Mabel. 'I wish they'd ask me.'

'Who were her special friends?' I asked.

'No one. She didn't have anybody.'

'I thought you were all friends here,' I said, a bit sardonically, perhaps.

'Louise was different.'

'Why was she different?'

'Because of what she was . . .' She stopped.

I frowned. '*What* was she then?' I asked. 'Tell me, Mabel, what was she?'

'She was . . . she was a sort of messenger.' Mabel looked frightened. 'Oh, no, don't take any notice of me. You know I'm always silly, dear.' And she gave a little laugh to show how silly she was. I found myself not believing in the laugh. 'Silly Mabel, silly Mabel.'

'What does that mean, Mabel? Never mind the silly Mabel. What sort of messenger was Louise?'

'I hate messengers, don't you? They never hear any good of themselves, do they?' Mabel was fidgeting from one foot to another.

The twin girl dancers were coming out on to the floor to start again: or perhaps they were not twins, just two girls as beautifully matched as a pair of carriage horses as they stood poised ready to dance. One of them smiled faintly. All the time her lips were curved in a smile; I suppose it was how you told her from her sister. Her mirror image stood facing her. The musicians began, the girls swung into the dance. This time it was not a polka, but a dance I had never seen before, perhaps their own invention.

Mrs Sanctuary walked round the room and joined us. I looked at her without a word.

'Visiting us are you then, Miss Lamont?'

'I came to see Mabel.'

'Ah yes.' Her gaze flickered to Mabel. 'Nancy was your first request, I believe.'

She had a sort of fiddling precise way of speaking. It had crossed my mind that she might, in the past, have been one of my ilk; a teacher, in short. I could see her in front of a class of country girls teaching them reading and elementary arithmetic, always with that reserved smile on her face.

Now I came to think of it there were a lot of smiles on faces in this room, perhaps including my own; but none of them seemed to offer much promise of real joy.

'Nancy is out, I was told.'

'She's back now, I understand.'

'Then I could see her?' Perhaps I didn't want to see Nancy; I was just testing the ground.

'I don't see why not. Shall I lead the way?' Smoothly she moved ahead. In a little while she would have moved out of sight round a corner without looking back, so confident was she I would follow her; but I called her back.

'I shan't see Nancy now, Mrs Sanctuary.'

'No?' She turned and raised her thin eyebrows; I fancy she was near-sighted, there were the lines of a frown between the brows and it seemed to me that she didn't really read my expression from where she stood. In her profession it was no doubt a decided advantage to be short-sighted.

'No, I am leaving.'

The girls were dancing again, grave and gay at the same time. The music was beautiful, a sort of mazurka. I supposed it derived remotely from a piece by Chopin, but some extra quality had been added.

'But I think Nancy would like to see you,' said Mrs Sanctuary, still in that well controlled voice.

'Then I'd like to see Nancy,' I said, thoughtfully. Nancy was cleverer than Mabel and much harder. She had a wonderful appearance, with black hair and a pale white skin; my father said she posed beautifully and had been one of the best models he had ever used. He said also that she was a girl of some education. On the other hand, she had never had much to say to me. I turned. 'Goodbye, Mabel.'

Mabel grasped my hand in her soft white one. 'Oh, goodbye. Everything works out, you know, I've often noticed it.'

'I'll remember that, Mabel.'

'Oh, do.' But she still stood there.

'Run away and finish your rest now, Amabel.'

'Just going, Mrs Sanctuary.' And she moved away with a drift of swansdown.

I watched her retreating back, wondering if she was, indeed, as she so inelegantly phrased it, 'knapped', and what would happen to her and the child if so. But there wouldn't be a child. She'd made that clear enough.

'I'll just get Nancy,' said Mrs Sanctuary, and she led me back into the room where I had met Mabel. The contrast between this room and the fantasy of the room I had just left was extreme. In this room I was back in the familiar scenery of my own era. The other room had reached backward, and yet forward to a world evolving.

I sat down on a green plush seat and waited for Nancy.

I wondered what Nancy wanted from me or why she wanted to see me. I could visualize that proud dark face. My father had painted her as Queen Dido, then destroyed the painting. He said he hadn't liked what had looked out at him from the canvas. I could see Nancy full of self-destruction, in despair, like Dido after Aeneas had left her. It would be an act of self-murder if there ever was one. It was my belief, although I never said so to my father, that Nancy's life here *was* a life of self-destruction, embarked on to avenge herself on all men because of the act of one man. I had seen her look at my father in a way, ironic and mocking, that did not make me think she liked the opposite sex. I used to think that there must have been a bitter taste to any pleasure they got from her.

The small gilt clock over the fireplace said five o'clock. It was later than I had meant to stay. I must soon hurry back to Sarsen Place.

123

I walked over to the door and grasped the gilt handle. It turned, but the door did not yield.

I was locked in.

I rattled the handle and pushed against the door. Stupid behaviour, for which I now reproach myself, but the truth is I was as frightened as any little country mouse caught in a trap. I *was* a little country mouse caught in a trap.

The cheese had been offered me and I had walked in.

For a few minutes I was too flustered to do anything except stand by the door and rattle the handle and call. No one answered, although I had a feeling that someone was standing just outside the door, listening. Then the presence seemed to move away and I was alone. Hardly a comforting solitude, however, as it allowed me to consider where I was and wonder for what purpose I had been locked in.

There were several possibilities, all of which boiled down to the fact that I had been stupid. I hesitated to use the word silly, because that implies a sort of simplicity, and I had not acted so because I was simple, but because I thought I knew the rules of the game. One of the rules was that Mary Lamont would always win. It was an unconscious rule and, I saw now, a mistaken one.

The fire was still burning in the basket grate and I went to sit by it, comforted by its heat and light. My thoughts were less cosy.

A possible reason why the lock had been turned on me was that I had been caught as a prize object for the collection, to add to the Mabels and Nancys and Roses. This possibility I dismissed straight away. The establishment was run, I was convinced, on hardheaded business lines, and I was unlikely to be good for business. Was I like Mabel? Was I like Nancy? And the answer was, no. In short, they did not need me. More, I was a dangerous captive, on whose behalf forces would be rallied which would bring the whole house down upon them. I had not particularly taken to the detective in Oxford but I had no doubt he would be capable of finding where I was in a short space of time and without much difficulty. No, I was no Turkish captive incarcerated in a harem. (Was it my dream to be? I sincerely hoped not.)

The other possibility was that my inquiries about Louise de la Vallière had touched a tender spot. As she was dead and had probably been killed, then I was in danger. Great danger, I was inclined to think. I had a strong chance of being found floating in the Thames myself.

There remained one other thought: Christian Ableman. Supposing the door should open and he should walk through? He had walked away once, but he had not finished talking to me. In the sort of world he lived in a man could not afford to be worsted by a woman. Jessie would say that in this world no man ever could.

And yet, of course, they were cheated all the time at Tinker's, whether they knew it or not. They were swindled, because, whatever price they were paying for the pleasure and amusement at Tinker's, it was higher than they knew. Mabel and her colleagues weren't getting paid in quite the gold coin they supposed, either; they were a lot of false moneyers in this house, paying in false coin to everyone. Nothing was true or real, not the pleasures offered, not the pain received.

And here I was, in the house of the women, where they knew all the secrets. I suddenly realized I was living out the phrases in my classical texts.

I stared in the fire, silently assessing the thought. It changed the texture of my experience. I was neither a mouse in a cage nor a free agent. I was a word staring out of a page.

My mood was broken into by the sound of voices. I moved across to the door. Outside I could hear quiet speech. I tried to listen through the crack, but all I could hear was an occasional muttered word.

I drew back. There was something familiar about the tones of one muttered voice. I was sure I knew it. There was a quality about this muttered voice which both irritated and alarmed me. Of course, I was considerably alarmed and irritated already, as I was discovering there is always room in the human cup for one drop more of discomfort.

I hammered on the door and shouted, 'Let me out, let me out.' But all that happened was that the muttering stopped and the feeling of a human presence disappeared and I was alone again.

I went to the window. It was locked, immovable.

I went back to the fire and sat down again. It was stuffy by the fire but I was unaccountably warm and yet shivering at the same time. On a small round table was a decanter on a silver tray with a flask. A silver label round the neck read 'Brandy' in an ornamental script. With a decided hand I poured some and drank it down quickly.

Probably it was under the influence of the brandy that I suddenly rose and went over to the door and put my eye to the keyhole. At first I could see nothing except a patch of the corridor wall opposite. There was also a decided draught. I stared for a minute, but I could see very little, and went back to sit moodily by the fire. Next to the brandy was a small leather box. I opened it and saw, not to my surprise, that it contained cigarettes. I took one out and held it between my fingers. I had never smoked one, although my father did so constantly, and I was accustomed to see Mrs Demarest puff away delicately in the quietness of her boudoir. I lit the thin cylinder with a spill from the fire, then I put it to my mouth and drew one or two quick breaths to keep it alight, as I had seen my father do. A puff of smoke went down my throat, and I choked, but after this I managed quite well. A thin fragrance hung on the air. I began to see that the process might be enjoyable. I leaned back in the little green velvet chair, which soon seemed of surpassing comfort. Dreamily I thought that I wasn't really wasting my time shut up in this room. I had drunk some brandy and I was smoking my first cigarette. The little clock chimed the quarter hour.

The fire in the grate had died down and the whole room was bathed in a rosy glow. I thought how attractive it was and how clever they were at Tinker's, so that even the fires obeyed the rule of pleasing. I lay there, enjoying the colour, which seemed to rise and fall delicately, as if the fire was breathing.

Just at the edge of my vision, the room faded into shadow,

and the shadow wavered. In the depths of such a shadow I saw the door move. Had I turned my head I could have stared straight into the opening door, but I stayed still.

Then Christian Ableman came into my vision. He was dressed exactly as I had seen him before, in neat plain clothes that could have been worn by any man.

'So it's you,' I said, my voice calm. 'Was it you I heard whispering outside the door?'

'Not whispering,' he said.

'Stupid,' I said.

'Many things are stupid. But not me.'

'I suppose I knew it was you all the time.'

'And *I* suppose that is why you came here.'

'A monstrous thought.'

'I know when people are looking for me.'

'I came here . . .' I found I didn't quite know how to finish the sentence. 'I came here to see a friend. To make an inquiry.'

He laughed. 'Get up from the chair.'

'No, certainly not.'

'Then I shall make you.'

I put my hands over my eyes. The colour from the walls was sinking into my eyes and entering into my brain. Everything about me felt warm. Without any more prompting from Christian Ableman I should rise from my chair and sink into his arms. I felt weakness mounting within me.

Then there was a gap in my self-knowledge, and suddenly I was standing in front of him, and my eyes were open.

'I knew you'd come here.' He sounded triumphant.

'But that's impossible. I didn't know you were here,' I said.

'Of course you knew I was here. I sent you a message.'

'I had no message.'

'I sent it by a secret messenger, and you got it secretly.'

I put my hands to my head. 'This is madness.'

'People usually come to my messages, and if they don't I have ways of ensuring it.' This was his first hint of violence. Then I think he put his hand round my waist. I don't remember this very clearly, but then I think he kissed me.

It was not my first kiss. William Train had kissed me once,

behind a big clock, slyly, and to my astonishment. But that had been a cold, dry, experimental kiss; and this one had warmth, with a strength which carried me away. Perhaps it was a fancy of mine, but we seemed to stand there a long time. Outside, distantly, I heard the music start up again. The tune I could not detect, only a resonant beat.

'Last time we met you taught me a lesson,' he said. 'Now I have taught you one, and a good little pupil you are going to be.' His hand caught at my dress.

How strange words are. Now, when I write this down, 'grip' means nothing – a short, dull word. Then, it was a gesture of infinite promise.

I looked up and saw his eyes. They were large and bright and round, hardly touched with emotion at all. They seemed, in that moment, eyes which knew nothing of control or discipline, eyes which looked as they would, never veiled, never pretending to emotions they did not feel. I saw that his was a gaze that did not look forward and could not look back.

'No,' I said.

'You don't say that to me. No one does.' He managed to make it a proud statement. Probably for him it was. People have strange sources of pride. I quite liked him for saying it, really, it seemed in character. No doubt he thought it was true. It was the sort of thing people always believe of themselves. Never mind that No as big as a house had been said to him the second he was born. Birth, none; fortune none; education, very little. I would lay hazard that he was a bastard by a servant girl or a dancer like Mabel, but from whom? No father had dandled that fierce poppet on his knee.

'Neither a borrower nor a lender be,' he said. 'Just a taker.' He looked at me. 'Go on, you're the same.'

Yes, I was a taker, I knew it. If it had not been for my father and the money his painting earned and the education it had bought for me, if it had not been for these things, I should be what Christian Ableman was now: a lost soul.

'No,' I repeated.

'A lesson has to be learnt,' he said.

'That isn't why I came,' I whispered.

'It's what everyone comes *here* for.'

'I came because of Louise de la Vallière.' The words seemed to echo round the room.

All the pleasure faded from his face. 'You blower. You flammer,' he said.

I didn't know I knew such words. And then he said something which I was not sure I could hear. 'A witch hunt. You're wrong to do it, wrong to do it.'

Wrong to do it. Wrong to do it. The colour from the fire seemed to get into my eyes. I felt them watering, almost like tears. The room began to spin around me, and I moved to the chair by the fire, and closed my eyes. I no longer felt drawn to Christian Ableman or even noticed his presence. When I touched my cheek, it was as wet as if I had been crying for a long time. I put my hand down to my bodice and fastened the buttons which had come undone.

The clock chimed six silver strokes. The fire looked dim. I was alone. Christian Ableman had gone. He must have left the room at the moment I ceased to feel his presence. I'm sure he knew he was banished, we seemed strangely bound together in our thoughts.

I stood by the dying fire, and tried to get my bearings. My head ached and I was very thirsty, but I shuddered away from the decanter of brandy. 'I must have been mad,' I said to myself, 'or drunk'. It may be salutary to know that one has the weaknesses of one's sex, and I now knew that Mabel and I were sisters beneath the skin, but I felt I had had enough of home truths for the moment. What I needed to feel was the old Mary Lamont back again. Time, which, as we all know, changes its speed according to the principle of pleasure, had passed with the quickness of a dream while I was with Christian Ableman. It was a sinister fact, but true. It showed me that I was in danger of falling into a pit, perhaps had already done so, and must dig myself out again. I took some deep breaths of air, and was pleased to notice that I was steadier. The dizziness, whether of emotional or physical origin, had passed.

I walked over to the door and pulled; to my surprise, it was still locked. For the first time I was really frightened.

Perhaps I was in the pit and should never get out. What was it Christian Ableman had said? The words were coming back to me. 'I ought to dewskitch you.' I pressed my lips together to stop them trembling. It was a weakness in me, I admit it, but I do fear violence. I am not physically brave. The thought of pain and humiliation is not something I can approach without flinching. The intensity of my fear startled me.

I walked twice round the room, more for something to do than for any other reason – or so I thought; but perhaps I had already quietly observed something of interest, and was now seeking to find it again. I think we often take in more than we know, feel more than we admit, face facts even when we appear to be burying our heads.

On the panelled wall beside the fire was a tall mirror framed in gold. It ran almost from floor to ceiling. The mirror was most elaborately edged in scroll-work of gilded wood. I put my fingers on a particularly prominent golden curl and pulled. The mirror moved slowly out towards me.

I had opened a door.

Straight ahead of me ran a narrow corridor, with doors opening off it on either side. The end of the corridor was crossed by another hall. I could see no one, nor was there any sound.

I had no hesitation about what to do. I picked up my mantle, which was lying across a chair, and stepped through the door, closing it silently behind me.

Tinker's was a house in which there were secrets inside secrets. I had now penetrated one step further into the mystery.

I paused cautiously. I had remembered that there were dogs in this place, and dogs hear you and bark. But wherever the dogs lived it was far from this passage. There was neither sound nor daylight here. The carpet beneath my feet felt thick and soft, as if I was walking on fur. I looked down, and saw that it was a sort of coarse fur, like bearskin. My feet moved across it silently. I could not help wondering about the other feet that might have moved across it. Bare feet, were they? Why should I think that? But I did.

I padded forward. Three doors lay to my left, and all of them stood open. Anyone could be inside, watching and waiting. Anyone or no one. I moved silently onward.

The first door was pushed right back against the wall, and it would have been almost impossible not to see inside, even if I hadn't been curious. My own curiosity surprised me. I began to realize the deep validity of the Pandora myth. Fleetingly, I remembered La Grande Pandore, the big doll belonging to Madame Blanche. It seemed a strange name to give to a doll, but no doubt La Grande Pandore had been the cause of other people's opening boxes: money boxes. The clothes the doll displayed were all highly priced.

The room I gazed at was tiny, but its size was increased by the mirrors that surrounded it and covered the ceiling. It was all mirror, a mirrored padded box receding into endless distances. I stood there, looking around me, and I noticed that one of the mirrors had the curious property of reflecting the body with a wavering reflection, as if through water. Another one of the walls was set with many little mirrors, so that dozens of reflections came back.

I felt the very strongest temptation to break each and every mirror with the heel of my shoe. I did get so far as to take my shoe off. Then, overcome with the ridiculousness of it, I giggled. 'Well,' I thought, 'if they want mirrors, let them have mirrors.' Jessie wouldn't have giggled, though, and she might very probably have broken a mirror. But between Jessie and me, as I was coming to realize, there was a gulf.

Yet I closed the door quietly, with something of repulsion, after all. There were so many eyes looking back at me.

The room next door was clearly visible to me as I passed it. It was all hung about with black and had a huge bed. I didn't like it. It was a dark, hungry room, like an empty mouth.

The last door was almost closed. I caught a glimpse, though, and was puzzled. It seemed strangely furnished for pleasure, with a rack of wood and a wheel of shining steel. Altogether a sort of torture room without the Iron Maiden.

I was standing there, looking, when I heard a noise. I turned to see Nancy, standing there watching me. Her hair was flowing loosely over her shoulders, and her arms were akimbo. Not for the first time I thought that she was indeed striking-looking, both sullen and powerful. I was sure that, unlike Mabel, she did not rouge, and that the colour on those lips was natural.

'Well,' she said. 'Looking at our playthings?'

'Is that what they are?' I was thrown off balance by her appearance and her ironic comment.

'Someone's playthings, at all events,' she said. When she was older she would be a heavy woman. She looked at me angrily.

'I was just looking.' My explanation stumbled to a halt. She had never been so hostile to me before. Nancy had never been friendly, I doubt if she was friendly to anyone, but she had never shown me such dislike.

'Not what you expected, eh?'

'Well, I didn't know . . .' I fell silent.

'You know nothing about it. Nothing. You don't even understand what you see.'

I shrugged.

'You don't even know about yourself –' she broke off.

For a moment, I pondered my father's relationship with her. But no, I believed they had only met in his studio, and the studio was such an austere place.

'I'm just leaving,' I said.

'You'll never get out on your own.'

'Will you show me?' I didn't believe what she said, of course. This is the last quarter of the nineteenth century, not the eighteenth, and I should certainly extricate myself from Tinker's. Even the locked door no longer alarmed me. It had meant nothing. They always locked doors at Tinker's, I knew. However, there might be a certain amount of unpleasantness in the process of freeing myself, and I would prefer to spare myself this if possible. I had another motive also. I thought Nancy might tell me things I wanted to know. I have seen people before in that state of strung-up emotion I read in her now and I have noticed that it loosens their tongues like wine. (I wondered if Nancy had taken a little too much wine now? I couldn't detect it on her breath, but there was a strong odour of sandalwood and patchouli coming from her person which would mask it.)

'Yes, I'll show you. I'm not on the side of this lot here, any-hows. I like my freedom, myself.'

'Of course you do.'

'Don't you reassure me, miss. You're the one that needs to look to herself.'

There it was again, that note of warning, coming again from Nancy as it had from Jack the chestnut-seller. Was she too warning me against Christian Ableman?

'Brazen, some might say, coming here.'

'I hope none will know,' I said mildly. From the mood Nancy was in I thought she would as soon clout me as help me, that the one action would relieve her passion as well as the other. I knew she did attack the other girls. Mabel once had a bruise across her face which Nancy gave her. Or so she said it was.

One of the little dogs came trotting round the corner to Nancy. She picked it up and held it cradled against her breast, stroking its soft coat with her free hand. Over its white head she looked at me defiantly. 'I shan't say. I can keep a still tongue.'

'Can you, Nancy? Is that what Christian Ableman likes?'

'Don't know him,' she said sullenly.

'By another name, perhaps? He's tall and dark.'

'Good-looking, is he?'

'Some would say so.'

'Would *you* say so, miss?' She knew how to be impertinent.

'Do you say so, Nancy?' I asked softly.

'I told you. I never saw him.'

'He is here today,' I said.

'What, here? Never.' She stroked the little dog and held it up to lick her cheek. Her bright colour never wavered. She did not buy the pink on her cheeks from Madame Blanche. I wondered if that vivid colour was healthy. I have known people with a fever to look like that.

'I saw him.'

'You saw him?' She repeated the words, spacing them widely. 'You saw nothing. You couldn't have.'

'Saw him and spoke to him.'

'Well, you're mad, then,' she said. 'Touched up here.' Satirically, she pointed a finger at her head.

'Was Louise de la Vallière a friend of yours?'

She shook her head. 'How could she be? She didn't have no friends. She was strange, that one.'

'Did *she* know Christian Ableman?'

'I don't know what you're talking about.' She was exasperated. 'She might have done.'

'I can't ask her, you know. She's dead.'

'So I've heard,' she said sullenly. 'So I've heard.'

'Don't you wonder why she drowned?'

'I don't go round asking questions. And, if you want to go on happily, nor should you, either. Has it done you any good? No, it hasn't.'

'So far, I'm not harmed,' I said stoutly.

She looked at me without a word, and if a girl like Nancy could be said to give an enigmatic glance (a word which I doubt if she knew), then this was what she did. Call it appraising or assessing if you like. She looked at me as if she knew where my wound was and soon so would I.

'You were angry with me just now, weren't you?'

'Because I see how you look about you: so *superior*. You looked as though you can't ever be touched by what you see. Drawing your skirts aside from us, you were. It riled me.'

'Well, I'm sorry, Nancy.'

'I'll take you out now.' She swung round, skirts flying. The little dog stared over her shoulder. I followed.

We turned left down the corridor and then through a door which opened on to a flight of steps. She nodded her head. 'Down there,' she said. 'Then out the door at the bottom and up the area steps. You come out at the back and you'll have to go round the shrubbery.'

'What about the door?'

'It's all right. It bolts on this side and the bolts are well oiled. I see to that. I often go that way myself.'

'I'll close it after me,' I said.

'It's dark outside. And raining. You'll get wet.'

She watched me from the top of the stairs, still clutching the little dog to her.

'How will you get back to Oxford?' she said.

'The same way as I came. I walked.'

'They say you're a clever girl,' she said suddenly. 'A proper scholar.'

I was silent.

'All right, if you're so clever, I'll tell you something: look round your friends and see whom you can trust. That's my advice to you.'

'Good advice,' I said.

'And more, I don't know much about that grand household where you live, but we have a visitor from there, I can tell you, oh we do. Try and guess *his* name.'

'You could tell me if you wanted to,' I observed.

'So I shall one day, if it suits me,' she said. 'I'll work out what is best for *me*.'

'I don't blame you.'

'Oh, blame!' She shrugged. 'Who cares for blame? I have to think of pounds, shillings and pence. However, I'll give you some information *free*. It's free to a girl like you.' And she gave me an angry stare.

'It's about Louise, isn't it?'

'Yes.' I had surprised her. 'How do you know that?'

I shook my head. I hardly knew myself, but sometimes minds do reach out and touch other minds, and between me and Nancy there was a kind of sympathy, somewhat malignant on her part, perhaps. 'Just a guess.'

'I'd like you to know about her. She talked to me more than I let you think. She trusted me and you can't trust most of the girls here, silly tattle-heads.'

I waited.

'She wasn't called Louise de la Vallière, really,' said Nancy.

'I never supposed she was.'

'Oh, it was near enough. Louise Vallon she was, and her grandparents were French, he was a waiter at Romanée's in Soho. Louise changed her name later. And how did she come to change her name, you might ask?'

'I can guess,' I said drily.

'Not so, not how you think. She was a respectable girl and in service when one of the sons of the house took a fancy to her. What could a girl like her do? Who took her word that it was no fault of hers? And who helped her when she was turned from the house without a reference? Who *does* help girls like that?' Nancy glared at me, almost as if she was telling her own story, as perhaps she was. 'And so by degrees she came to be at Tinker's and calling herself Louise de la Vallière. But she was never one of us. She helped with our clothes, and then she travelled to and fro on business.'

'What sort of business?'

Nancy shrugged. 'She could speak French, Louise could, after a fashion. I reckon she was useful to those that hired her. But she was frightened of them. She was always frightened, poor Louise was. She was ruined from the word go. I knew it. She knew it, and now you know it, Miss Lamont.'

I didn't answer and she watched me, intently.

'She wasn't the only one either. At Sarsen Place, are you? Well, watch your step, miss. Ah, that's driven you away. Shut the door behind you as you go,' she said.

'I will.' I was already withdrawing into the night, which was as unwelcoming as she had promised.

'One last thing,' she called after me. 'If you're so clever, how come you're walking all the way home when even I go in a carriage?'

She had had the last word. You could expect that with Nancy.

I returned from Tinker's wet and bedraggled. In fact I had not walked all the way back. There was a horse bus to Folly Bridge, as there had been on the way out. I had been guilty of a small untruth to Nancy.

It was past seven o'clock. I hurried up the stairs at Sarsen Place, hoping I would meet nobody. None of the Demarests, I suppose that meant, because when I met one of the maids I was delighted and asked her at once for some hot water.

'Oh yes, miss, at once, you look drenched,' she said with sympathetic horror. 'I'll get a hip bath ready for you.'

I demurred. I was going to be late for dinner, a sin in the eyes of Mrs Demarest.

'Oh yes, miss, I should indeed, dinner's to be an hour late

tonight, anyway.' She giggled. 'Mrs Ceffery's quite put about. Looking for an early night, she was. But I don't mind, I like a bit of excitement.'

'Oh?' I raised my eyes in query.

'Yes. The lawyer from London, a barrister, miss, with a *lovely* voice. He's been with the master and the Captain all afternoon. I couldn't hear anything, though,' she said regretfully, 'although I passed the door several times. Very quiet voice the lawyer has.'

'Anything about Ellen?'

She shook her head, the smile wiped off her face. 'Poor Nelly. The police have been searching about the gardens and in the coach house. They think she was spirited off from there.'

She came into my room and drew the curtains and lit the gas lamps with a pop, and helped me off with my wet cloak.

Sitting before the fire in my hot tub with the big screen drawn round to form a protective alcove, and feeling warm and relaxed, I was able to think again.

I soaped myself with the carnation soap which came from Madame Blanche's shop in boxes printed with tiny red carnations and was a present from my employer. I think she liked those about her to smell nice. Even the servants in this house smelt of fresh print dresses and lavender.

I assembled my thoughts. Whether I had done good or harm by going to Tinker's I was still not sure. I had learnt nothing about Ellen's whereabouts, but I had confirmed my knowledge that the drowned woman, Louise de la Vallière, had a mystery in her life. I suspected this mystery was connected with Tinker's. And now, because of what Nancy had said to me, I was able to connect Tinker's with Sarsen Place. Or perhaps I should put it the other way round, since someone from Sarsen Place was visiting Tinker's. I wondered who it could be and could see only one candidate myself: Captain Demarest.

I could just see the Captain disporting himself under the mirrors. Hastily I turned my mind from the subject; I was used to study human forms but between the objects of Greek art in the Ashmolean Museum and the Captain's limbs there must be a gulf fixed. It was essential to my composure and purpose that the gulf remained. Indeed, it was only due to my father's desire to teach me to draw that I knew as much as I did about the antique Greek muscles. He had obliged me to copy several of the bronzes in crayon; I never became very good at drawing but I learnt a great deal about anatomy and became very interested in Greece.

There was another name in my mind, that of Christian Ableman, and the strange thing was that the episode with him was rapidly retreating in my memory and seeming less and less real every minute. It was taking on the elusive quality of a dream. I could hardly believe it had really taken place.

Perhaps it never had.

The thought came into mind oddly, before I gave a startled burst of laughter and went to dress.

I wore a new dress of azure merino and swansdown. I was doubtful about it. As I entered the drawing-room I saw Mrs Demarest flick her eyes over me and so I knew I looked wrong. She herself looked charming in an antique moiré brocade with panels of embroidery.

We were alone. The visitor from London, the barrister, indeed that was what he was, had departed. I stood by Mrs Demarest for a moment, then she patted the sofa beside her. It was upholstered in gold damask and her green dress made a wonderful contrast, of which I thought she was not unconscious.

'You spent a pleasant afternoon, Mary?' she remarked agreeably. If she was reproving me for being so long away from my pupil, she was doing it gently.

'I was away longer than I meant.' I felt a little nervous.

'Alice slept.' Yes, it *had* been a mild reproof. 'She needs a change of scene, I believe.'

Once uttered, that would be enough. Mrs Demarest would say nothing more, although I always had the feeling that she kept pretty good accounts, and that I would find this absence debited there. Adelaide Demarest liked to profess a well-bred inability to show surprise, but I thought that if she knew where I had really been this afternoon, she would hardly have been able to suppress astonishment; and, of course, it would be the last of me as Alice's teacher. But I had long ago learnt to repress the side of myself that did not fit in with Sarsen Place (when I was there, anyway), and to look at me sitting quietly by my employer on the sofa you would never have supposed I had gone further than the Botanical Gardens to look at the hothouses.

Mrs Demarest looked at the enamelled French clock on the table by her elbow (it was one of Will Train's greatest treasures). 'Late,' she grumbled. 'My sons expect to live here as if it was "en garçonnière".' Then, as if the word reminded her, 'Where is your father staying in Paris?'

'He addresses his letters from the Rue St André des Arts,' I said cautiously.

'The Quartier Latin, I suppose? Not a part of Paris I know.'

'No.' I bowed my head submissively. Probably just as well, I thought. I sincerely hoped that my father's Paris and hers never coincided.

At that moment both her sons came in. With them came a breath of Cuir de Russie. The daughter of one of them might have been attacked, a servant abducted, the police might this moment be prowling round the shrubberies, but both were dressed in a magnificence of starched linen and fine broadcloth. Captain Demarest even had sapphire shirt studs. I supposed the Cuir de Russie was his, too. And the smell of brandy.

'There was a boy here this afternoon asking after Ellen,' said Mark Demarest at dinner. 'Do you know him?'

'I think so.' I supposed it was Jack with the chestnuts.

He frowned. 'Yes, he spoke as if he knew you. He seemed upset. I let him talk with the policemen who were here. I fancy I know his face.'

'You will do if you have ever bought chestnuts in St Giles,' I said.

'No, I've never done that.'

'It's ice cream in summer, I believe.'

'No, not even that.' He laughed. 'All the same, I've seen him somewhere.'

'Have the police ...? Do the police ...?' I could only start the question.

'No. Nothing.' He spoke in a clear, hard voice. 'They have no idea what has become of the girl.'

'There is a connection,' began Mrs Demarest. 'That is, we were told . . .'

'A suspected connection,' broke in her son. 'London criminals at work in Oxford.'

'"Suspected" means "is thought to be". It's the same thing.' She was tetchy.

'Not precisely, my dear mother.'

She shrugged. 'Put it how you will.'

'I understand you are a classical scholar, Miss Lamont,' said Charles Demarest, cracking a walnut. 'Beyond me, I'm afraid I never could get beyond amo, amas, amat.' He laughed easily.

'A little more would have done you no harm,' said his brother sharply.

Charles smiled and stroked his beautifully pomaded moustaches. I could see he was watching his image in the big mirror which faced him on the wall beyond. A modern-day Hyacinthus, if I ever saw one. Just as well he was not acquainted with the Greek myths, I thought. 'A lady scholar, eh?' he said. 'That's a good one.'

'Just a scholar,' I said, unable to keep the tartness out of my voice.

Mark Demarest looked at me. 'I admire your effort, Miss Lamont.'

I looked at him carefully, to see if he was being pompous or patronizing, but he wasn't. To my surprise, I felt myself blushing. The Captain noted that, all right, preoccupied with himself as he was. I suppose it confirmed his belief that all women are soft little creatures at heart. I was ashamed to sense a definite aggressive dislike of the Captain growing up inside me.

'I believe Queen Elizabeth was a great scholar, and knew both Latin and Greek.' Mrs Demarest thought dinner-table conversation should be smooth and impersonal.

'And look what happened to her, by jove,' said Captain Demarest, roaring with laughter. 'The Virgin Queen.'

'Charles!' Mrs Demarest's reproof stopped his laughter, and he returned to his walnuts.

After that, I said no more. We had a decanter of blood-red burgundy to drink that night, and perhaps I took more wine than I usually did and was a little drunk, but it didn't make me gay or talkative, only forced me in on myself, so that I sat there without saying much, and all the the time conscious that out there in the shadows the police were still at work.

I am very ambitious, you must have noticed that; it runs like a vein of gold (or dross, according to how you value the quality) through my story. But until now I had hardly known what my ambition meant. I saw now that it meant status. Status to silence the gallantries of Charles Demarest, status to meet men like Mark Demarest on equal terms. I was beginning to recognize clearly that Mark Demarest was worth the challenge. His ideas about my sex were more subtle and sophisticated than those of his mother and brother. It was too much to hope that he might be a 'sympathizer' like Humphrey Ward, my friend Mary's husband, but he seemed rational in his approach, open-minded and fair. So many of the opponents of women's equality are irrational bigots; and so, alas, are many of its supporters. I saw that we attracted the lunatics as well as the enlightened. And this, of course, is what gives us momentum; revolutions need their fanatics.

I was very proud of myself at that stage of my life, slim and taut and proud. I thought the pride did not show, that it was all wrapped up inside me, well tucked in, but I think now it did show and that men like Mark Demarest saw it, and perhaps were touched by it. I didn't know it was pride. I believe I thought it was rationality, intellect, even a belief in the human spirit. But it was pride. Later, I became less proud.

I came out of the drawing-room that night and Prince gave the sort of cough butlers do give to attract attention, and told me in a quiet voice that a lad was looking for me.

'The one that was here this afternoon?' I asked. 'He saw Mr Demarest.'

He nodded. 'He's been hanging about ever since.'

'Where is he?'

'The back kitchen.'

'I'll come out.'

The back kitchen was a bleak place where the laundry was done, and in this early spring evening it was dark and chill.

141

Jack was sitting on an upright chair by the window. A single lamp, high on a shelf, lit the room and cast long shadows.

He stood up when he saw me. 'The old woman wouldn't let me in any further. She said I smelt of cinders.'

It was true, there was a perpetual smell of smoke and charred wood about Jack, inevitable to his trade, I suppose. Still it wasn't like Mrs Demarest to be rude, even to someone as low in the social scale as Jack. Oblivion was more the style she went in for.

'So you do, a little,' I said. 'I don't dislike it.'

'*She* smells of hot meat fat,' he said resentfully, and then I knew he was talking of Mrs Ceffery, so I grinned. They could take each other on, those two, I thought, and be well matched.

'I dare say you said so.'

He nodded. 'And she said I could sit out here for my pains. We could move now,' he said hopefully. 'It's warmer in the other kitchen and there's vittles there, besides.'

His lips looked dry and pinched and I thought: here this afternoon to see Mark Demarest, then waiting to see me, he's probably been hanging about all day without much to eat. 'Come into the kitchen,' I said, and led the way in.

'Eh!' said Mrs Ceffery, who was sitting at the huge kitchen table, reading a book. 'So there you are, then, sneaking into my kitchen behind a lady's skirts.'

'Let him have something to eat and drink,' I said. I looked round the kitchen. There was a big bowl of dripping on the table and a fresh loaf near by. 'I'm sure he'd enjoy some hot toast with some of your good beef dripping on it and salt, freshly ground, and some pepper, the way you do it for Belcher after a cold drive.'

'And I'm told I smell of it,' she said, with a sniff.

'It's a lovely smell, missus,' said Jack, suddenly looking young and cold.

She got up with a dignified gait, went to the loaf, cut two thick slices, stuck one on a toasting fork embellished with Charles Dickens's head as a handle, and thrust them at him. 'Take yourself off to the fire and get on with it,' she said, nodding towards the huge kitchen range, which glared out at the kitchen with great red eyes, like some well blackened and polished monster.

When the smell of toasting bread was filling the kitchen she carved a slice of cold beef and put it on a plate, together with a couple of dark brown pickled onions the like of which never saw the dining-room table. I saw that she had two styles of cooking, just as she had two styles of living, one for upstairs and one for below the stairs. 'Here, make a start on that while you're waiting. And you can have a mug of porter when you've finished.'

'Oh, thank you, Mrs Ceffery, mum.' He knew her name, of course.

'Smell of beef, indeed,' she said, sitting down again at the table and taking up her book. I could read the title, which was *Lady Audley's Secret*, by Mrs Braddon.

Jack ate neatly, but with gusto. When he had finished he patted his mouth with a ragged check handkerchief. 'That was good,' he said. 'That *was* something.'

'Glad you enjoyed it,' said Mrs Ceffery sedately; she had only been pretending to read. 'Nice appetite you've got.'

'Oh, I have.'

'A bit of something sweet to finish with?' She got up and, taking a tin out of a cupboard, cut him a slice of rich fruit cake.

I judged he was about eight years short of any real interest for her.

'Now,' I said. 'What is it you want? Why do you want to talk to me?'

Jack looked cautiously at Mrs Ceffery.

'It's all right. I don't suppose any of us have any secrets from Mrs Ceffery.'

She gave a hoot of laughter. 'One or two I expect, one or two. Same as me.'

'Come now,' I said. 'What did you want to ask?'

Jack held up his mug, to see that no last drops remained, then stood up. 'Well, you two have got it wrong. I didn't come up here to seek information but to have a look at your master. I wanted to make up my mind what sort of a man he is.' He squared his shoulders. 'I've never seen him. I wanted to weigh him up, see if he is a straight 'un, or not.'

'And is he?' said Mrs Ceffery.

'I dare say. Yes, I dare say. He ain't the sort of cove you can sum up easy, but on the whole I'd say what I saw was to his credit.'

'Good,' I said. 'And me, did you come to assess me, too?'

'No, I know *you*.' He paused. 'No, I come to *tell* you something.'

'Well, go on.'

He walked up the room, turned, and came back to face us. 'No,' he continued grandly. 'I haven't come here to seek but to lay information.' He paused. 'I accuse someone in this house of causing harm to my Ellen.'

'And Miss Alice?' said Mrs Ceffery.

'Yes, I dare say. I don't feel entitled to speak for Miss Alice, her being gentry, but I *am* my Ellen's voice, and I do speak for her.'

'The two can't be separated, in my opinion,' said Mrs Ceffery. 'They are entwined.'

'It's a serious thing you are saying.' I had risen and was walking restlessly round the room in my turn. 'Why do you say it?'

'Ellen told me.'

'Go on,' said Mrs Ceffery. 'Which is it? The master? The Captain?' There was something engaging about her readiness to believe her employers capable of any crime. 'And who was the *real* victim? Ask yourself that.'

'I don't know what you're talking about,' said Jack. 'But Ellen told me she was frightened of someone here, and Miss Alice the same. Miss Alice was the worse frightened.'

'Poor little thing,' said Mrs Ceffery, with jovial sympathy.

'And didn't she tell you who they were frightened of?'

'We don't meet all that often. Conversations between us isn't all that easy to come by.' He gave me a cool look.

'Still ...'

'Ellen told me, in a manner of speaking,' he said deliberately. 'A snake in the grass, she said.'

'Ah,' said Mrs Ceffery, nodding her head.

'No more?' I said sceptically. It wasn't like Ellen to be vague, a certain blunt explicitness was more like her.

'She wouldn't tell more.' He set his lips firmly. 'And that's why I must find her, see. She wouldn't tell me more, because she said it wasn't safe for me to know more. Me.' He was indignant. 'Me, that's floored many a chap twice my size, for I'm wiry, though I am thin.'

'Let's feel your muscles, boy,' offered Mrs Ceffery.

He ignored the remark.

'I pressed her, but she wouldn't tell.'

'She was protecting you.'

'Yes.' He was outraged. 'And that's not right. That's man's work. I'm to protect Nelly, not her me.'

Mrs Ceffery began laughing again. She had been putting away porter at a fair rate all this while and was by now far from sober. She could still have cooked an excellent meal, had she been obliged to do so, but she was in an exuberant, cheerful mood. A happy state, no doubt, if you can achieve it that way: I cannot.

'So I came up here,' he continued, 'to have a look round and to warn you.'

'Me?'

'Yes, you, miss.' He was severe. He would be a formidable paterfamilias. 'I've told you before and I tells you again: you mix with the wrong people.'

'What does he mean?' asked Mrs Ceffery hopefully.

'A man called Christian Ableman,' I said, wishing Jack had never seen or heard of him. 'It's nothing, nothing at all.'

'Do you or don't you mix?' she said, somewhat belligerently.

'It's nothing to you, Mrs Ceffery.'

'Right, Miss Lamont. So you says, and in some ways you're right. But I'm a woman and you're a woman and I call upon a woman's right to advise.'

A meeting between Mrs Ceffery and my friend Jessie would be interesting to arrange. Jessie was always talking about liberating the working class, but it struck me that a working woman who earned her own wage was about as free as she could be. Certainly I had never seen any sign of bondage about Mrs Ceffery, either to men or her employers. Such as Mrs Ceffery did not need emancipation.

'I'm tired,' I said, putting my hands to my head. 'Tired and bewildered.'

'So will you help me search for Ellen?' said Jack.

'Yes,' I said. 'Yes and yes. I'll go to someone I think must know the answer.'

'That was a policeman they had in the library,' announced Mrs Ceffery. 'Not a lawyer, but a policeman, a big man down from London.'

Oh yes, she knew everything, everything. The house of the women knows all the secrets. She was a household of women in herself, a whole regiment. I had to catch hold of my thoughts, they were spinning out in all directions. I suppose it was fatigue.

'What did he say?' demanded Jack.

'I couldn't hear much,' Mrs Ceffery said regretfully, 'although as chance would have it I passed the door more than once. I fancy I heard the word smuggled.'

'What was being smuggled, then?' asked Jack.

'If Christian Ableman is involved then it's not what, but who. The child knapper has another trade: in people,' I said.

'Then my poor Ellen's done for,' said Jack, white-faced.

'No, wait,' I said. 'There must be more to it than we believe. Who could drag a girl like Alice Demarest into a kidnapping plot like that?'

'Unless they hated her,' said Mrs Ceffery.

'Who could hate Alice?'

'Someone close to her,' said the relentless Mrs Ceffery. 'Just like Ellen said,' and she nodded towards Jack. 'Best find Ellen. If you can.'

Chapter Seven

By the time we had locked and bolted the back door behind Jack, and I had dragged myself up to bed, we had talked it over and formed an alliance, the stronger for being spontaneous and unpremeditated. Mrs Ceffery and I sealed our part of it by a long, quiet look passed between us as we closed the door behind the boy.

'You say nothing and I'll say nothing,' said Mrs Ceffery.

I nodded.

'But we'll watch. Watch and observe,' she went on.

'Yes, that's it.'

'I hope the lad will be all right,' she said heavily. She seemed quite sober now.

'I think he will sink into the background and no one will see he is there. Except when he chooses.' I was beginning to know Jack.

'Do you think he will find Ellen?'

I shook my head. 'If she's alive. How can we tell?'

Mrs Ceffery gave me a little push. 'He'll try. Up to bed, my lass, you look worn out.'

He'd try, and the police would try, and I would try to find Christian Ableman. That seemed the only solution left to me, as I turned wearily away.

In my room I drew back the heavy lace curtain from my window and looked out on the moonlit world below. There was something missing in what Mrs Ceffery had told Jack and me, which suggested she was not quite so well informed as she imagined. There had been two men in the drawing-room calling on Mark Demarest, not one. I had stood where I was now, face pressed to the cold window pane, and looked down on the scene illuminated by the flaming gas jets which flanked the front door. Two men had got into a waiting cab and been driven off. And one, at least, wearing a checked ulster, had looked like neither a lawyer nor a policeman.

I tried to imagine the interview in the drawing-room. The Demarests lounging on the elegant French furniture, and their two visitors, one seated, the other perhaps standing by the fire. The voices hushed, but full of significance: the voices of men at the height of their profession. The phrases they used – 'We have reason to suspect a connection' – and then perhaps they would use the name Louise de la Vallière, and say 'We suspect a connection between the death of Louise de la Vallière by drowning and the attack on your daughter'.

Had one of them indeed said this? And what had the man who looked so unlike a policeman said? Had he spoken at all or kept very quiet? I had the feeling that one man only had spoken, while the other remained the silent observer.

And had the conversation then moved on to the London criminals – 'a matter of grave importance'? A cry from Mrs Demarest, perhaps, at this point. Or had she long since collapsed into silent tears? But no, I had seen her later and her cheeks were smooth and pink. No sign there of grief and sorrow.

There was something badly wrong with the scene as I was imagining it.

A man in that room, one of the men, had used the word 'smuggling'. I tried to fit the word into its context. 'We fear that your maidservant Ellen has been abducted, smuggled out of Oxford, away from London, into another country. Your maidservant or your natural daughter, your suspected grand-daughter, your putative niece'. But they did not know of these suspected relationships, unless Mrs Ceffery had slipped them a word through a chain of contacts.

All the actors in this scene had emerged calm, some to eat a good dinner – those who should have minded most. This was a fact I had to hang on to. It was the one thing I knew, the one solid fact.

And then, at some point, had one of the visitors suggested special protection for Alice? Or possibly a removal elsewhere? 'May I suggest a change of scene?' Were those words used? It could be imagined that they were.

Two men had arrived, a long interview had taken place in the library, while Alice, mute heroine, slept above. Then the two men had entered a cab and driven away. The rest was silence.

I turned away from the window. The fire in my grate was burning down, and the room was grey.

I must find Christian Ableman tomorrow. Only a direct confrontation between the two of us would serve. Or so it seemed, as I moved restlessly in my cold cold bed.

The house was awake early. The little housemaid was in the room starting my fire and lighting it before I was really awake. I stared at her from my bed pillows.

'Mrs Ceffery thought you'd want to be woken early. You're all to go to London today. Word came down last night.'

'All?' I said, wondering.

'Well, the family, that is, not *us*. You're going to a hotel.'

She disappeared, then came clattering into the room with a tray, and on it a coffee pot and a cup. 'Mrs Ceffery said you'd want a cup early, and that before the family breakfast, as you'd want to go out to your house to collect some things for the stay.'

She wrapped a shawl round my shoulders. 'And how long do we stay in London?'

'Ah, that I don't know. Mr Prince heard 'em talking in the billiard room, you see, and he didn't hear no more.' She threw some sticks on the fire to make it blaze, and smiled.

I drank my coffee. Mrs Ceffery had read my thoughts. I would indeed be out early this morning.

I looked in Alice's room before I left. She smiled at me sleepily. 'Breakfast in bed for you, and I will be back in an hour,' I said.

Or two hours, I thought, not longer. Mrs Demarest breakfasted late and in her own room. She never knew where Alice and I were before luncheon.

All the doors were closed in Rosemary Court that morning; and there was no sign of life behind any of the unwashed windows. I paused for a moment outside the door where I had seen

149

Christian Ableman stand in the sun. There was no sun this morning and the door was locked. I knocked once.

Binny was in the dark little cave she called her shop, where her goods for sale hung on hooks and racks all around the walls and you had to push past the clothes to get to Binny behind her counter at the end. It always made me shudder. The presence of the past owners of the clothes was so pungently real. She shrugged when I asked for Christian Ableman.

'Like a nice grey and black silk mantle, only had three owners and is good for three more? I'll take a tanner for it. I don't know where Ableman is. I'm not his keeper. He was off somewhere yesterday, that I do know!'

'Where was he, then?' I thought I knew the answer, though: Tinker's.

'Dunno. You don't ask that one. But the way he was dressed he was off to London to see the nobs.' She gave a short laugh. 'He was in a rotten bad mood when he got back.'

I thought I knew the cause of his bad mood, too.

'What's the smile for?' asked Binny.

'I didn't know I smiled.'

'Must have been wind, then. That's what they say about babies when they smile: wind, they say.' She was in an evil temper herself this morning; it crackled through her bright eyes and curly hair. Normally I stayed clear of Binny when she was like this; she did you no good.

'Binny, about my cloak, the old dark grey check I gave you, what became of it?'

She shrugged. 'How do I know? I don't keep track of every old object I take in. Lord, I'd have a fine job if I did. Want it back, do you?'

'I could have it back if I wanted it. I found it hanging in the back lobby at Sarsen Place.'

'You never gave it me, then.'

'It smelt strange, Binny. As if something pungent and strong had been on to it.'

'Strong enough to take your breath away?' She gave a laugh, then realized what she had said, and clapped a hand over her mouth.

'Yes, you sold it to Louise de la Vallière, didn't you, Binny?'

'I'm not saying.'

'She was wearing it when she died. And then, somehow, it came back to Sarsen Place.'

'That "somehow" would be interesting to watch, wouldn't it,' said Binny, sarcastically. 'Got legs on it, I suppose, walked up on its own, I dare say.'

She had put her finger on a problem. I had wondered myself how and why the cloak had been returned to Sarsen Place. I thought if I could find the answer to that one I might have a solution to the mystery of a great deal else.

'Why did Louise buy my cloak?' I asked. To buy Binny's old clothes wasn't the style of things at all from the girls of Tinker's. Binny was a buyer there, not a seller.

'She wanted to look like a governess,' said Binny, with a snigger. I flushed.

A tall figure pushed through the clothes and stood there, outlined against the door by the gaslight. Christian Ableman stood still, carrying, oddly out of character, a round wooden tray with a cup and saucer and a tea-pot on it.

'Thanks for the cant, Binny.' He handed over the tray. So far, he appeared not to have seen me.

'Pleasure.' She gave me a glance full of sulky triumph. She had known where he was all the time; probably they had passed the night together. Well matched, I thought, Binny being ruthless and without love. If she had soft feelings for any man, it was my father, and God knew why.

He turned then and saw me, and a look of surprise crossed his face. 'So it's you, Miss Lamont.'

'I came to see you.'

'The last thing I should have expected.'

'To talk to you,' I said, looking straight at him. He was wearing a silk handkerchief round his neck and a dark waistcoat, but no jacket.

He laughed. 'That lay is coopered before it starts.'

I made an involuntary sound of dissent.

'Look here, Miss Lamont, I came into this town meaning no harm to you or yours, and before I could say Jack Robinson you were laying information against me with the police. And then when I call on you, in an unorthodox way, I admit, but it's well to be sure of an entrance, you savage me like a tiger cat. I'd like another meeting with you, Miss Lamont, I admit it, but I'll choose my own way and time, not yours. So that's that, and I'll say good morning to you.' He turned to Binny. 'I'm off.'

'Good morning, Ableman, my dear,' said Binny agreeably.

'And what about yesterday at Tinker's?' I demanded, blocking his way.

He stopped short. 'So what about Tinker's? A fine place for you to be naming, Miss Incorruptible.' Binny laughed.

'You know what happened there.' To my fury, I felt myself blushing, but it was so dark in Binny's shop that not even she saw.

'What did happen?' He gripped my wrists, the two together, imprisoning me.

'Nothing, I suppose,' I said slowly. Now I faced my memories and tried to formulate them, I was confused and at a loss. It was like trying to take hold of a reflection in a mirror.

'You,' I began. 'You . . .'

'Me again?' He laughed and threw my hands back at me. 'You must not think I am so simple but know the devil himself will not eat a woman.'

I leaned against the counter, rubbing my wrists, aware that Binny was watching and listening with sardonic interest. Outside, the heavy bell of the Christ Church clock sounded the hour.

'I'm off,' he said.

'No, wait,' I said. 'I haven't finished.'

He strode off with me following and Binny giving a screech of laughter in the background. There was nothing civilized or mirthful about Binny's laughter; it was her sharp comment on the irreconcilables in life, and I knew it.

He crossed Rosemary Court, whose inhabitants were now coming sleepily to life, pushing aside a dog that leapt at him and ignoring a man with a tousled head leaning out of a window. At his door he barred my way.

'No, no further.'

'But I must talk to you.'

He looked at me without speaking, only a slight smile. I was beginning to see myself that my behaviour was irrational and strangely persistent. Seeing him now against the background of Rosemary Court, I noticed that, although the place was untidy and dirty, he looked clean and neat. Only the lines at the side of his mouth and the hard way he had of holding it reminded me of the criminal.

'Surely you see after yesterday I *must* talk to you?'

He dropped his arm. 'Come inside, then, and stop this prating of yesterday.'

The room inside was the first, except Binny's, I had ever entered in Rosemary Court, and even in the state I was in then I could not repress the prick of curiosity. It was a square-shaped box with a shuttered window, against which bars had been fixed, but it had been swept clean and the boards scrubbed. A low truckle bed stood against one wall. It was neatly made up with a dark blanket folded at the foot. A looking-glass stood on a low table with a basin and a towel. Propped up against the wall was a coloured lithograph of a woman in flowing robes. I have sharp eyes and could read the inscription on it: 'Mrs Kenly as Lady Macbeth.'

I remembered I had heard of him that he had been an actor once, but this picture was old. The style and the clothes bespoke at least a generation ago.

He saw me looking at the picture and turned to stare at it for a moment himself, a strange look settling over his features.

'You quoted Shakespeare to me just now,' I said.

'Even the devil can quote Scripture.' He stared at me moodily.

'You have been an actor, though. I was told so.'

'Was *born* an actor, born in the lodgings of a poor slut of an actress and taken around with her until she died. Yes, I can quote you *Antony and Cleopatra*, but there's no living in it. I'm dying, Egypt, dying.'

'And there *is* a good living in what you do?'

He stroked the linen of his sleeve and looked down at his cravat, which was of fine watered silk. 'None so badly, things come and go, some days are better than others. I don't beg, though, and I don't jump to anyone's orders. Is this what we came to talk about, miss, the state of my wages?'

'No, but of the drowning of a woman called Louise de la Vallière and the kidnapping of a girl called Ellen Sweeting.'

He was silent for a moment. 'Your reasons, miss?'

'You're a professional criminal,' I said coolly. 'I have no need to give reasons. You have bars on your windows, and new ones too. Are they to keep people in or out?'

He scowled. His temper was rising as mine came under my control. 'Hardly. Even in this cursed country a man is innocent till he is found guilty. We suck that dictum in with our milk, we of the criminal classes, most keenly of all.'

'And yesterday you attacked me.'

'Yesterday I did not see you,' he said angrily. 'And the bars are to keep people out.'

The effrontery of it took my breath away. 'It may suit you to deny that you were at Tinker's but I saw you there, we were in the same room, as real as we are now.'

'I have a phantom then, and you saw him.' He slumped down on the bed.

'Rubbish.'

'Either you or I are mad, Miss Lamont. I say I was not there, and you say you saw me. Did you see me as you see me now?' He moved close and invited me to look at him.

'The room was smokier,' I said.

'Ay, very smoky.'

The sneer angered me. I took a deep breath. 'Where is Ellen now?'

'I never saw her.'

'You came here looking for children,' I said, shouting a little.

'What sort of lay did you think mine was?' he said.

'A kidsman, a corruptor of children, a trainer of little thieves.'

For a moment I thought he would strike me across the face. Then he drew back, suddenly cool again. 'What should you know of it all?' he said. 'Perhaps I did train up one or two snakesmen and a dragsman or two, and perhaps we did work together, but we were all family people, and what had we got in front of us,

154

them and me? Was it not better for us to steal than to starve? The clever ones steal, and end up with fine linen shirts, and the soft ones die. That's the way of it, Miss Lamont, and now you know.'

'But to use children . . .'

'And how old do you guess I was when I started? Seven when my mother died, nine when I first walked the boards, twelve when I played Octavius, thirteen when I first starved. Starved! What had it been before but greasy stew in someone else's kitchen?'

I was quite silent, my anger put out, like a light doused with water.

'Oh, why do I tell you all these things?' He turned away. 'Except that you look like Ophelia and talk like Regan.'

'I see it very clearly,' I said sadly. 'Very clearly. You make me understand.' Never before had I been more aware of the two worlds in which I moved. On the one hand the intellectual and social world of Miss Clough and Mrs Demarest, on the other the lower world of Tinker's, which the accident of my father's profession and way of life had acquainted me with. I had thought that I could, somehow, walk easily in the two. I saw now it could never be so.

I leaned against the wall and found that I was trembling. My body was hot as if I had a fever, and yet my cheeks felt cold.

'Silly little miss,' he said, almost fondly. 'What a pity we had to meet. We're different sorts of goods, you and me. You're lighter stuff. Brush against me and you'll be broken.'

'Perhaps already,' I said to myself. 'Perhaps broken already.' Because, after all, what is it to a woman to be broken, but to lose that essential wholeness of spirit, a sort of virginity, which once lost can never be restored? A woman can lose it in so many ways, within marriage and without. We now have a Married Women's Property Act, but the spirit is a property which cannot be locked up.

'I'm going now,' I said. I had meant to find out the truth about Louise de la Vallière, about Ellen, about Alice's fears. I was still convinced he knew the truth about them all, but he had worsted me. I had come away with a truth about myself. The usual sort of

155

truth: that I was weaker, by far, than I had thought, less strongly planted in my hopes and ambitions than I had believed. He was an avowed criminal, a man without respect, an outlaw, but he was stronger than me. He fought his battles with a firm belief in a sort of natural justice.

I looked at him now, sitting on the edge of the bed, dark head bent, momentarily downcast. My generation flies so easily to quotation, all the best things have been said for us. 'A man's a man for a' that,' I thought.

'I'm going,' I said again, wrapping my cloak around me. I opened the door. Outside it was bright day, and Rosemary Court had come fully to life.

He raised his head. 'The woman in the picture,' he said, 'in case you are interested, is reputed to be my grandmother. Reputed. Nothing is sure in this world.'

I had got to the mouth of the narrow alley which debouched near my father's studio when I heard footsteps hurrying after me. I suppose I was not in the least surprised.

'I'll walk with you,' said Christian Ableman. He was still dragging on his coat.

I smiled demurely and walked on.

'I'm only going to St Giles, then a cab back to Sarsen Place.' Still demure, still meekly provocative.

Such behaviour is not natural to me. It was a measure of how far I had been blown off my course.

He did not speak, but walked along beside me, awkwardly adapting his long strides to my shorter ones.

At the corner which turns into St Aldate's I stopped. 'We must part here.'

'Ashamed to be seen with me, then?'

'No.' That was true enough. Except for his breadth of shoulder and his height he would not stand out on the crowded pavements. No, my reason was entirely instinctive and emotional, a feeling that I must extricate myself now before I became too deeply committed. As it was, every step by his side seemed an avowal I did not wish to make.

'Don't know what to make of me, do you?'

'No.'

'I'll tell you, then: take the best you can see and leave the worst. That's what you're told to do, isn't it? That's your Christian morality.'

I didn't answer him, but he answered me, in any case.

'No, where I come from we're neither Christians nor pagans like your old Greeks and Romans. Perhaps we have a few household gods we touch our caps to, but that's about it.'

'Heathen,' I said. 'That's what being a heathen means.'

'Yes, we're naturally heathen, it's to be expected,' he said seriously. 'Well, say goodbye to the heathen, then. If you can.'

'Goodbye.'

'It's not the end, you know,' he said, still seriously. 'Not while I'm living and breathing. I'll take my Elijah's oath on it.'

'So you do know some gods.'

'Prophets,' he said.

'You're laughing at me.'

'I'm allowed a little of that, Mary Lamont, seeing you take yourself so seriously.'

It was true enough. I took myself very very seriously. Too seriously to linger here on the corner with him with the red mail van marked with a giant V.R. loading from the Post Office and the errand boys pushing past.

This part of the town was always crowded by women going to market and men and boys hurrying to work. The shops were starting to trade. I had to remember it was still quite early in the day. There were stalls selling vegetables on the kerb just ahead of us and others selling meat – I could see a bleeding carcase being hoisted on to a hook. An omnibus was stopping on the further side of the road to let off passengers. All about me was the bustle of a beginning day.

A policeman watched a group of schoolboys hustling to school. He frowned as they pushed against each other.

I had already drawn away from Christian Ableman a little. Hidden cords still bound us, but the onlooker, knowing nothing of the game, might not have guessed that we had any connection with each other. Yet the game was real and the ties, although new, were of a strength as yet unassessed by me, and might hold. I took another step away.

157

Between me and Christian Ableman a gap had opened up, into which a fat old woman in black, intent on buying apples, had inserted herself. I was grateful to her for the intrusion. She was shuffling rapidly towards the apples, and then she turned her back towards me. Although she was so fat she didn't look soft and bouncy, but solid, like a wall, and her face, when I could see it, was round but not benign. Then she swung towards Christian. For a moment she was still, then I saw the back ripple, and she started to scream. Shout, really. She was pummelling at Christian with a fist like a man's and yelling at the top of her voice.

'Thief! Thief!'

Standing where I was, I saw that as her right fist banged him, her left hand was unobtrusively sliding into his pocket. Christian stood back from her with an angry word, but she followed him, shouting.

'Pickpocket! Thief!'

A small crowd soon clustered around them; the policeman advanced solemnly. She turned towards him and beckoned furiously, hanging on to Christian Ableman by his sleeve.

'Here's a thief, constable. He's had my purse. I felt him take it, so I did, the villain.'

'I have not touched her purse.' Christian Ableman spoke angrily.

I stood my ground, watching. A cab had halted in the road and the cabby was watching the scene, entranced. The schoolboys were jumping up and down to get a good view of events. On the edge of the crowd I saw Grace Stableton, another of Miss Clough's students, and destined to be my contemporary at the new women's college. She was watching with fascinated eyes.

'She's a liar.' Ableman again spoke.

'Search him,' commanded the old woman. 'You have a look and see if you don't find my purse. Got it in his pocket, I don't doubt.'

Christian dragged his arm away with a controlled force that told me how angry he was. He took a step sideways, as if he might push his way through the crowd.

'Hot beef, hot beef,' cried the schoolboys. 'Catch him and see, catch him and see.'

'What's this?' said the policeman. 'You're laying an accusation, are you, ma'am?'

'Yes, I am,' said the fat woman. Beneath her great skirts she had surprisingly neat small boots. I've often noticed fat women have delicate feet. 'Against *him*. He's had my purse. Search him.'

'I can't do that on the street, ma'am. But, of course, if the gentleman,' he looked doubtfully at Christian Ableman, who was looking fiercer and fiercer, 'would turn out his pockets voluntarily ...' He dragged out every syllable of the last word.

Ableman set his jaw, but the old woman flew at him like a great angry bird and drew her purse from his pocket with a triumphant screech.

There was a murmur from the crowd.

'So,' said the policeman. 'Well, come along now, my man.'

'Watch or he'll mizzle,' said one onlooker, who was straddling the gutter and eating a banana.

After a moment in which I hesitated, I knew what I had to do. 'No,' I said. 'No.' I moved forward. 'He didn't take it. I was watching. She put it in his pocket.'

'Liar,' said the fat woman. 'Watch what you're a-saying, miss, or you'll be in trouble. They're a pair, constable, both in it together, I dare say.'

I flushed. 'Ask her where she lives and her name,' I said solidly to the policeman. 'I can give you my name and the names of people to vouch for me.'

Out of the corner of my eye I was observing the furious face of Christian Ableman.

'A gammon,' he groaned. 'The old dumplin' trick and on *me*, too.' He seemed to feel the shame of it more than anything else, but I could see a more sinister picture. If the old woman's accusation held, then the policeman would be obliged to take Ableman into the police station (provided he could get him there, I thought with fleeting amusement). Once inside, he would not easily get out again. A notorious criminal had no real chance of escape. I did not know whether Christian Ableman had ever yet served a term in prison. Somehow I thought not. He had not the look or manner of a man who had known incarceration. He looked free. A wicked look now came over his face, and he grabbed the old woman in his turn. 'This isn't chance,' he said. 'Who put you up to it?'

Now that I studied his accuser's face, there was something alien about it. She stood out from the rather rustic characters around her.

'I don't believe she even lives in Oxford,' I said. Grace Stableton's eyes were on me, round with amazement. I remembered that she wasn't a clever girl but was celebrated for her retentive memory and sharp observation. She was now exercising both on me.

The policeman was looking interested. He turned to the fat woman. 'Can I have your name and address, madam?'

'Got my purse back,' she muttered. 'Won't press anything. Leave it there.' She was already beginning to efface herself in the crowd.

'Ask her where she *does* come from,' I said. 'London, I believe.'

But the woman's neat, agile feet were already carrying her rapidly down a side alley. She had pushed through the crowd and was now hurrying away.

'Well, I never,' said the policeman, slowly assessing the situation. 'She's a wrong 'un.'

So we all were in this scene, in our different ways, only he did not know it. Christian Ableman was a criminal; the fat woman was a faker, and I was as much a deceiver as if I was playing under-and-over in some fairground game. None of this was guessed by the policeman, a simple man with a Banbury accent. Without knowing it, he had caught a big fish in his net, but now it was going to swim away. I saw a bead of sweat on Christian Ableman's forehead and guessed that he was one of those people who could never tolerate the loss of his liberty. For him that way would lie madness.

'Thank you for speaking out,' he said, his voice thick.

'An embarrassment for you, sir,' said the policeman, the

politeness coming easily to his lips now, although it wouldn't have done a minute ago. 'You have to thank the young lady.'

'I do thank her.' Slowly he bent his head and kissed me on the lips. Spontaneously, tears sprang into my eyes. I stood quite still. 'It is time for me to go,' he said quietly. 'I am in danger here.' He stood away a little and I saw him smile. 'You think all the danger has been for you and yours, but I can tell you that in this jungle I, too, am hunted.'

'We must never meet again,' I said. 'Never meet, never speak, never touch.'

'I don't accept that. Not after what you just did for me.'

'It meant nothing, nothing at all.'

He reached out to grip my arm, but I turned resolutely away.

'Mary.' I didn't answer. 'I'll follow you. You shan't say me no.'

The crowd was melting away, the boys running to school, the women back to their shopping at the stalls. The policeman touched his helmet and took up his beat. Grace Stableton gave me one last fascinated look, as of one who had missed no aspect of interest, and moved on.

The cab which had halted came nearer. William Train leaned out of the window.

'I'll give you a lift back to Sarsen Place, I am on my way there now,' he said, with some austerity. 'Strange company you keep. Get in.'

I left Christian Ableman standing with his hand held out.

As the cab swung across Magdalen Bridge I could hear a newsboy shouting. There was a little hunch-backed lad who had a stand by the church there and called the news with a thin high nasal wail that never could be missed.

GIRL'S BODY FOUND IN SEWER, he called. GIRL'S BODY FOUND IN SEWER; and then again GIRL'S BODY FOUND IN SEWER.

Oh God, I thought, Ellen.

William Train saw my face, studied it for a moment, then turned away to look out of the window, his features drawn and tired.

'No, no one you know,' he said. 'Not the maidservant. A woman called Stella Darley; a milliner.'

'I *do* know her. She works at Madame Blanche's.'

'And the boy exaggerates; not a sewer,' he said. 'Her body was found in a small stream that runs into the Thames.'

'Drowned?' I said.

'Drowned,' he said.

Chapter Eight

Back at Sarsen Place the day was just beginning. A Sèvres china tray decorated with rosebuds and violets was being carried up to Mrs Demarest with her breakfast chocolate as I arrived. That it was going up the front stairs was an indication of the mild disorder in the house; the luggage for London was going down the back. Two great valises and one trunk, covered outside in dark blue upholsterer's velvet and inside in striped silk, were standing by Mrs Demarest's door.

'Are we going for long?' I asked. Yet I need not have asked. We were not going for long, but Adelaide Demarest could not travel, even to London for a few days, without many changes of dresses and all the accessories that went with them, the thin silk underbodices, the embroidered silk petticoats, the wrappers edged with lace and swansdown, the velvet slippers with rosettes on the toes. I didn't exactly envy her them, her style of dressing was not truly mine, any more than her heavy scent of heliotrope and sandalwood would have been; but I suppose I envied her the freshness and elegance of it all. To be economical about dress usually means to wear things not in the very first state of newness. This was how it was with my clothes, but I had packed my best Liberty dresses for London and hoped to peacock in them with the best. And I thought that their unusual colours and flowing simple lines were both more romantic and more becoming than those stiffer garments from Madame Blanche.

I walked into my room and saw Alice standing by the window. Her hair was shining and new-brushed, her face calm. Did she know about Stella Darley? But how could she, and, if she did, what could it mean to her?

Alice turned and smiled at me. I saw that all the night fears were washed away. She was no longer a frightened little creature, but a child again.

'We're off soon,' she said brightly. I realized she was happy at the thought of a holiday. 'Are you packed and ready?'

'Soon,' I said. I walked past her to my little Davenport desk. 'I have a letter to write.'

I must write to the boy Jack and tell him that I had found out nothing at all positive and let him know we were on the move. I did not want him to think I had deserted him, although what I was doing came very close to it. I picked up my pen and dipped it in the ink. I hoped he could read.

'Can Jack read?' I said, turning to Alice, who was still standing there.

'Oh *yes*, he and Ellen write to each other all the time.'

I might have known it. 'He's looking for Ellen,' I said abruptly. 'You feel strong enough to talk about it now? What did happen? Please tell me.'

She swallowed. 'I don't remember so *very* clearly, Mary. I remember going out with Ellen. I remember the wind being cold. Then someone hit me. And I remember Ellen screaming.'

'It was you screaming,' I said coldly. What she was telling me was less than she knew, I was positive of it.

Her eyes fell.

'Come, Alice,' I said impatiently. 'I've known for a long time there was something worrying you. Why not tell? You trust me?'

'Yes, yes, I *think* so.'

'Thank you, Alice,' I said, in a voice full of adult anger.

She raised her eyes to me, and when I saw the look in them I was ashamed. I read in them the fears of a pygmy in the forest for the giants, of someone who, however treasured and loved, knew her powers to be ultimately puny. I had forgotten the defencelessness of the child against adult society.

'It's a secret,' she said huskily.

'So?' I waited.

'It started before you came.'

'I knew that.'

164

'One day Nurse Mackenzie and I were in the Parks, walking...'

I wondered about Nurse Mackenzie. No one mentioned her much, and she seemed to have left no friends behind. A nonentity, I decided.

'Yes, Alice,' I prompted.

'Well, we saw, that is I saw...' She stopped and her eyes went to the door. 'She met a friend from Madame Blanche's...' Her voice trailed away.

'Forgive me for disturbing you, ladies.' William stood hesitantly at the door. 'May I come in and attend to the clock on the table?'

'Oh, come in.' I was hardly welcoming, but I knew the clock to be a valuable one, which needed delicate care.

He picked up the blue enamel and gold clock, and carried it to the window.

'Ah, yes.' He looked up from the clock, and gave us a serious look. 'I'm afraid I shall be some time.' He laid a selection of feathers and a bottle of oil on the table and drew a chair up. Over his sober work-clothes he had tied on a big white overall. It was hard to remember that this was the man who dreamed of fantastic jewellery, rich with yellow gold and studded with living jewels.

I was irritated by him but prepared to forgive him. I knew he loved the clocks. I stood up: I would soon make an opportunity to speak to Alice again.

'You treasure these clocks, don't you?' I said to William Train.

'More than their owners.' He held the clock up to the light, and squinted inside it. 'Never let an owner wind a clock, if you can help it. Death, it is.'

Alice had departed sedately, not unsorry, I thought, to get away without any further confidences.

I looked at his bent head. I was at a loose end till the carriage came round to the front of the house at eleven. My packing was done. 'I suppose you really know this house better than anyone, William.'

'In a very superficial way. I suppose you could say I know the furnishings.' He had a tart tongue.

'Did you know Nurse Mackenzie?'

He bent over the clock again, humming. 'Naturally.'

'Why did she leave?'

'No one told me.'

'But you listen to gossip. I know you do, I've seen you.'

He smiled a little. He could be like a great tabby cat at times. 'I suppose Alice outgrew her.'

'Where did she go?'

He shrugged.

'I expect Mrs Ceffery knows,' I went on.

'She may do.'

'I'd like to talk to Nurse Mackenzie. Yes, I'll ask Mrs Ceffery. She'll know her address. She's supposed to have married. If that's true, she may just have retired. Would Mrs Demarest have pensioned her?'

'Retired?' For the first time there was emotion in his voice: surprise. 'Pension?'

'Yes. She was quite old, I suppose?' I had an image of a plump, elderly, comfortable person.

'Old? Nurse Mackenzie? Not her. She was a young woman and a raving black-haired beauty into the bargain.'

I ought to have remembered that he had an eye for the girls.

'Well . . .' I drew a long breath. 'That certainly changes my picture of things.'

'I thought it might do,' he said, sardonically. 'So perhaps it might be as well not to inquire where she's gone, eh?'

The name that at once flashed into my mind, of course, was Captain Charles Demarest. He was in trouble of some sort, and perhaps it concerned Nurse Mackenzie. From what I had seen he was unlikely to have ignored a black-haired beauty in the same house. It was surprising, indeed, that Mrs Demarest should have engaged such a nurse for Alice, but she was a lady who liked to have things beautiful about her, and Miss Mackenzie may have captured her eyes. Like mother like son, I thought.

I finished my letter to Jack and handed it to Belcher for

delivery. Where Jack lived was unknown to me, but he must surely reappear by his chestnut stall sooner or later, in order to live, and then Belcher would hand over the note. In an odd kind of way I trusted Belcher to be efficient and practical, in his own grumbling fashion.

The moment I had finished, I received an urgent summons to Mrs Demarest, and expected a reproof for my absence. She said not a word. All my recent comings and goings appeared to have passed unnoticed, which confirmed my belief that the Demarest household was preoccupied with itself.

She was sitting up in bed, surrounded by all the equipment of a rich and idle life: her letters, several samples of new silks for her embroidery (which she did with superb taste and delicacy; one could never underestimate Mrs Demarest – had she been born poor, infallibly she would have surrounded herself with lovely objects of her own construction), two French novels, and her dog.

'Oh Mary, dearest,' she began. I was always Mary Dearest when she wanted me to do some task beyond the strict call of my duties as Alice's 'gouvernante'. Secretly, it amused me, because these were usually the errands I enjoyed most. 'I want you to go to Madame Blanche and collect my new violet hat to wear in London.'

One of the things that diverted me most about Mrs Demarest was the way she ordered special clothes in Oxford to wear to London and then when in London selected other choice garments in which to appear in Oxford. One city was constantly dressing her for the other, with, always, the spirit of Paris the presiding genius over all: although she assured me that for gloves and shoes and all soft and beautiful leathers Vienna was in every way superior. She attributed that to the taste of the Empress Elizabeth. ('You know she wears an undergarment of soft, soft leather against her skin, always?')

'The hat may not be ready,' I said.

'Oh, they'll get it ready for *me*.' She spoke with the utmost confidence. Clearly she did not know about Stella Darley and I decided not to tell her. She wouldn't regard it as a reason for not getting her hat. 'You know about our plans? My son has decided we shall all go to London, and that you and Alice are to come too. We shall have a delightful time. Shopping, the opera, Madame Tussaud's for Alice.'

'She won't like that,' I said promptly. 'She can't bear that wax doll of Madame Blanche's.'

Mrs Demarest stiffened. You might have thought, for a moment, that La Grande Pandore was a close friend of the family instead of a horrid stuffed creature with a painted wax face. Then she relaxed and smiled. 'I don't really like her myself, and I think it ridiculously old-fashioned of Madame Blanche to continue to use her. They are beginning to use real girls for showing clothes nowadays. In Paris Monsieur Worth always does so. Don't you think that an improvement?'

'It must always be better to give a job to a woman than a doll,' I said. 'Although, regrettably, women sometimes get mistaken for dolls.'

Women's emancipation was not a subject it did to embark on with Mrs Demarest, and now she made a little purring noise of dissent. 'We women would have a sad time of it if our clothes and our way of life were left to you to arbitrate upon, May.' There it was, the sting and the soft name May (which, incidentally, I hated) all cast up together in one sentence. She knew how to wound and bind in one breath. She was what society called 'a proper woman'.

'I'll get your bonnet,' I said. 'I'll bring it back in person.' If it kills me, I thought, that hat shall be fetched by me and deck your head in London.

'Take Alice with you,' she called after me. 'The air will do her good. And tell Belcher to use the brougham.'

I doubted if the scented hot air at Madame Blanche's could do anyone good and Alice had certainly glowered at the thought, but we neither of us, emancipated women in embryo that we both were, ever disobeyed a direct order given by that gentle tyrant Mrs Demarest.

My hopes of a continuation of the talk with Alice on the way down there were dashed by the appearance in the carriage of a toothache-stricken housemaid to be delivered to the dentist.

We were crowded together in the brougham; the big carriage was being cleaned for the trip to London.

I remember I looked at Alice across the tearful swollen face of the housemaid, and said: 'We'll talk later.'

I suppose it sounded like a threat, because she went white and nodded. Poor child, she must even then have been debating what lie to tell me.

Belcher dropped us at Madame Blanche's house in St Giles and muttered that he'd be back after he'd delivered 'this one to the dentist'. I gave him a meaning look, hoping he would understand I wished him to try to give my letter to Jack. He returned me a blank stare, but with Belcher that meant nothing. He habitually turned a dull face to the world. Over the years he had found it paid him better.

Alice and I went through the dark red front door, an eccentric colour among the black and dark brown of the others, but one which marked Madame Blanche's house for her own. We had come too early, the place had an air of only sleepily waking to life. With Alice standing beside me, wearing a set face, we waited in the pink and gold salon. For a moment I thought the establishment was untouched by the violent death that had come so close to it, but by and by I saw I was wrong. The room was subtly untidy. Always it was scattered with delightful and elegant objects, but the litter was planned to please. Now I was looking at disorder. We were left to wait a little too long as well, and when Madame Blanche arrived, although perfectly tidy, her colour was high and her manner jerky. She was never very pleased to see me. I suppose she sensed unconsciously that I was a saboteur of her world of indulged and pampered women. She was quick to recognize a threat to her livelihood. I suppose I should have respected Madame Blanche as an independent woman who supported herself, but to me she seemed a parasite on an aspect of society I detested.

I did not mention Stella Darley; neither did she. Another girl appeared through the heavy curtains, carrying a box with the promised violet hat. She looked as though she had been crying.

The little hat came out to be shown to me. It was a tiny thing, to be worn right at the back of the head with the curled hair falling forward. The ribbon was velvet, tied on one side with a small looped bow. I doubted if even Paris could produce anything more delicious. Madame Blanche certainly had genius of a kind. One half of me liked it very very much, and wanted to wear it.

I stood there frowning at it, caught up in a tangle of emotions, not noticing Alice.

'Agreeable, is it not?' said Madame Blanche. 'You think it will please Mrs Demarest?'

'Yes, indeed.' She wasn't truly interested in my opinion, what she was really doing was distracting my attention from her trembling hands as she twirled the hat. When I looked round, I saw that Alice had moved forward and was talking quietly to the girl assistant.

So now she knows about Stella Darley, I thought. She has asked the girl why she has been in tears and the girl has told her about Stella Darley's death. The two girls looked at me with the same guilty expression of those who have been talking about forbidden things.

The real truth did not, I swear, occur to me then.

Madame Blanche saw them too.

'Oh, I have your usual treat for you, miss,' she said to Alice. She twitched a curtain with a trembling hand. There, seated on a low chair in an alcove, dressed in a silk gauze ball dress, was Pandora. Only, where there should have been curls and pink and white simpers, was emptiness, a gaping void. Someone had taken Pandora's head off.

'Detestable,' said Alice in a low voice. 'Horrid thing.'

'Oh, she can see just as well without her head as with it, and vice versa, you know,' said Madame Blanche brightly. 'Dolls don't really have an independent life of their own.'

I thought Pandora looked as if she might have, and not a very nice one, either.

Madame Blanche reached behind the chair, retrieved Pandora's head, and fixed it on. 'There she is,' said Madame. 'I know little girls like dolls.' She smiled at Alice brightly. I thought the words 'detestable' and 'horrid creature' could have been applied as aptly to her as to her doll.

Belcher brought the carriage up as we came out into the street. He gave me a meaning wink, which certainly would not have been missed by even a less keen observer than Alice. She saw.

'Delivered your note,' he said hoarsely. 'Party you're interested in hangs out at 23 Walton Street. Basement premises, one room. Snug little billet.'

'He meant Jack?' said Alice as she stepped into the carriage.

'Yes.'

'I guessed.'

'You couldn't fail to,' I said repressively. I didn't wish her to enter into the subject. She saw this at once.

'I know where Jack lives. You could have asked me.'

'And how do you know?'

'Ellen told me.' She gave me a satisfied look and settled into her seat, but when we were moving, she wound the window up and turned to me with a movement so like her grandmother that I caught my breath.

Alice said to me soberly: 'One of the girls who works at Madame Blanche's has died. She's drowned.'

'Yes, I know.'

'You didn't tell me.' She said it objectively, calmly, not making an accusation of it, although it was one.

I didn't answer.

'You expect me to tell you things, but you don't tell me anything,' she said, reflectively. 'That doesn't seem fair.'

'I suppose I do it for your protection.'

She gave me a wintry smile, as one who knew all about *that*. 'Safe is better than sorry,' she remarked.

'Is that something your Nurse Mackenzie taught you?' I said irritably. It was such a nursery remark, the sort of warning nurses all over the world give their charges as they go near the flames or cross the road or walk near a river.

'Yes,' said Alice, turning away and looking out of the window of the carriage. She spoke not another word. For the moment I let it go. I would make my opportunity and talk to her some other time. Inside I felt the curious anger that all teachers feel, I suppose, when their pupils are difficult to control. Alice, usually so polite, was never really docile. Inside was a watchful alert observer.

'A hot drink for you before we set off,' I said, feeling her hand. 'You're cold.'

There was a great debate going on in Sarsen Place when we got back, on the subject of whether we should go to London by train or by carriage. Both were at our service. A compartment was reserved for us in the train and the carriage had been specially warmed, cleaned and aired for the occasion.

In the end things were arranged as I could have predicted from the beginning: the gentlemen went by train and Mrs Demarest, Alice and I travelled in the carriage, with arrangements to stop at High Wycombe for a late luncheon. I would have preferred the train as being quicker but there was a certain delicious enjoyment attached to travelling in the luxurious carriage. I had plenty to think about as the carriage rolled on, including some news from Mrs Ceffery that I put aside for the moment.

I knew what would happen at luncheon at the Red Lion. Mrs Demarest would find fault with the flavour of soup, the quality of the roast beef and the brew of the coffee. And she did. I, being hungry, ate all with relish. Alice picked at her food and complained of gristle in the meat. In this matter she and her grandmother saw eye to eye, and both looked at me doubtfully as I ate. I could see that in Mrs Demarest's eyes it demonstrated my lack of breeding. A lady should be like the princess in the fairy story and feel a pea beneath six mattresses.

I felt a sense of exhilaration as we bowled down the main road to London. I was leaving mysteries and terrors behind and going on holiday. I was young enough and silly enough to feel this way at the thought of pleasure. Of course, I covered it up for myself with a layer of earnest intentions. How I would visit the British Museum and study the Elgin Marbles and the little Greek temple they have there. How I would pay great attention to the opera and really try to understand the music for once, instead of just listening with my mind entranced. How I would visit the London Library and do some serious

172

reading every afternoon. I put all these virtuous thoughts in the front of my mind, but really I was lying back in my seat, bouncing along with the carriage springs, feeling the sun on my cheek and given up to the sheer animal pleasure of an outing.

I was happy in this manner until we had passed through Beaconsfield and picked up the main road to Slough, and thence London. Then I glanced at Alice and saw the pinched look around her mouth and knew that all our terrors had packed up and come with us. Do you know that story about the family that is haunted by a ghost, so they pack up and move house, and as they move off with all their goods and chattels disposed around them they hear the voice of the ghost from the top of the coach? He has packed up and moved off with them, too. So it was with us, our ghost had packed up and joined the party on its travels.

'What are you doing, Alice?' said Mrs Demarest, her voice quick. She was always irritable on a journey. I think she felt sick with the motion of the carriage but would not admit it.

'Playing solitaire.' Alice was fiddling with the tiny ivory toy balanced on her lap.

'It never comes out,' said her grandmother fretfully.

'It does sometimes.'

'I expect you cheat.'

'No, grandmamma.'

'Unconsciously. Everyone cheats unconsciously.' She was in a bad mood, a sad worried look tilting her lips downward.

The horses trotted on and we in the carriage rolled behind them. Every swing of the wheels was taking me farther away from the world of Tinker's and Madame Blanche, and equally from my own world of scholarship and learning where I talked with Mary Ward and Frances Pattison. The Great West Road, Slough, Kensington, Hyde Park, we had arrived.

In a quiet street near the Park our hotel greeted us with cheerful welcome. Mrs Demarest was an old and valued visitor. The doors were opened with a flourish, there was a scent of flowers and cigar smoke. A lady with a sable cap and muff went past, leaning languidly on the arm of her bearded stout companion.

She had enormous pearls and very pink cheeks. 'An actress,' said Mrs Demarest, with one look at her complexion. Then actresses have very august friends, I thought, but, of course, I might have been wrong in identifying her escort. Impossible not to believe that Mrs Demarest had not recognized him also, but she had passed on without another look.

The hotel was very modern and had a tiny gilt cage in which one ascended to the next floor. Mrs Demarest stood up very straight and still and thus betrayed her nerves, but Alice laughed and openly enjoyed the sensation.

'What a mercy we can't fly,' said Mrs Demarest, with a sigh of relief, as the lift stopped. 'Suppose there was such a machine. We should be obliged to use it, you know, because it would be fashionable and expensive; but just think how unpleasant.'

'But fast,' said Alice gleefully. 'I love to go fast. Faster and faster.' She was whirling round in the corridor.

Once inside the comfortable set of rooms arranged for us, Mrs Demarest was absorbed into the sybaritic way of life that suited her. Tea and delicate sponge fingers arrived to refresh her.

'Some tea, Mary?'

I accepted the tea, poured by a thin wrist and a long beautiful hand. The sponge finger was lemon-flavoured and both crisp and light. Alice sat on a footstool and ate shortbread. She was absorbed by the view from the window, paying the rest of us little attention.

The characteristic sweet fragrance that I always associated with Adelaide Demarest had already spread over the room. In an adjoining room her maid was preparing her bath and putting out the eau de toilette scented with sandalwood that would be rubbed into her body. As I watched I saw the maid light the spirit lamp which heated the curling tongs.

Adelaide Demarest touched the Alexandra fringes which she wore across her forehead. 'Yes, Marie, my hair does need a little crimping up, but no scorching me this time, mind.' Impossible to believe that her neat-fingered French maid had ever done her job other than deftly. What Adelaide Demarest was really saying was: 'I am different from you and my skin is more delicate and more sensitive than that of an ordinary person like you'. It was at moments like this that I felt as far away from her as I could possibly be.

She lit a cigarette, which she held in her pink-tipped fingers. Then she saw me looking, and laughed.

'You always look slightly shocked when I smoke, Mary, as if you have never seen a lady smoke before. I believe you *are* shocked.'

'No, my friend Mrs Mark Pattison smokes . . .'

'The wife of the Rector of Lincoln College?'

'Yes. But it always seems as though ordinary rules could never bind her.'

Mrs Demarest shrugged. 'Worldly ambitious women have always lived worldly ambitious lives.'

'Surely she is not that?' Now I was shocked.

'Pre-eminently, I should say. And well on the way to achieving her ambitions, I should speculate.' She laughed and arched her eyebrows.

I guessed she must be referring to some gossip or scandal I knew nothing of. I felt a flush rise in my cheeks. I couldn't bear to think of anything polluting or marring the elegant image of Frances Pattison. I didn't want to know more, and I was glad when Mrs Demarest rose and swept over to where the maid was arranging her dresses. Perhaps she thought she had gone too far and was glad to be quiet. I had noticed before that her cigarettes loosened her tongue, rather as drink sometimes did my father's.

Now she leaned towards me confidentially. 'I was glad to get Alice away from Sarsen Place. Such an intense child. I sometimes think the house does not suit her. Indeed, I have sometimes thought she positively dislikes it. A great shame, when it is so charming. It will fall into neglect in her possession, I dare say.' She sounded vexed at the prospect.

I raised my eyebrows. 'But surely her father . . .' I began.

'The house is, in fact, dear Alice's,' she said, breathing perfumed cigarette smoke over me. 'The place in Dorset is my son's. Sarsen Place is Alice's property.' She smoked some more. 'It comes to her from her maternal grandfather as part of her mother's marriage settlement. *Devolved* upon Alice, as the lawyers say.' She smiled blandly into the smoke haze she was creating. 'Alice will inherit great wealth.'

I knew I had heard something of great importance. The whole position of Alice was changed. She was not just a vulnerable child, she was also an heiress. I did not doubt that money had come together with Sarsen Place, probably a very large capital sum. Alice was rich.

Mrs Demarest had drawn away to talk to her maid. Alice turned from the window to join us.

'Yes, my hair now, Marie, and I am going to drive these two away.' My employer smiled at me charmingly. 'A rest is prescribed for you both.'

'A rest, nothing,' said Charles Demarest, coming into the room at that moment. 'Or rather, a rest now, in order to be at your best later.' He gave Alice and me a small bow. 'We are going to the opera. I have tickets.' He threw them on the table with a grand gesture.

I was learning to read Captain Charles, and I knew that in taking us to the opera he was postponing an evil hour elsewhere. I thought I could probably even name the spot where the evil hour might take place.

I looked at him without a smile as Alice and I departed at Mrs Demarest's gentle nod, and wondered what he would say if he knew the gossip already circulating in the servants' hall about him.

Mrs Ceffery had told me, as she prepared Alice a hot drink before our setting out.

'I expect there'll be fine doings in London and that you're being taken there to be a proper witness to them and to make it all seem above board. Or there again, you may never be told. I dare say the old lady' (Mrs Demarest would surely not have relished the title, she was only a few years older than Mrs Ceffery, but certainly lacked the other's sexual vigour) 'will snuff it all out if she can.'

'What has he done?'

I shouldn't have asked, of course, but I did. She expected me to, and she wanted me to.

'A married man, my dear, would you believe it? Married secretly for three years, got three sons.'

'Captain Demarest is married?' I found it hard to believe, no one looked less married.

'Got an establishment out at Kew. A lady wife and a family. But he won't own to them. Pretends they don't exist. Acts the bachelor. Married in Kew. Not married in Knightsbridge Barracks.'

'How do you know?'

'We're not supposed to know, but try keeping anything from us.'

I accepted this statement. I knew the servants' hall to be excellently informed, within certain narrow limits.

'We've known longer than the master and madam. Now *they* know, and, oh, the fuss. I could have told 'em weeks ago. My sister's husband's cousin has a grocery business and he's been serving Mrs Charles since they moved there, which they did after Christmas. But I kept a still tongue.' She looked virtuous.

As I sat in my room, I wondered if this was indeed why we had been brought to London. It could be so, but it was not how the Demarests arranged things. And, in any case, I was not sure Mrs Demarest knew of her son's marriage, even if the servants' hall did. There was exasperation in her manner to him, but none of the outrage I thought she might have felt at the story of a secret wife and a hidden family. Three sons, I thought, how long is he planning to keep them quiet? Until they are grown up and ready to join his regiment?

I had the strong feeling, that no reasoning could dispel, that the Demarest family were closely connected with the deaths of the women. Two women who had moved on the edge of my world had died by violence. Louise had died mysteriously, perhaps by drowning, perhaps by some other method that mimicked it. I guessed that Stella Darley had died in the same fashion. Behind both deaths I sensed a killer who had no taste for violence, just a cold-blooded ability to use murder as it suited his ends. Some women attract violence. I did not need Tinker's to teach me that lesson. Perhaps the protagonists spilled out of the underworld of cockney London, with its poverty spurring them to come, but the Demarests had their part to play. But which Demarest? I summoned them in turn before my eyes. First, the one I knew best, my clever, bewildering Alice. Sometimes I did not know what to make of her. She had it in her to become what Jessie and I might never achieve, a 'new woman', emancipated, educated, free. But all might founder yet, if she was not properly educated in these crucial years of her girlhood. Here I distrusted Adelaide Demarest, whose ambitions for her grand-daughter could hardly include a serious education. The question was whether she ruled her sons, in particular Mark Demarest. I suspected he found it difficult to resist her warmth and charm. Was he a man softened by women? He was hard for me to weigh up; of all the Demarests I found him the most difficult to know. He teased me. I did not waste much time in worrying over Captain Charles Demarest, who seemed a shallow, selfish man with all his mother's faults and none of her virtues. No doubt he resembled his father, the creator of the original scandal which still seemed to hang over the family. Charles was only carrying on the family tradition.

Among these three adults might be one unnatural soul who desired to destroy Alice Demarest. The servants thought so, and divided their suspicions between them. Mark Demarest, they conjectured, might wish to replace his legitimate daughter with his natural child, Ellen. If Ellen *was* indeed his daughter. Or alternatively, Charles Demarest, the classic wicked uncle, could be plotting to become his brother's heir. Adelaide Demarest's position was more ambiguous. I liked her, and even admired her. But I saw strange lax traits in her character.

I brushed aside these suspicions as the barbarous products of uneducated minds. The servants read too many stories from the Newgate Calendar. At the same time, I knew them to be sharp observers of their employers. They were wrong, yet not entirely wrong.

I walked to my window and looked out. Below was the London street. Evening was here, and there were few pedestrians, but cabs and carriages rolled by every minute. Two red-coated soldiers strutted past. We were not so far from Knightsbridge Barracks. A policeman paced sedately along the pavement. I felt far away from Tinker's and the house of women which 'knew all the secrets'. But I knew there was a link between that world and Soho and its itinerant population of pleasure-seekers and light women. A figure moved in the dusk below me. Something in the stance and the build reminded me of Christian Ableman. Then the figure was gone. I dropped the curtain and went back into the room.

With some care I dressed for the evening. I couldn't do much about my hair, which had its own way of settling into waves, whatever style I tried. In any case it suited me best if worn plainly. I looked at my image in the looking glass, and saw that my skin was pale by nature, but with the faint pink of health discernible beneath the creaminess. I never had a bright colour, but I was not sallow. My eyes are my best feature, deep blue and wide, giving me a gentler, more innocent look than I deserve to own.

I wore my best Liberty dress of blue and white. I thought its simple, flowing lines, with its neck cut square, and the skirt with 'Watteau pleats' infinitely more aesthetic than the contrived elegances of Mrs Demarest's smart London dress with its low décolletage.

When I was dressed, I peacocked up and down before the mirror before spraying my hair with some Florentine water.

There was a quiet knock at the door and, holding my skirt, I moved across to open it.

Mark Demarest stood there. He had dressed for the evening in formal dark broadcloth and starched linen. We stared at each other, then he came in and closed the door behind him.

'I wanted to talk to you on your own, Miss Lamont. You must be wondering why we have all come to London.'

I waited. I spared him the thought that the servants believed he had a terrible family scandal on his hands.

'There is some legal business to attend to,' he said, making the admission with difficulty. All the Demarests preferred to behave as if their life was conducted on an Olympian height.

179

'But I brought Alice away, and you with her, Miss Lamont, because the police advised me she was in some danger at home.' He took a few steps up and down the room. 'I wanted to keep it from her.'

'She knows it,' I said.

He stopped short. 'You think so? She's only a child.'

'A very alert, clever one.'

'She can't know everything.' He resumed his pacing.

'She knows enough.' And more than you think, I told myself.

'You will have seen that the body of a woman has been found in a stream at Oxford? The police make a connection between what happened to Alice and Ellen and what happened to this woman. Also the death of another woman earlier.' He sighed heavily. 'It seems Ellen knew both women. I think that must mean that Alice, too . . .' He stopped.

'That Alice also knew them. I think so,' I said. 'She must certainly have known Stella Darley.'

I could see him fumbling with the idea that Alice might not be the innocent bystander, but, in some way, an active participant.

'I am concerned about the missing girl, Ellen. You must not think . . .' He paused. 'She's a good girl. I have seen her with Alice.' I suppose something in my silence got through to him. 'I know it is said (oh yes, I *do* know, Miss Lamont, gossip gets around),' he gave a slight smile, 'that she is my natural daughter, but that is not so. She is not *mine*.'

I thought of his smooth-skinned bright-eyed manservant, and I knew the channel by which gossip got through to Mark Demarest.

'She is indeed the daughter of someone I was fond of, a boy I grew up with in Dorset and who died at the battle of Kandahar. His widow moved to a village in Oxfordshire.'

'You didn't have to tell me, Mr Demarest.' I felt myself flushing.

'I found I wished to do so.' We stared at each other in silence. Then he spoke in a voice deeper than I had heard. 'You know, Miss Lamont, charming as you look tonight, I believe you mistake your style. You don't really belong to the world of Mr

William Morris and Mr Rossetti. You should wear clothes of great elegance and richness. Truly, you belong to the great world, Mary Lamont, whether you know it or not.'

He was gone before I could answer. I went to stare at myself in the mirror on the wall. I tried to imagine myself in the formal splendour of a dress from Worth or Doucet. I smoothed my hair back from the forehead, straightening the waves, imagining jewels here and on my throat. But all I could see was a very tired girl, wearing the only dress she could afford.

We were joined at the opera by a third man, who was introduced to me as Sir Henry Russell, and I knew him for a lawyer before he ever opened his mouth. You can usually tell a sailor by the lines around his eyes, and a lawyer by his mouth, with its careful, neutral, give-away-nothing set. He had such a mouth, and as soon as he spoke in that resonant beautiful voice I knew he must be a barrister. I was an innocent then, and did not know that he was a barrister in the Queen's Bench and specialized in civil cases, those concerned with property and marriage.

I sat in the box with Alice, neat in blue velvet, between me and Mrs Demarest, and listened to the flowing melodies of Gounod's *Faust*. The house was darkened, but I could see the bare shoulders and jewels of the ladies in the stalls below and smell the faint but perceptible perfume of flowers floating up to me. I watched Alice enjoy the prettiness of the ballet and I sympathized, heartily, with the plight of the heroine Marguerite when she bewailed her love for the damned Faust. I discussed the opera with Alice in the interval, but all the time I was really straining to hear the conversation of the men behind me. A word here, a word there filtered through to me.

Part of it was about an earlier meeting between them all, which had apparently taken place in Oxford and confirmed my belief that Sir Henry Russell had been the lawyer present in the library the day before we all left for London.

Sir Henry seemed to be giving advice that the brothers found unpalatable. Or possibly it was just Charles who was reluctant. His was the uneasy answering rumble. What Sir Henry said, time and time again, was 'It must be done'. He said it different ways, trust a lawyer for that, but he always said the same thing. Truth will out, he was saying, you must set the record straight.

Mark Demarest hardly spoke at all. I caught one phrase. 'Coming on top of my business,' he said, and his voice sounded weary. Sir Henry, in reply, was brisk and cheerful. 'Families survive,' he said. 'It's their job to.' And then I heard him move, as if leaning forward, and say, in a kindly way, 'You must marry again.' Behind my back I heard Mark Demarest murmur what sounded like 'There has been too much marrying in this family'. And beside me, it seemed to me, Adelaide Demarest drew in her breath sharply. I glanced at her. She, too, was listening. Only Alice sat with wide eyes and parted lips, looking at Covent Garden, and full of excitement.

Mrs Demarest got up. 'Mark, Charles, let's walk down the stairs and show Alice the portraits that hang in the foyer.' She turned to me. 'Portraits of past singers and dancers. Not good in themselves, but interesting.'

'I'd rather stay here,' said Alice. 'I like looking down on it all.' She spoke dreamily, as if the scene had mesmerized her. But we persuaded her to come with us, and walked through the anteroom, out into the corridor, and down the wide red-carpeted stairs. The staircase was crowded with other opera goers. Sir Henry Russell was still continuing his low-voiced conversation with Mark Demarest. His visit to the opera was pretence: it was business all the time with him. Probably he was always the same. I saw him bow in a languid way once or twice to acquaintances as he passed them. But this, too, was pretence. His back was straight and his eyes bright and untired. Languor and indifference were his game.

'My friend Norris assured us yesterday . . .' I heard him begin to Mark Demarest.

'Your friend Norris is a policeman,' said Mark Demarest bluntly.

Good, I thought to myself, now I know that the two men visiting Sarsen Place yesterday were Sir Henry Russell and a distinguished London policeman called Norris. I was a better detective than Mrs Ceffery. I also knew that Sir Henry had talked about 'family matters' with Mark Demarest and his brother. But what had the policeman talked about and why had he been there? Had Sir Henry brought him down? At the request of Mark Demarest? The Demarests were the sort of people who might expect important policemen to come to their aid when they needed help, and Sir Henry was just the man to have a tame policeman in his pocket.

But the subject, I thought, what did they discuss? The attack on Alice, the disappearance of Ellen, the involvement of professional crime? Did the policeman Norris really believe that out of the alleys and tenements of London's slums had come a plot which touched the Demarests, wealthy, cultivated and protected as they were?

I walked sedately down the steps behind the three men, Alice by my side. At the foot of the staircase a large concourse of people were strolling around. It was an occasion to see and be seen. I observed one or two dresses in the loose simple style I was wearing but I had to agree with Mark Demarest that they did not appear to advantage in these sumptuous surroundings, which were made for formality. I was almost at the bottom of the staircase, with Alice on my right, when I saw Christian Ableman.

He looked up and saw me. He knew I was there, had probably been looking out for me. There was nothing chance about this meeting. He was well dressed, wearing the same dark cloth and white linen that the other men wore, and with something more of a flourish than most. His dark skin was flushed, as if he had been drinking. He looked raffish, but with a glitter about him. Beside him, Mark Demarest seemed quiet and unassuming.

He had a companion. The woman on his arm was wearing black satin and no jewellery except a plain jet necklace; she had a plain, good-natured face, now looking ill at ease, as if she wished herself elsewhere. She had her arm linked with his and showed an appearance of wanting to withdraw. They stood out in the crowd as people who were different, and the crowd parted around them to let them through as if they were Hottentots.

'In the same world at last, Miss Lamont,' he said, sweeping me a bow. 'We meet on an equal footing.'

'I hope you enjoyed the opera.'

'Lovely music,' said the woman, dabbing at her forehead with a handkerchief. 'Lord, upon my word, it's hot in here.'

'Quiet, Maudie, speak when you're spoken to.' He *was* drunk. 'I enjoyed the opera as much as you did, Miss Lamont, which wasn't so much. I'm thinking. I watched your face.'

I felt a suffocating feeling, as if the walls were closing in on me. Alice, who was watching me, moved closer and clutched my hand. 'Are you all right?' she said urgently. 'Are you all right?'

'I like to watch you,' said Christian Ableman. 'I do watch and always will, when I am able. Or others will do it for me. I am all eyes.'

'Go away,' I said in a low voice. 'Go away. Never let me see you again.'

His face darkened. 'Take care what you say, my darling.'

'Go away.' I turned. The Demarests were politely pretending not to notice any strangeness, but there was no doubt that they had heard everything.

'Be my angel or my devil, but stay with me,' he said, rocking on his heels.

I turned away, taking Alice by the hand. The Demarests, polite as ever, moved on with me without a word. But behind me I heard Sir Henry say in a quiet voice to Charles: 'Strange friends Miss Lamont has.'

Odious man, I thought, horrid patronizing snobbish man.

I sat rigidly still during the next part of the opera, hardly hearing the music, staring straight ahead, knowing that from somewhere in the house Christian Ableman was studying me.

In the second interval the others remained seated, but I made my way to the ante-chamber behind our box, where a carafe of wine and one of water had been placed for us on a table. Thirstily I drank some wine and water.

I heard a footstep behind me, then I felt an arm go round my waist. Surprised, I turned round and found myself pressed into Charles Demarest's arms and his lips on mine. I remained quite motionless, sternly resisting the impulse to kick him.

'Just a little kiss,' he said, raising his head. 'You're so dev'lish pretty.'

'Charles!' His brother's voice was crisp.

'Hello, Mark, just having a little breather, don't you know.' He gave me a sheepish look, which I returned with a blank stare. 'Must go back now. Hear the music starting up.'

His brother stood aside and held the curtain back for me to take my seat. 'I apologize for my brother,' he said softly as I passed. I did not answer. I knew now where I stood with at least one Demarest brother. I was an object to be fondled and patronized. Never had I felt closer in spirit to my friend Jessie. I was furiously angry. I wanted to spit, snarl and scratch.

Nevertheless, it was not I who needed a restorative. On the way home, Mrs Demarest, who had been increasingly restless and irritable, demanded her smelling salts. I held the small rounded bottle, decorated with Madame Blanche's Golden Rose, to her nostrils, as she leaned back against the pillows of the carriage.

My nose pricked with the stinging smell of ammonia.

I was ill-humoured all the next day and took Alice around to see the sights of London with a poor grace. Normally, I think I might have enjoyed myself. I like a holiday as well as anyone. Alice did not wish to visit the Waxworks or the Zoo or any of the usual childish treats, but said she wished she might go to the Natural Science Museum in Kensington. There was the skeleton of a pterodactyl she was anxious to see. It had a dull-looking face with a tiny brain. Not an animal that it would have been interesting to meet, I felt.

All the time, as I went through the streets, I seemed to be more conscious of that other world that people like the Demarests hardly knew existed, the world of the poor and the criminal. I seemed to see members of it all around me. The boy who swept the crossing outside the entrance to the Museum. The old woman selling flowers on the kerb. The man wheeling a barrow of stinking fish along the road. They were poor people, probably not professional criminals, but who could blame them if they were not fussy about how they turned their next halfpenny? Not I. They walked on wild pavements.

I looked too at the sharp-featured man lounging on the corner by the hotel, and wondered if he had rubbed shoulders with Christian Ableman and was his friend or his rival. And there was the girl I saw standing with her shawl dipping across her stained satin dress and the safety pin joining together her bodice. Had she once been known at Tinker's? I remembered Jessie saying that the poor and women were equally exploited and maltreated by society, and ought to join together. 'The poor and the women together, that *would* be a revolution,' she exclaimed enthusiastically. I could just imagine Jessie, with her American ideas of hygiene, subjecting some of her unwashed revolutionaries to hot baths before she allowed them to proceed with the change of government.

Alice and I did not speak much to each other. I no longer wanted to question her about Ellen, from which I thought I would only get prevarication or lies. Alice wasn't a girl whose mind I could control and that's all there was to it. She had her own standards and she lived by them and judged others by them. I suspected she judged me by them. Once or twice I had seen her looking at me in an old-fashioned way, half affectionate, half indulgent, as if she was immeasurably more mature than I was.

They were a baffling family, the Demarests. Except Charles. He did not baffle me. Even his little secret life had been displayed in the open for me. Spread out for me to see, with sighs by his brother.

Mark Demarest sat by, while Alice drew some of the things that she had seen that day, and he talked to me.

'He has been married three years and kept it from us all this time. Three sons, Miss Lamont, and his wife ...' He shook his head. 'Poor woman. Never acknowledged. A married man in Surrey and an unmarried man in Knightsbridge. Even when rumours got to his Colonel he assured him he was an unmarried man. But we've had it all out now. He may have to leave the Guards, of course.'

'I suppose that's why he kept quiet.'

'Not so.' He shook his head. 'He hates being a soldier, although his Colonel says he makes a good officer. Charles always wanted to be a diplomat or a politician.' He smiled ruefully. 'Poor Charles, he was cut out to be an elder son and has always felt the lack of it.'

Your servants think he is by way of remedying that defect, I thought. They believe he has engaged a professional criminal to help him. Only it was I, Mary Lamont, not Mrs Ceffery, who could supply his hireling's name – Christian Ableman.

But it was Mrs Demarest who told me about Mark Demarest, and did so in an awkward and stiff manner that I wondered if it was her son who had asked her to do it.

'This has not been entirely a pleasure expedition,' she said. 'Of course, I know there was the matter of Ellen . . .' Her hands fluttered. 'But we had other business here in London. Or rather, my son had.'

I waited.

'The fact is . . .' Again a pause. She hated telling me this. 'It is not true, as you have been told, that Alice's mother is dead. She is far from dead. She left my son in company with another man when Alice was two years old. They were all on holiday in Italy, and she eloped with a man she had got to know out there. They moved in very artistic, literary circles, unwisely, in my opinion, and this is what came of it.' She closed her eyes for a second and then opened them again. 'Last year my son started a suit for divorce and under Sir Henry's guidance this has recently been brought to a successful conclusion.' She took a deep breath and seemed glad to have done with it. But I had a question.

'Does Alice know?'

'No, certainly not. It has not been necessary to tell her.'

'She ought to know. She has a right to know.'

'How can a child of twelve have such rights?'

I shrugged.

'Pass me my cigarettes before you go, please, Mary.' Her apricot-coloured tea gown fell away from her arm. I passed her the box.

'May I try one?'

'I shouldn't.'

'I *have* smoked,' I said, remembering the cigarette at Tinker's.

'And did you enjoy it?'

'It had a strange effect,' I said.

She laughed, and took out a cigarette. 'Oh, you were a novice.' She puffed lazily, closing her eyes to enjoy it.

A dark-faced woman appeared from her dressing-room. 'Mrs Demarest?'

My employer opened her eyes. 'Ah, there you are, Teresa.' She smiled at me and our interview was over. 'You and Alice can have tomorrow morning all to yourselves,' said Adelaide Demarest, as we parted. 'I have fittings at my dressmaker's and my son has an appointment with his lawyers. Mr Champion has come up from Oxford specially for it.' Naturally, for such an important client as Mark Demarest the Oxford lawyer would leave his humbler clients and travel up in the train to Paddington. Probably, too, he enjoyed being in the secrets of the smart world.

As I sat alone in my room after leaving Mrs Demarest, I wondered why Mrs Ceffery had not told me about the elopement and the divorce. I could only suppose that the Demarests were able to keep secrets even from their servants. But, then, they could afford to pay people like Sir Henry Russell to help them do it.

I sat there in my corsets and wrapper and reflected that a kind of bastard *noblesse oblige* would prevent me telling Mrs Ceffery what I now knew. It was a shame, because I could imagine the speed with which she would have hastened to tell such things to me.

I smiled, and drew off my stockings.

Alice was sitting up in bed in the room adjoining, reading one of her stiff books on science. From the door I said: 'Who is Teresa, Alice?'

She looked up. 'Miss Mackenzie was called Teresa.'

'There's someone called Teresa here now, with your grandmother,' I said.

'What's she like?'

'Handsome,' I said. 'Young. Not a bit like a children's nurse.'

'Then it's her,' said Alice, and lowered her eyes to her book. I waited for her to say something more, but this was the end, apparently.

We still had another day in London. I woke up early and found my room full of sunlight. A sunny day is still enough to make me happy. I am very easily affected by my surroundings. I was influenced now by the comfort and luxury of my hotel room. I felt pleased and soothed. The wellborn ease of the Demarests was rubbing off on me. I stretched back on the big down pillows and wondered what it felt like to be Mrs Demarest. But that way of thought was dangerous, so I got up, splashed my face with cold water, and thought of my friend Jessie.

I knew by the colour of the sunlight that I had overslept, but perhaps it wouldn't matter very much. Alice and I had all day to idle through. Alice too must still be drowsy, for all was quiet in the room which adjoined mine. Or perhaps she was reading in bed.

I dressed quickly and went through the door which linked our two rooms.

Alice was not there.

Alarm did not immediately sweep over me. All Alice's girlish possessions were still scattered about the room, her books, her ivory-backed hairbrushes, her discarded hair ribbon. It looked as though she had just got up from the bed, dressed, and walked out of the room.

Then I saw that her heavy walking boots were gone and her tweed skirt and jacket and her plaid cloak with the hood. I walked over to her dressing table. Her little purse had gone, too, and so had a small brown case.

I could read the signs. Alice had packed a bag and gone. She hadn't been kidnapped and she wasn't lost, except to us. Some time this morning, of her own free will, she had departed.

If I sound cold and hard in my reactions, it was not so; it was just that I never had a moment's doubt where she had gone. I had known from the beginning that the three children, Ellen, Alice and Jack were as thick as thieves. Alice knew where Jack lived and she surely must have gone there. Why she had gone was one thing to worry about. Her state of mind as she fled was another.

I went into the corridor in search of the maid. I found her bringing my breakfast tray, assisted by a waiter. I followed them back into my room and watched them place the tray on a round table in the sunlight. Then I let the man go, and asked the girl to stay. I poured some coffee and drank it while I considered what to say. It might be wiser not to be too explicit.

'Did you see the young lady go out?' I said.

'Miss Demarest?' She sounded surprised. 'Yes, she went down the stairs at a run, carrying a small bag, and I thought she had gone to catch her grandmother up. Mrs Demarest and her two sons had just gone off.' Now she was getting nervous. 'I hope there is nothing wrong?'

Clever, clever Alice, I thought, to time your departure to give the impression you were running after your grandmother, for, of course, you were not.

'No, nothing is wrong.' I drank some more coffee. 'But she didn't tell me she was going.'

'She hasn't run away?' Now she was interested and curious.

I didn't answer. In my opinion Alice had done just that. I stood up. 'Thank you,' I said. 'Is anyone in Mrs Demarest's room?'

'I don't know, miss.'

I walked in, the rooms were empty. I suppose I had thought, in my heart, that Teresa Mackenzie might be sitting there waiting for me to accuse her. For I certainly had a desire to accuse her: of mistreating Alice, mistreating her so seriously that Alice had fled from this place as soon as Teresa Mackenzie appeared in it.

I went through all the rooms given over to Mrs Demarest. The first two were clean and empty. But on the dressing table I saw Mrs Demarest's little gold mesh purse lying open and empty. I suspected that Alice had not gone to Oxford with an empty purse, she had emptied her grandmother's.

In the third room, the dressing-room, her maid was sitting at a table sewing. She glanced up with an unfriendly look.

'Madam's out, miss.'

'Is Teresa Mackenzie here?'

She pursed her lips. 'She is not.'

'She was here yesterday.'

'I dare say. Nurse Mackenzie's behaviour is no concern of mine.'

Spleen and envy were written all over her face.

'What is Teresa Mackenzie?' I said.

'That's not for me to say,' she answered repressively, and bent her head over her sewing. 'But she's not a good woman.'

'I wish I could speak to her myself.' I was pacing the room restlessly.

'I shouldn't advise it, Miss Lamont. Teresa Mackenzie is better left alone.'

I thought *she* was better left alone, at all events, and I had decided what I must do. Conscious thought was hardly necessary, there was no moment when I sat down to think things out, what I must do seemed already planned in my mind.

'But you know where she is?'

The woman gave me a tight sour smile; she was so eaten up with envy and hatred of Teresa Mackenzie that she did not fear to show it. 'She's not far away. Mrs Demarest requested her to stay. Teresa Mackenzie has a room on the top floor next to mine.' She hissed the words out in her fury. 'Requested!' She almost spat the words. 'I think Madam dare not refuse.'

'Tell me how to find her room.'

'You walk up the stairs, two flights. On the top floor are the rooms for the ladies' maids and valets. We have to sleep somewhere, you know, even such as us. Teresa Mackenzie has room 8.' She turned away with an angry shift of her shoulders. 'Madam gave her Madam's third best cashmere shawl, which if it *was* to be disposed of, *I* had a right to.' She couldn't help spewing out that last bit of spite.

I found room 8 and knocked on the door.

'Come in.' The voice was deep, but very feminine. Teresa Mackenzie was seated in a low chair; the cashmere was thrown over the bed in front of her as if she had been studying it.

She stared at me. It was a strange face, full of the elements of beauty, a broad white brow, rich lips, a noble curve of cheek, but not achieving loveliness. She frightened me.

'Well, Miss Lamont?' she said.

'You know me?'

'Of course.' She was calm, but I felt instinctively it was not the calm of indifference.

I shut the door behind me. It was a brave act. I would have chosen to run away if I could. I believed I saw the evil genius who had organized the series of episodes directed against Alice. I had expected to find a figure that repelled me. Reality always shames imaginings with its richness. She did not repel me; I saw her fascination, but as she came towards me, and I saw the strange light in her eyes, I knew she was mad. Not with the madness that would send her to an asylum, although that might come, but with a deep abnormality. Somewhere within her human reason had been overthrown and something alien and irrational had taken its place. Can you tell all that at a glance? And yet, I thought I did.

'Yes,' I said, as I stood there, back against the door. 'I suppose you have always known all about me, and I have known a very little about you.'

Her eyes stared at me as if I had been impertinent.

'I have found your traces, though.' Unconsciously, I was talking of her as if she was an animal, a terrible thing to do. 'The rattle of your baby; his grave; your photograph of Charles Demarest.'

She repaid me with a look of anger. 'I *hoped* they would be found,' she said in her deep voice. 'I had a *right* they should be seen.'

I wondered if she spoke in this manner to Adelaide Demarest. Then I thought that she did not need to be arrogant with that lady because she had a hold of another sort over *her*, the exact nature of which I did not yet know for sure, but began to suspect.

'Oh yes, I know you, Mary Lamont,' she said. 'We all knew all about you before you came to Sarsen Place. Your cleverness and your kindness, your education and your elegance. Add to them your fancies and your follies and I reckon I know you.'

I thought we knew each other; and there was a battle on between us, my weapons against hers. My heart sank. All I had to use was reason, logic, the intuitive processes of the human mind. Opposing me was demoniac force; she seemed larger than life. All the time I was talking to her I could see that her feet were never still, the right one was rubbing restlessly, incessantly, against the other. It was like the motion of an animal waiting for the moment to attack.

I never doubted that her cruelty and hatred had assembled all the terrible assaults on Alice's body and mind. Teresa Mackenzie took pleasure in pain: it was as simple and awful as that.

'I came to you to plead for Alice Demarest,' I said in a low voice. 'I see now it is of no use.'

As I walked down the corridor I heard her laughter in my ears.

It had been a false move to see Teresa Mackenzie, for I had both alerted her and made her angry. But I too could be clever and quick and passionate. I decided to act.

Before leaving, I wrote two short notes, one to Mrs Demarest, the other to Mark Demarest, telling them where I was going and why. I left these to be given to them as soon as they returned.

I descended in the lift, the only passenger, and demanded a cab from the hotel porter. One soon arrived, the usual weather-beaten, blasé London cabby holding the whip. 'Where to, miss?' He waited for directions.

I stepped in. 'Take me to Scotland Yard,' I said. I hoped he was impressed, but it was impossible to tell, with such a lined and seamy face as his was.

He drove me with despatch to that area in the old Palace of Whitehall known as Scotland Yard. 'Going to be a move here soon,' he said gruffly, as he let me out. 'Got too big and grand, they has, for this old place, and so the government has bought them a site on the Embankment and is a-going to have a great new big building there for to watch over us and keep us all happy.' He gave a cynical low rumble that passed for a laugh.

'Will you wait for me? I don't expect to be long.'

'I charges for waiting,' he said at once.

'Ten minutes,' I said firmly.

I marched through the door. A uniformed but bareheaded constable stood there. He held the door for me politely enough, but also effectively blocking my way.

'Yes, miss?'

I had decided what I should say: 'I want to speak to Mr Norris,' I said, in as firm a voice as I could manage.

'Mr Norris, miss? We haven't got a Mr Norris here.'

'He's an important policeman.' I had decided that if he was a friend of Sir Henry Russell he must be a very important police-man indeed.

He looked at me keenly, but I stood my ground. 'Lord love me, miss,' he said. 'I believe you mean Mr Norris Vincent.'

193

I realize now that I was privileged to see John Norris Vincent at the height of his powers and in the full flourish of his great position at the head of Scotland Yard. As a young barrister he had been summoned by the Home Secretary, Robert Lowe, to take hold of the Metropolitan Police at a time of crisis and scandal. He was the virtual creator of the Criminal Investigation Department, which he modelled on the centralized French system, of which he had made a special study.

He was standing with his back to the window when I was ushered in, and my first impression was of height, a commanding head, and broad shoulders. Later, as my eyes adjusted themselves, after the darkness of the corridor, to the sunlit brightness of the room, I saw he had blue eyes and dark brown hair. Across one chair was the check overcoat I had already noticed as he stepped into the car at Sarsen Place.

He looked at me without speaking. I was worldly enough to realize that there was something surprising in the ease with which I had got to see this important man. As he studied my face, I understood that my name, taken in to him, meant something to him and that he wished to see me.

'So you are Miss Lamont,' he said, drawing up a chair for me. I sank into it, my legs suddenly weak. 'I have wanted to meet you.'

'You know me?'

He smiled. 'You are the young lady who laid the information that sent me scurrying down to Oxford.'

'With Sir Henry Russell?'

'That was one occasion. But not the first.' He was still smiling, and unlike many smiles on official faces this smile gave the impression of genuine compassion and good humour.

'You are a remarkable young lady.' He sounded admiring. 'Are you going to make a habit of calling on policemen?'

Such was his charm that I could laugh with him. 'I hope not, sir.'

'And so you thought I was called Norris?' He leaned back in his chair, and looked amused.

'I heard Sir Henry talk about you.'

'Oh, Harry Russell.' He was playing with a pencil on his desk. I was properly impressed with a man who could call the great Sir Henry 'Harry'. 'In the same chambers once, we were. A devilish good advocate, Sir Harry. Melt your heart he would, when he leads for the defence, and freeze your marrow when he attacks for the prosecution, a regular tiger, but on the whole I would say he was at his best as a defence counsel, and that's where the money is.' He had a pleasant voice with a trace of some country accent: Leicestershire, I thought. All the time he was speaking he was watching my face.

'You're a teller of tales, young lady, are you not? Quite a Scheherazade.'

Scheherazade had a meaning for me he could not know. She was to be given her life provided she kept her lord amused. All her energies, all her vivid intelligence, all her grace, everything that made her a person was turned into a toy. I hated the society that found charm in this fable. I had an idea that Scheherazade and I had a lot in common. She was the first modern woman struggling to survive.

'Only your stories can be believed,' he went on.

'I did not realize that anyone took seriously what I had to say,' I said to him.

'It fitted in with other information we were receiving, Miss Lamont. An organization like this has many sources, as you may imagine. The task is to relate them, and assess their truth. We assessed your information, Miss Lamont, and found it interesting.' He was still playing with his pencil. 'We have been fearful, from certain things we know, that organized French crime is coming into this country. Our criminals are not organized, Miss Lamont,' he laughed. 'Free-lances all. But we have reason to believe that certain continental criminals are trying to work over here as they are accustomed to do at home.' He looked as though he would give them short shrift. 'Mr William Stead has alerted us to the possibility of certain directions these criminal activities may take.' He was looking severe and serious now, and not at all amused. 'Traffic in young girls. Your information, Miss Lamont, seemed to fit in with that fearful theory.'

I looked at him anxiously.

'That particular fear,' he said frankly, 'we now believe is false.'

I took a deep breath of relief.

'But *some* criminal traffic is going on between England and the continent.' He held up a hand. 'You will understand that I can enter into no details as to its nature. But we here have had inquiries from the French police. If I was the criminal concerned, I should be very alarmed; French law is primitive. Hulks and prison colonies and the guillotine. I believe these people *are* alarmed, Miss Lamont.'

I thought he might have told me something more, in fact, as I had apparently been so helpful to them.

'Now we come, at last, Miss Lamont, having cleared away one or two preliminary points, to ask why you came to see me today?'

'I came to see you to tell you, because you are a policeman and a friend of the Demarests . . .' He held up a hand as if he wanted to protest that he was not a friend of the Demarests, but I swept on. 'Alice Demarest has left her family, has run away, back to Oxford, I think, and I am going after her.'

'I will send a telegram to the police in Oxford at once,' he said, ringing a little bell which stood on his desk.

'Yes, do that. But I am going, anyway.'

He bowed assent, preparing his telegram with one hand as he did so. I would have been glad to see what he wrote, but it was quite impossible. Soon a uniformed constable appeared and bore the message away.

'Can you tell me if any progress has been made in finding Ellen Sweeting?'

He looked at me thoughtfully, playing with an ivory paper-knife on his desk. He had a number of nervous tricks of this sort, so behind the calm face must be a considerable degree of nervous tension. I judged him to be an ambitious and persistent man, with a good deal of physical energy. It would not have surprised me to learn that he fenced and boxed, and rode to hounds in an energetic, countryman's kind of way. These were the sports he would go for, not billiards and a little gentlemanly shooting like Charles Demarest.

'I cannot tell you much. I mean I may not. We are on her track. We are watching a certain establishment. You understand I cannot tell you which one or where.'

'She is alive?'

'I believe her to be.' He nodded.

'I hope you are right. I think I could tell you that I believe the cause of Alice leaving today was the appearance with her grandmother yesterday of a woman called Teresa Mackenzie who used to be her nurse. That is the *cause*. The reason I do not know. But I am convinced that the woman frightened Alice.'

He listened to me carefully. 'The name is familiar to me.'

'She is supposed to have come to London to be married. I do not believe that to be true.'

'You could have questioned Mrs Demarest.'

'Nevertheless, I did not do so.' I stood up and looked him straight in the face. In my face he read what I would not say: that I did not trust Adelaide Demarest.

'Don't worry too much, Miss Lamont,' he said. 'And don't underestimate the police, we know a great deal. We know about the gang that is operating, and indeed, we have been in touch with the French police for months now. We know who are most of the band of accomplices, we know what they are trading in.'

I swallowed, my throat suddenly felt constricted.

'We know about Madame Blanche, we know what the doll Pandora carries. We even know that there is more than one Pandora. That startles you? Oh yes, the dolls come and go and it's not always the same doll. We have been watching. That is what police work is, Miss Lamont, watching and noting detail and matching one fact against another. So you see, we have been at work and we do know many things. What we lacked was the identity of one person. That person you have led us to, Miss Lamont.'

'I have?'

He bowed. 'For this we have to thank you. We lacked one name, one man, and your activities have flushed him up. We have much to be grateful to you for, Miss Lamont.'

My cabby was waiting for me still, his eyes were closed and he appeared to be asleep. I was escorted to the door by Norris Vincent himself. One or two young constables followed behind in humble procession.

I turned to ask the question I had wanted to ask all the time. 'Does the name Christian Ableman mean anything to you?'

'In connection with this case? It does.'

'Is he . . .' I hesitated. Is he guilty, I wanted to say, but I could not form the words. But he understood me.

'He is a professional criminal, a trainer of criminals. It looks as though an attempt was made to use him, hire him, engage his services, and that he quarrelled with his employers – if we can call them that. At all events, attempts have been made in one form or another to draw our attention to him, as if someone wanted him behind bars.'

Like getting accused of being a pickpocket, I thought.

'What sort of man is he?' I asked, impulsively.

'Well, a criminal's a criminal, my dear lady, we mustn't be sentimental, must we? Once a man's been on the treadmill, he's not the same as you and me.'

'*Has* he been on the treadmill?' I felt sick.

'It's no longer used, my dear lady, but if anyone could stand it physically, Ableman could. There's a physique for you! Amazing in a criminal, poor stock usually, I'm afraid, as a consequence of bad breeding. A devil among the ladies, my dear.' He gave me a keen look.

'I heardhe'd been an actor,' I said.

He looked at his watch. 'You have forty minutes, I calculate, in which to catch the next fast train to Oxford. Cabby, take Miss Lamont to Paddington by way of the old Devonshire. It's where he acted. Goodbye, Miss Lamont.'

He touched my hand and was gone.

We soon came to where the Devonshire Theatre stood, with some of the worst slums in the world behind it. The façade of Corinthian pillars was dirty and stained with bird droppings. The windows were broken and the doors boarded up.

'Well, there it is,' said the cabby, leaning on his whip. 'It's coming down and all the alleys behind. A good thing, too, proper thieves' kitchen it was.'

'What will take its place?'

'Driving a new horse road through, they are. It'll run from Oxford Street down towards the city. Fine new road with new buildings. Not before time. They say the police daren't go in that district as it now stands.'

We got to Paddington just in time for my train. I paid the cabby, tipping him well. He accepted it graciously, buttoning the money into his inner waistcoat. As he moved off, he called out, 'There's been a cab a following us on and off, thought you ought to know.'

I hurried to the train. As far as I could see, there was no one following me.

On the train I collected my mind and considered Teresa Mackenzie. As soon as I saw her proud passionate face and saw how intimate she was with Mrs Demarest I knew that I had found the answer to much of the mystery of Sarsen Place. Alice had been right to run: Teresa Mackenzie could bring her nothing but harm. She looked a woman who had great powers of seduction. Mrs Demarest was in her thrall. Had one of the Demarest brothers also felt her powers? And if this were so, what ambitions might he have stirred in Teresa's mind? Ambitions to which Alice, the heiress of Sarsen Place, might be a check.

The train rattled and jolted me to Oxford as I pondered.

At Oxford I was still in a hurry and sped on my way on foot. I was sure I knew where to find Alice. She had Jack's address in her head, and would go to him before doing anything else. What she would do then or what plans she had in her mind I did not know, but I made sure I should find her at Jack's in Walton Street. I think she trusted him and Ellen in a way she trusted no one else.

There was a policeman pacing up and down the road by the station, but he gave me no more than a glance, and was obviously not alerted to look out for me. For which I was glad and yet not glad. I wanted to be free to go to Alice as I chose, but I felt the breath of danger coming close, and would have been grateful, in a way, to have had the protection of the police.

I turned towards the main road and halted to avoid a cart, when to my surprise I saw Jack and his barrow set down across the road. He had his brazier alight, some nuts roasting on a long shovel, and was intent on cutting up the squares of newspaper he used to serve the roasted nuts in. It was business as usual with him.

'Jack!'

He looked round to see me coming. 'Thought you was gone,' he said, in an unfriendly way. In his view I had deserted him, and he wanted me to know it.

'Have you any news of Ellen?' I said, before I asked him anything else.

'I'm still looking,' he said keenly. 'There's a good many places I know she isn't. She's not dead, though. I know she isn't. I'd know it here,' and he placed his hand on his heart.

'And Alice, where's Alice?'

He stared. 'I dunno.'

'I made sure she was here with you. I thought she would come straight here.'

'You'd best explain to me what you're talking about.'

I did so quickly, standing by his fire, feeling the warmth and smell of the nuts and burning coal. I shall never forget that smell. 'I was so sure she would come straight to you,' I said.

'And so she may have done,' he said slowly. 'I ain't been in my room much. I'm out looking for Ellen most of the time. I walk up and down the roads calling. One day she'll hear and answer.'

I could see now that he was thinner than ever, with two lines from nostril to mouth that had aged him by ten years. He had a muffler round his throat and his jacket, trim but thin with age, was buttoned tight.

'Where can we talk together?'

'Here,' he said, giving his fire a stir, so that a little cloud of sparks rose up and disappeared into the sunlight.

'Somewhere more private,' I said.

'This is my patch. This is private to me.' He squared his shoulders. Here I am and here I stand, he was saying. Not only was an Englishman's home his castle, but his stretch of pavement was his kingdom.

So we stood by the brazier and I told him almost all of the story as I knew it, even of my visit to Scotland Yard. All I kept back were some details of my meeting with Christian Ableman. He had thoughts of his own in any case, as well I knew, about

Ableman. He didn't say anything now. He was too preoccupied with the intensity of his own feelings for Ellen, the lost girl.

He listened intently. 'And the man at Scotland Yard, this great policeman feller, said they were watching "a certain establishment". Why couldn't he talk English, why couldn't he say what he meant?'

Why indeed, I thought, except to stop just what we are going to do now, invade such an establishment and try to find Ellen.

'There's two places it could be,' he said. 'One's Tinker's and the other is Madame Blanche's.'

'Yes,' I said doubtfully, 'unless . . .'

'There's no unless about it.' His voice was imperious. 'Which first?'

'Not Tinker's,' I said. 'Because if Alice couldn't find you at home, she may have gone to where she believes Ellen to be. And I don't think she's even aware of the existence of Tinker's.'

'We're not in the way of knowing what she's aware of and what not,' he said. He was packing up his barrow as he spoke. 'Right, we're off.'

'Where to? Madame Blanche's?'

'You're not thinking,' he said over his shoulder as he moved off. 'To my place first. If Alice ain't got nowhere to go she may be there waiting.'

It was a matter of four hundred yards or so from where I had met him to where he lived and we covered them in a few minutes, Jack pushing the barrow fast and talking as he went, and me rushing along behind. The grey walls of the Radcliffe Infirmary stood on our right. I wondered briefly how the girl Fenny was recovering.

There was a covered archway beside one house in Walton Street and here Jack pushed the barrow. 'This is me,' he said. 'Down the steps and we're home. The door's locked, though, and she couldn't get in without a key, no one can, I make sure of that.'

I stared down the steep flight of steps, which led down to a little paved yard, a locked door and a shuttered window. No sign of life to be seen there. I felt a pang as I remembered the cosy picture I had been nourishing all the way to Oxford, of finding Alice sitting by the fire with Jack, and both surprised faces turning towards me at the door as I opened it. I had even imagined the room clean-swept and polished, as probably no room connected with Jack had ever been.

In its place another picture soon came. A picture of Alice, arriving lonely and frightened at the station, and meeting there with someone to whom I dared hardly put a face and did not wish to put a name, someone who took Alice away to a place I was frightened to imagine. My picture became clearer and more alarming every minute.

'Not a sign, eh? I never thought there would be.'

'I was *so* sure.'

'Oh, she was here, right enough.' Jack stooped down and picked up a piece of paper which was lying on the top step, and straightened it out. 'THE GREAT WESTERN RAILWAY', it said. 'Excursions to Leamington Spa, Cheltenham Spa and Malvern Spa.' 'She left this on purpose,' said Jack.

'Yes, that's Alice,' I said sadly. 'Yes, she's clever enough.'

I was standing there at the head of the stairs, my eyes not focused on the street scene in front of me.

Alice was well within vision before I realized that I had seen her. She was walking sedately down the road, side by side with another girl.

'Alice, thank goodness we've found you.'

'Oh, Miss Lamont, so you've come. I feared you might, but I wish you hadn't. I'm not lost, you know, in fact, in a sense you could say I've found *you*, since I was coming here, anyway.' She was her coolest, most provoking Demarest self. 'I left a letter to my father.'

'You amaze me sometimes, Alice.'

She shrugged. 'I've been with Fenny here. I went straight to the hospital to see her and the nurses let me stay with her. You're much better, aren't you, Fenny?'

'Convalescent, the doctor says.' Fenny, whom I hardly knew in her new look of health and good humour, smiled. 'I'm to take a little walk every day. I shall leave the hospital before very long.'

'I was very comfortable sitting with Fenny,' said Alice calmly. 'And, of course, I knew I would find Jacky here eventually.'

In short, granted the premise that she had to flee from her family, she had behaved sensibly. To hear her now you would not have known that any element of panic had entered into her behaviour, but I knew enough to understand that there must have been a quiet desperation inside.

'Who are you running away from, Alice? Me?'

She shook her head.

'No, not me. Your grandmother?'

She did not answer.

'Your grandmother together with Teresa Mackenzie?'

'Yes.' A tremor passed across her face.

'Why?'

'Nurse Mackenzie frightens me.'

'I know that, Alice, but there must be a reason. *Why* does she frighten you?'

'She frightens me because she wishes to frighten me.'

'You mean she threatens you? Was it she who sent you the stuffed cat from Paris?'

'She had my own cat killed,' said Alice. 'She wanted me to know she could do more if she had to.'

For a moment I wondered if she was really telling me the truth and if any woman could really be as evil as Teresa Mackenzie would have had to be. And then I remembered Alice's nightmares, her moments of fear both at home and outside, the way she watched the open window of her bedroom as if she thought a face or a body might appear at it; and I realized that someone had terrorized her.

'Are you going to tell me why Teresa Mackenzie should behave like this?' I said, deliberately keeping my tone dry.

'I know something about her,' said Alice, in an equally matter-of-fact way. 'Something I heard. Something I must never say.'

My lips tightened. I was beginning to feel both hate and contempt for a woman who could intimidate a child put in her care. And to conceal what must, at worst, have been some

203

sexual transgression. In my mind I indicted Charles Demarest. But then there was Adelaide Demarest to remember. What had she done? And what part had she played in all this?

Jack was standing there with a cynical expression on his face. Fenny wore a slight smile of sympathy. It came as a shock to realize that they both knew more than I did, that what Alice was saying was no news to them.

'You've heard this before?' I said sharply to Jack.

'What do you think Ellen and I are?' he said. 'We've talked. This much I know but not much more, because Ellen wouldn't say. But she knew.'

'Yes, Ellen knew,' said Alice. 'I told her. And she was there.'

And look at what happened to Ellen, I thought. She disappeared. Poor Ellen, she seemed to have been turned into a surrogate Alice, to suffer in her place.

'Perhaps you should go back to the hospital,' I said, turning to Fenny.

'I'm not tired,' she said unresentfully. 'But I suppose I'd better go.'

'Yes, can you go back alone or shall we come with you?'

She shook her head. 'I can go in that gate there,' she pointed. 'And anyway, there's a nurse I know. I'll walk with her.'

I watched her catch up a uniformed figure and then the two of them turn into a nearby gate. 'Now Fenny has gone,' I said to Alice, 'you must tell me what you know about Teresa Mackenzie.' She didn't speak. 'Come on, now, two women have died and Ellen has disappeared. It would be madness not to tell me what you know.'

'Tell me one thing first, Alice, and speak the truth. Teresa Mackenzie used to come back to Sarsen Place, didn't she?'

'Yes. I told you so.'

'You did. But in such a way I did not see the significance.'

She hung her head. 'I was frightened.'

'And it was she who turned on the gas in your room?'

'She meant to frighten me so that I would not talk of her to you.'

'And yet the next night you watched for her from the window?'

'She didn't come,' whispered Alice. 'Not then. But she hated

204

me when her baby died. I knew about the baby, you see. She used to tell me she would turn me out of Sarsen Place and reign there in my place.'

'She meant to marry Charles Demarest,' said Jack.

'He's married already.'

'Any fool could have told her she'd never be Mrs Demarest or reign in Sarsen Place. There's the old lady and Alice's father for a start, but Teresa thought one would die and the other stay without a wife and she'd be queen of all she saw.'

'Poor girl,' I said. I could not stop myself. Between me and Teresa Mackenzie was a terrible chain and it was made up of my hopes and her hopes, and her dreams and my dreams, my fears and her fears. They interlocked.

Teresa Mackenzie had been seduced by Charles Demarest and bore him a son. This was why she had left the house. But the child had died and impudently, yet tragically, she had come secretly back and buried the little body in Sarsen Place. I suppose almost everyone there among the servants had guessed the truth, but would they ever say? No, not they.

But Teresa's ambitions had extended to marrying Charles and taking her position in Sarsen Place as his wife. It had to be remembered that when she formed these plans Mark Demarest was abroad, Mrs Demarest under her thumb, and Alice only a child.

And yet I could not find it in my heart to condemn Teresa without admitting I understood a little of her heart.

'She had an accomplice in the household?' I said.

Alice nodded. 'She used to talk to someone who used to come to the nursery when she thought I was in bed and asleep in the room beyond. But the door between was not quite shut and I could hear. She's very stupid really, is Teresa,' said Alice in a terrifyingly adult way. 'At first it was just silly loverlike talk, but eventually she started to talk loudly as though she was frightened, and it was then she said about the woman in France being killed. She cried and said she didn't want her head cut off. But she also said Mrs Demarest would always stand her friend. I didn't like that much.'

Jack said: 'And wasn't Madame Blanche all part of it?'

Alice nodded. 'Teresa used to talk to her also when we called with Grandma, and carry messages for her. And they would both look at me as if I wasn't there. And one day Madame Blanche said, "The child will have to be silenced". Then I started to dream.'

'She's worse than Teresa,' I said vindictively. 'Her motives are purely mercenary.'

Alice shivered. 'She pretended to send the doll, Pandora, to keep an eye on me. Of course I knew she couldn't really, but it was horribly real, and I used to dream of Pandora lying next to me in bed, stifling me with her softness,' she shuddered. 'Sometimes, too, Teresa would talk to her friend about Pandora almost as if she *was* alive and was helping them in their schemes to become very rich. I would lie there in the dark and hear them laughing and talking.'

'I take it that the friend Teresa laughed and giggled with was a man?' I said.

Alice gave me an odd look. 'I think so. But I only heard him speak in whispers and never saw him ... sometimes, I used to wonder ...'

'Yes?'

'No, I won't say.' Her mouth set in its obstinate lines. She didn't yet altogether trust me. She didn't want to commit herself wholly to me. I wondered how much of Alice's tale was solid fact and how much was childlike imagination. Yet no one was less childish than Alice.

'And Ellen?' I said. 'What of Ellen?'

'What I knew, she knew,' said Alice simply. 'But Ellen is braver than I am.'

'I think you're brave enough,' I said, looking at her.

'Ellen wanted to find out more, so that we could frighten Teresa for ourselves. When those notes came telling us to be good and keep quiet, I wanted to burn them, I was so frightened, but Ellen said keep them and one day we could show them to the police.'

'I got one of those notes,' I said.

'Ellen has a head on her shoulders,' said Jack.

'She used to slip out of the house and watch Madame

Blanche's, and once she talked to one of the girls there, the one with the sad face.'

'Stella Darley.'

'I don't know her name,' Alice said, and shook her head, 'but she was frightened as much as we were, and said one of her friends had already been killed for wanting to talk. Everyone seemed to be frightened.'

'Ellen doesn't seem to have been frightened,' I said.

Jack made a sort of strangled noise at the back of his throat, expressive of rage.

'I think she was,' said Alice, after a pause. 'We both were, because, you see, whatever we did and however we acted, it seemed to us that Teresa Mackenzie would always win, because she had powers over my grandmother. She made my grandmother happy. That's how it seemed to us and so we *were* frightened. We expected, as I did, to be attacked. I wasn't surprised when the man rushed at us in the garden. I'm glad I don't really remember how it happened at the time.'

'You must have learnt something more of what was going on than you've said,' I asked Alice.

'What they seemed to say,' she said, 'was that every time Pandora went to Paris to be dressed in new fashions to bring back for Madame Blanche to copy, she brought something else back with her. She didn't come back empty-handed, that's what they said. Pandora is always full, they said.'

'They?' I prompted.

'This man,' said Alice, giving me her blue opaque stare. 'If you don't know who he was, I can't tell you. I only heard his voice. I never saw his face. It was always voices from another room.'

'*She* knows who it must be,' said Jack. 'Man with a criminal connection, man with a way with women, a violent man, only one man it could be.' He stared at me.

I knew he meant Christian Ableman. I stared at the busy midday street scene, as the pieces fell into place like *tessere* in a mosaic. What other purpose could Christian Ableman have in seeking my company except in some way to control me. Suddenly it seemed very plain. He wanted me to jump to his tune because I was close to Alice, and might otherwise threaten his criminal plan. I could imagine that he must have sought out Teresa Mackenzie for this purpose originally, and then, when I succeeded her in Alice's life, he transferred his interest to me.

'Yes, I know,' I said sadly. 'I know what you mean.' However it was, Teresa Mackenzie and I were sisters beneath the skin.

I was hearing all this in the open street with the wind on my cheeks and my hair untidy. I wanted a mirror, I wanted to look at my face, and see if there was anything there at all to love.

And then, in the way in which a more superficial worry often finds expression in place of a more deep-seated fear, I found myself saying: 'I don't understand what you meant by Teresa making your grandmother "happy".'

Jack gave one of his bursts of laughter. 'That's easy, that one is. I caught on to that as soon as she spoke. Happiness like that can be bought and paid for. You know that you can buy an ounce of laudanum over the counter as easily as buying a pennyworth of brandyballs, and there's plenty of poor people as *do* buy it, for it's cheaper than gin and lasts you longer. And if thinking yourself warm and comfortable when you ain't is what you want, then laudanum's the stuff. That's liquid happiness that is, and I've tried it myself.'

'Jack, you haven't?'

He brushed me aside. 'It comes your way sometimes, if you're poor and tired, you see if it doesn't. But grand ladies don't like to take laudanum to cheer themselves up, there's a prejudice against it, the feeling that it's for poor people. So they gets their maid to buy them the special cigarettes and they smoke them. Tofferkins, I've heard them called, and some smart Frenchie invented them. They're opium, all the same, though. I don't know what Mrs Demarest calls them, but that's where she's getting her happiness from, I lay.'

I didn't disbelieve him. I had noticed for myself the strange effect the cigarettes she smoked had on Adelaide Demarest. And it came to me now that I had probably smoked one myself, at Tinker's, and that my meeting with Christian Ableman had been a smoke-created fantasy, a dream out of my own mind. It was too late to blush.

'Do you think she knows what she smokes?' I said. Jack said nothing, but laughed harshly again. He knew what he thought, and no proper respect for his betters prevented him thinking it.

It was a strange conversation to be taking place in the open street, but nothing in my life was ordinary or normal any longer. From the moment I saw Louise de la Vallière I had crossed the road from where the ordinary pedestrians walked and joined the wild marchers on the other side, the wild pavements.

'Now that I've found you, or, at any rate, have you in my company,' I said to Alice, 'I will take you to Sarsen Place.'

'No,' she said, sitting down comfortably on Jack's top step. 'I'll stay here until my father comes to fetch me.'

'You may find the police come to fetch you, miss,' I said irritably. 'I, at any rate, have more sense than you and I have spoken to the police and told them everything I know. They're looking for you, and me, too, I expect.'

'You may stay here if you want,' said Jack, handing over to Alice a large key. 'The fire's out down there and 'tis none too clean for someone like you, but there you may sit, if it pleases you. You too, Miss Lamont. I'm off to get Ellen out of Madame Blanche's, for that's where she is, I do believe now.' He was making preparation as he spoke, picking up a large stick from under the archway, and going to his barrow and removing a rope and winding it round his waist.

'No, not Madame Blanche's,' I said. 'An artist's daughter picks up lots of stray information. She learns things about chemistry and the human body. And then I'm a student of ancient texts. I know the value of detail. I have learnt to put minute facts together. On my train journey here I began to do this, Jack, and I have put my facts into one whole.'

Do you know that feeling when the mind takes a jump forward and suddenly says, 'This is how it was, this is the truth'? It comes to us all at times. So with me now. All the thoughts that had occupied me on my journey assumed a coherent and logical shape.

'What we must do first,' I said, 'is to find out what is protecting Ellen.'

'Protecting Ellen?' Jack bristled at once at the idea of any slur on his girl.

'Ellen is not dead. We all believe that, even the police. But two women *have* died here in England and I believe a third has been killed in France. So why hesitate to kill Ellen if she is a threat? The answer is that she has protection of some sort. What sort, then, we ask? Is she protected by a *person*? Someone close to her who has a special relationship to her?'

Jack again made that enraged noise in the back of his throat.

'There has been some reason to believe she has a special protector,' I said, casting a sidelong look at Alice. 'I won't go into that now but I reject it. It is false. Ellen is what she appears to be, a simple country girl working in a family which wishes her well but has no closer relationship with her than that.' Alice looked puzzled and interested, and I knew I should have to explain this later. 'What then is the next step in logic?' I paused. 'If Ellen is not protected by a person, she is protected by a *thing*.'

'You can go on,' said Jack. He did not cease to look threatening.

'Did not Ellen keep a diary, Alice?' I asked.

'She wrote things in a notebook,' said Alice slowly. 'We both did. It was a game with us. But she wrote more.'

'Then I guess she wrote down all she knew, all she discovered of the strange and terrible things you were both involved in, and she hid the book. She must have used this book to record herself. She must have told whoever has imprisoned her that this record exists and will be found. They won't kill her until she says where it is.'

'But won't they make her tell?' This was Alice.

'Ellen would hold out,' said Jack. 'She's brave.'

'Do you know where it is hidden?'

'I can guess.'

'And won't other people, the people who have Ellen, try to guess too?'

'Oh, yes,' I said. 'And the person I'm thinking of has a logical and clever mind, and has everything to lose.'

Freedom, I thought, and the hope of wealth, and all the pleasures of the body, which I know he loves. A sensuous man who could not tolerate confinement.

'But I believe I may be ahead. I believe I have seen the place. I believe I have *seen*.'

There was nothing more natural than that Alice and I should return to Sarsen Place and we did so openly in a cab. Jack followed secretly and was to hide in the garden and join us if he thought it wise.

The servants were 'en fête' when we got back. There was nothing inherently surprising in this. Expecting, as they did, several days' absence of their employers, they had arranged to enjoy it. No one greeted us as we came in, and although the outward appearance of the house was polished and orderly I could read the signs. To begin with the smell of brandy was apparent even as I stepped into the hall. A great deal of it must have got spilt somewhere, I thought. Then I saw Prince lying quietly under the hall table, in sound and drunken sleep.

'Don't wake him,' I said to Alice. 'The fewer the people who see us for the moment, the better. Will you go to your room and lock yourself in?'

'I am coming with you.' Her voice was all Demarest.

'Then you must do *exactly* what I say. Follow me and be quiet.' I too knew how to command.

Followed by Alice, I moved quietly through the green baize doors to the kitchens. I needn't have worried about being heard. The noise of a fiddle playing was audible even at the end of the passage. It was early in the day for a ball, but it might have been going on sporadically all night, or ever since the family left.

The kitchen door opened and a burst of sound came from it. A footman appeared and staggered forward blindly. He wasn't a man I knew. I guessed the servants had visitors from some of the other big houses round about. I drew Alice into the housemaids' pantry, and with the smell of beeswax in our nostrils and

211

feather brooms tickling our necks, we heard him lumber up the passage and out through another door halfway down the corridor which led to the stillroom. Then, in a minute, we heard him come back. He seemed to be pushing something.

'He's rolling a barrel of beer,' said Alice, who could see through a crack.

'I hope for their sakes they haven't been at the wine,' I said grimly. On the whole the Demarests' servants were honest and although they might soak up the brandy and gin and steal a barrel of beer, they were too shrewd to touch the valuable and irreplaceable wine. But this party showed signs of having got out of hand.

'We have to get to the back kitchen,' I said to Alice. 'I think that's where Ellen kept her diary. When we have that, we have a powerful weapon.' I hoped it wasn't all guesswork and that I had not underrated Ellen's acumen. I didn't think so.

I heard a footstep outside and a voice saying softly. 'Miss Lamont?'

'Jack,' I said in relief, 'you've found us. How did you know we were in here?'

Alice and I emerged, I brushing lint off my dress and a feather off Alice's hair.

'I saw your dress sticking out.'

'Good job they're all drunk, then,' I said.

'As lords.' He sounded wistful. 'The sore heads there'll be all round town when this is done. There's more guests arriving, too. Heard a cab draw up soon after I got here.'

'We can get to the back kitchen if we go down to the cellars and up the small stairs in the second cellar,' said Alice. 'They lead directly to the laundry and the back kitchen.'

The stairs and the cellars were whitewashed and clean-smelling. I suppose the bottles of Montrachet and Château Yquem and Pol Roger that were housed down there in neat racks deserved the best treatment. Jack, holding a small lamp, led the way. We passed through the cellars, up the stairs and safely through the doors to the laundry.

From here another door led into the back kitchen, where I had found Ellen's box in which the anonymous and threatening notes were carefully preserved. This was where, in the same box, I felt sure she had buried her story. I poked my head round the door. One of the maids was sitting in a corner, but a quick glance showed me she was, in fact, sound asleep, with her hair all over her face. I couldn't even recognize this refugee from the bacchanalian revels going on near at hand, and I resisted the temptation to lift the fringe of hair and peep. Perhaps it was only one of the visiting servants anyway.

There was the cupboard and there, as I remembered it, was Ellen's box. 'Keep quiet,' I said to Alice. 'And, Jack, stay behind the door. We'll go back the way we came.'

Beyond the door there were voices, one or two of them familiar ones, and I knew I must be quick. One voice in particular I was listening for. I fancied I heard it.

I drew the box towards me and opened it. Everything was as I had left it. I saw the letters, which I took out. Beneath them was the slim blue notebook I had seen earlier. It was of the sort Alice used for her lessons. I opened it.

Ellen had written her name large and clear, and underneath she had written:

'This is a true story and not made up.'

I flipped through the pages, reading rapidly. She had it nearly all there. What a clever pair she and Alice had made, both so quick and observant. It all confirmed what I had begun to suspect. I read a name I knew and had begun to expect to find.

Then I heard a voice outside, talking to Jack, and I looked up as the speaker entered. I was not much surprised.

'So there you are,' I said to Christian Ableman. 'I thought it might be you who arrived in the cab that Jack heard. You followed me from Paddington.'

He didn't bother to answer. Already his eyes were travelling alertly round the room, taking it all in at a glance.

'Got here in time, eh? Led me quite a chase, you did, my lady. But I'm here, and I reckon I'm in time and that's all that counts.'

'Time for what?' I tried, unobtrusively, to slide the book behind the box.

Behind Christian Ableman I saw Jack standing. He was

unwinding the rope which had been looped round his waist. I shook my head at him slightly, hoping he would understand me. Tough and wiry as he was, he would be no match for Christian Ableman.

'Time for me and time for you,' he said ambiguously. 'I have something here in my pocket that I want you to consider, Mary.'

He put his hand to his side. I had seen a gun there once, perhaps there was one still. It might come in useful.

'I don't want to talk now,' was all I said. Alice, by my side, hardly seemed to breathe. She was composed, however, and I felt none of the terror emanating from her that I had felt on other occasions.

'Shall I tie him up?' said Jack.

Without even troubling to look round, Christian Ableman laughed. He was in a very confident, assured mood.

'Take no notice of the boy,' I said, as evenly as I could manage. I had seen enough of Ableman to desire not to ignite his temper. 'He means no harm.'

'Don't I, though,' said Jack. He was swinging the rope from his hand and moving on his toes like a boxer. 'Where's my Ellen?'

There was what seemed a long pause, till Ableman said, 'I haven't got your Ellen.'

'You know where she is, though.'

'I know where Ellen is,' I said, and my words were unexpected, even to myself. 'She is shut up in a small room with windows high on the walls and stone flagged floors. It's an old room, and it looks on a back yard. She can shout and no one will hear her, and perhaps there is a smell of ammonia there.'

'Did you read all that in the book you are hiding?' said Christian Ableman.

'No. No, not all. I have been in that room myself once.'

'Will you believe me, Mary, if I tell you that I have no idea where the girl is?' said Ableman in a quiet voice.

The door from the kitchen opened and a burst of sound came with it. The door closed again. I turned my head.

Like a stranger from another city, William Train stood there, holding his usual small black bag, as if he had come to wind the clocks.

William Train was Teresa's ally. He had helped in her scheme; she had been willing to aid him in his plans. Sensuality and greed and ambition had bound them together as strongly as love.

And yet I suffered with Teresa. She seemed to me my own dreadful reflection seen in a distorting mirror. Teresa was as proud, passionate and ambitious as I was. More, she was myself, limned by a hostile artist. We were women fighting for our lives. Her, me and Scheherazade.

Towards William Train, though, my heart was harder.

'Hello, Will,' I said. 'It's a strange world, isn't it, in which you have fallen into a life of crime and become a murderer?'

Some people say that murderers have a special sort of face and that you can read a criminal's past and future in the lines and features he was born with. I don't think you could have read anything in Will Train's. Yet there he was, with his usual bland smile and respectable dark suit, the man who had designed that lavish and beautiful room at Tinker's with its more than hint of decadence. Of all the people I knew connected with Tinker's only he could have created it. How could I fail to have read the message of the jewellery he designed, with its passionate appeal to the pleasures of the senses? I knew without being told that it was to escape from the world of his father's parsimony and create the way of life he desired, that he had turned to crime. And what better sort of crime for him than creating beautiful and untraceable jewels from stones wrenched from treasures stolen in France?

I don't say all this was written in Ellen's diary, but she had snatches of information that she had picked up and put together. She mentioned the doll, Pandora, being used to transport packets and had guessed there was something strange about them. I knew that the doll's head unscrewed and was hollow. Ellen mentioned 'Mr Train's French friends' and I remembered how he was learning to speak French and recalled the inscription 'L'Inconnue' on the back of a portrait of Louise de la Vallière. I wondered briefly what his relationship was with this French-speaking girl from Soho, had *he* and not my father painted her portrait, and had he already planned to kill her when he painted her portrait in my father's studio? And what mixture of jealousy and conscience had worked on Louise, that she wanted to confess all she knew to me or to my father? She had been the second victim killed. Not the first and not the last. But certainly it had been with her death that events had whirled to their climax.

Will Train did not answer my remark. He was not a man given to talking over much. But I saw Jack's eyes widen with amazement and knew he was ready to burst into eager speech. I held up my hand to silence him. Alice was staring at Will Train, her face white. *She* knew. Perhaps she had known all along. Ableman was dead silent.

'A dealer in stolen jewellery, and a murderer,' I said to Will Train.

'I heard you had arrived in Oxford,' he said in a conversational tone. 'I heard from my friend who is in the Oxford police. He came with me. He's getting very drunk now in the kitchen.' He smiled a small tight smile.

'I should think that's the end of him in the police force.'

'It was bound to happen anyway,' said Will. 'A most unreliable fellow.'

'In this book in my hand,' I said, 'are many interesting things observed about you, and Teresa Mackenzie, and Madame Blanche, by a keen young observer. I will give you this book if you will take me to Ellen and set her free. I guess you have her shut up in one of your sale rooms at the back of your father's shop.'

He considered, or appeared to do so.

'You have time probably to escape to France, if the police have not already got a warrant out for you. Which I think they have not.'

'It's a bargain,' he said, holding out his hand. 'What about you, Ableman, coming too?'

Christian Ableman scowled. 'I cut my knot with you before it was pulled tight. I never worked with you, you mincing scringing woman-twisting lot, that's not my lay at all. I spit on you.'

'I want to kill him,' said Jack in a voice I hardly recognized.

'Much good would that do you,' I said, my eyes on Will Train's face. So much of what I said had been guess and speculation. I really did not know where Ellen was.

We were a small group of people in a house full of drunken revellers, and except for Christian Ableman we offered no real threat to Will Train.

I knew that but for the protection of Ableman I might have joined Ellen in her prison, there to await the asphyxiation with ammonia and the watery grave that Louise and Stella (and perhaps that first girl in France, the Princess of Orléans's maid) had already experienced.

In a moment of weakness, I put my hand to my face. It seemed to me I could already smell the ammonia.

Will still had his hand held out. 'Give me the book, then.' He moved forward, fumbling in his bag.

'Back, friend,' said Christian Ableman loudly and in the same moment he kicked Will's bag away from him. It fell to the ground with a thud. There was a splintering of glass and a choking vapour arose in that corner of the room. I coughed and felt my eyes sting.

'Get that in your face,' said Ableman, 'as you nearly did, and you'll be blinded for life.' He was breathing deeply. 'Blue Vitriol. I'll lay my oath, or something like it.'

Will stood against the wall, glaring at us both. His face was white and furious. His left hand was rubbing his wrist, but I knew him well enough to guess that he had never been more dangerous. Then he dropped his hand quickly to his pocket and it came out again holding a pistol. He pointed it straight at me. I turned my head to look at Ableman and he reached out his hand towards me. It would not quite reach my own, our hands would not quite join.

Will said nothing, but still aimed the gun at me menacingly, and began to move quietly towards the door. Christian Ableman stood still.

'Don't move, Mary,' he said.

'A good idea,' said Will, speaking for the first time. 'Or I'll blow your head off.' He moved another furtive step towards the door, but he trod in the oily liquid which had spilled from his bag, his foot slipped, and for a second his eyes were off me.

The violence in Jack erupted and he sprang at Will, pummelling him with his fists and kicking him at the same time. Ableman pulled Jack back by his shoulder and himself hit Will hard in the face, so that the blood spouted from his mouth, and then gave him a great body blow which knocked him against the wall and on to the floor, where he lay still with eyes closed.

Into the moment of absolute stillness which fell upon us when we faced each other, there intruded the sound of loud knocking and louder voices from outside, and I realized that the police had arrived.

Christian Ableman heard it, too. 'Mary,' he said, seizing my hand, 'this isn't the time or the place, but there are the hounds of hell out there and I must speak to you. This is our moment, Mary, will you or won't you? It's what I followed you for. Join me. I'm going to emigrate to Australia. Come with me.' He patted his pocket. 'I have the berths booked. I'm a man with a future, Mary, believe that of me.' He was speaking rapidly and with all the force of his powerful nature in his voice. 'Come with me and I'll make you the Queen of Melbourne.'

I shook my head, my eyes streaming. 'No.'

'Oh, Mary, Mary.' He gripped my arm.

The noises outside increased. He heard them.

'I must go,' he said urgently. 'Come with me, Mary. Come now. Have me, Mary.'

I suppose he read my answer on my face, for he dropped my hand, and said with bitter self mockery, 'There is a world elsewhere.'

I did not see him go, nor the police enter the room. I was on my knees, eyes full of tears, with waves of nausea sweeping over me. Alice was safe, Ellen would be rescued, but I could hardly take it in. Heart and mind and body were totally engaged with the man who had just gone.

It was Mark Demarest who raised me from my knees, not only then, but in the months to come. He made a gentle, courteous suitor. If that is the way to describe him. In an old-fashioned way he was paying his suit to me. Only once did he press me, and this with good humour. 'For I should like to be married to you in this century, Mary,' he said drily.

218

So many things ran through my mind and had to be thought about.

My father came back from Paris eventually, and without Mrs Ely, who had gone to Baden Baden. 'But I had some good painting, Mary,' he said, much as another man might have said, 'The fishing was good.' He made little mention of the troubles I had been involved in, and indeed, seemed little interested, but this may have been pretence.

Shortly after his return he handed me a letter. 'Found this tucked under the door of my studio. It had slipped under a mat, so you must have missed it. Open it.'

I unsealed the letter. It was written in a flowing childish copper-plate, the hand of someone who had learnt to write well at school and not written much since.

It began: 'Dear Honoured Sir.'

I looked up and met my father's embarrassed eye. 'Reads like a testimonial, doesn't it? Suppose it is in a way, poor soul. Truth is, I knew the restaurant where her father worked, and used to talk to her about it sometimes.'

I turned back to the letter. There were a few sentences about hardly daring to write to him but feeling sure of his sympathy, and then it went on to dwell on the writer's longing to confess.

'I was born into the Church,' wrote the simple straightforward hand, 'and although I have long fallen away, the habit of confession does not die. I must confess, and to you I will tell my guilt. The beginning of my story you know already, but about what came afterwards I have been shamefully false. You knew I was lying, I dare say, when I told you that my journeys to Paris were concerned with the Young Ladies' clothes. They none of them dress in Paris, you did not need me to tell you. When I first fell into trouble I was helped out of it by a woman (now dead, as I soon may be) who proved a false friend. She took me in, fed and looked after me, she introduced me to a life of crime.'

The stilted phrases were all the writer had at hand to express a real emotion. I read on.

'All that happened to me I will not tell you, but by degrees I sank into the state I am in now: an associate and accomplice of jewel thieves. The jewels are stolen in France and then reset over here. The reason they are brought to England is that the French police have become too powerful since Leduc took charge and reorganized the Sûreté. But lately they and the British police have begun to work together. One after the other we have been picked off. My employers have begun to quarrel among themselves. In this country I am principally in touch with Madame Blanche (Mrs Bennett is her real name), William Train, and Mrs Sanctuary. I carry the jewels between France and England, using the doll Pandora. We called her La Jolie. There are other dolls and other messengers, but they tell me I am best at it.'

I paused in my reading. The writer had had her pride: she had been proud of being good at her job.

'If I turn Queen's Evidence I will be pardoned. I want to wipe the slate clean. But I am frightened. I fear William Train. He hates women, he is cruel. But his cruelty is nothing to that of Teresa's. Black Teresa, I call her in my heart. There is a sort of wickedness in her I cannot describe. Madness, it may be, for all I know. I could understand her ambitions, although I saw, as she did not, that they could come to nothing. But when her hopes were checked she turned her spite upon Alice Demarest, who seemed to be and to hold all that Teresa wanted for herself. Her hope was to possess the child's mind as she had begun to possess the grandmother's. "I have to break her little will first," she said to me. "But I can do it." I said to her that it would never serve to give the child drugs like the grandmother for it would surely be discovered and would only tell against her. Then she laughed and said she had not read fairy stories to the child without knowing those that frightened her. Did I not know the tale of the Sleeping Beauty terrified the child? She would let Alice have a taste of nursery tale horrors, she said. That is the sort of girl she is, Mr Lamont. I dare to call her girl. She and William . . .'

I handed my father the letter. Poor Louise de la Vallière. She had come into my life like a ghost and now was passing from it like a wraith.

'Explains a lot, doesn't it?' said my father, after a time.

'Was it all as she said?'

'More or less, poor thing. Perhaps she made herself out a little

more of a victim than she really was. But how can we know . . . ?
You didn't finish reading the letter.'

'I've read enough.' I waved the letter aside, and watched him
burn it.

In October I joined the group of women students in Norham
Gardens. They, at least, were well informed about my adventures
and regarded me with some awe and alarm. The arrest and trial of
William Train and Madame Blanche and Teresa Mackenzie and
the arrest of their French accomplices had received great pub-
licity. Jessie, too, drew away a little. I was, you see, no longer such
a useful recruit for her schemes since I had compromised myself.
Sadly, she gave me up as an ally. And for me too life was more
complex than I had guessed in my young ambitious dreams.
Christian Ableman had invited me into a world I could not now
shut the door on. 'Come unto these yellow sands and then take
hands,' was a song I had heard once and forever, a reluctant
Miranda.

So many things had to be tidied up, including the matter of my
old water-stained cloak which I took down to the gardener to be
burnt. I wanted nothing more of it. Will Train had admitted to
the police that he had returned it after taking it from the dead
body of Louise de la Vallière. He knew it was mine and did not
wish the police to trace it to me and thus make *any* connection
with Louise and Sarsen Place. Sometimes the best place to hide
an object is where it is habitually kept.

The Captain had returned to his regiment and, somewhat reluctantly, established his wife and family in Knightsbridge. Mark
Demarest had gone to Italy, to Florence, where I was told he had
a house. Before he went, he called on me to say goodbye.

'But I shall be back soon,' he said, holding my hand. 'I am
only going to Florence for a short while to see the house is ready
in case it should be needed for a longer visit. I should like you to
see it, Mary.' He pressed my hand. 'We could be there together.'

I did not meet his eyes, and turned away.

Alice had gone away to school. Her grandmother, all things
considered, was in no position to argue. What her son had said to

his mother about her addiction to the opium cigarettes which had placed his daughter in so much peril I do not know, but Mrs Demarest was quiet and chastened. Before we parted, at her son's request (or so she said), she told me the bare outline of the earlier family scandal concerning her husband. He had been an early friend of the Prince of Wales, and had been his companion in the escapade which had preyed on the mind of the Prince Consort in the days before his death. Anyone associated with the fatal illness of her beloved Albert was anathema to Victoria. She hardly forgave her son. Francis Demarest she could *never* forgive, and she had her own ways of making her displeasure felt. Mrs Demarest told me the story stiffly and with dignity. She hated the telling, but she knew, and I knew also, why Mark Demarest wanted me told. I was to be told all the Demarest family secrets. So Alice had departed in triumph to Cheltenham and Mrs Demarest to St Petersburg to visit her sister Countess Vronsky.

Ellen and her Jack came to see me only the other day, to say they were leaving Oxford and would be married. Ellen looked happy and well.

'And what will you do?'

'Nelly and I are going to London. We've got rooms with a relation of Mrs Ceffery's who lives in Greenwich.'

'Oh yes, I've heard of him.' They seemed likely to be a fertile couple. They would proliferate and in fifty years' time there would be descendants of Jack and Ellen all over London. Some would prosper and others would sink. Some would be on the right side of the law and a few, and perhaps the more prosperous, on the wrong.

'What will you actually do for your living?'

'I'm going to join the police. Mrs Ceffery's brother-in-law is a police sergeant and he's spoken for me. I need to grow another inch, which I think I will do, for I'm still filling out and then they'll have me.' He was clear and decided. I never doubted it would come about. 'Yes,' he said, 'London is the place for Jack Coffin.'

One tiny problem has continued to perturb me. Was the woman I saw walking in St Giles in the fog in any sense a ghost? Or merely a contrivance of my disturbed imagination? Or a real passer-by? I prefer to accept the last suggestion. Yet one question still remains. It was the way in which the phrases 'the house of the women' and again, 'the women know all the secrets', seemed to stare up at me so appositely from my reading during those days. There is an answer.

Old Dr Clough had died, and weeks afterwards his sister told me that he had arranged with a close friend to look out for certain words which he, from whatever after-life he had found, would transmit. The words were ordinary words, women, love, secrets. These words would be his way of proving that minds could speak to each other from beyond the grave.

'Who was there to receive the words?' I asked.

'Miss Playfair. But she heard nothing,' said Miss Clough. 'She did not know what words she was to look out for, mind. Only my brother knew the key words, which were in a sealed envelope to be opened by me. But weeks have passed and she has heard nothing.'

It is interesting, is it not? The message was to Miss Playfair, but she received none. I had been very close to her, and at the time was in a state of great sensitivity and emotion. Receptive, you might think. Can we believe that my mind plucked from the mind of the dying Dr Clough a message and fashioned it into something that made sense to me?

In spite of everything, there is an air of promise and happiness hanging over my relationship with Mark Demarest. Mabel at Tinker's promised to pray for me, and I have a picture of her praying all the time to her feministic hedgerow deity. I begin to think this divinity's name is Venus. Mabel is still in Paris where, I have heard, Nancy has joined her, in order, as she ambiguously puts it, 'to try to her luck'.

St Giles' Fair was held this late summer in Oxford. I went to it with Mark Demarest. Sweethearts always do take each other to it, and as I have grown a little older, so he seems to have grown younger and gayer. We walked by the merry-go-rounds and gay booths and where the hurly-burly ended and the cloistered calm of St John's College began, he took my hand and kissed it.

'Love me? You *do* love me, Mary?'

'With all my heart and for ever and ever.'

'You made it sound like a prayer.'

It *is* a prayer. I thought, a prayer; you will never find out how much of that love you owe to Christian Ableman. And I turned to Mark Demarest with a bright and confident smile.

I am going to be painted in my wedding clothes. It is to be my father's wedding present to me. The present is likely to be a valuable one, for his price has risen lately. And I wonder if people in future generations will look on my portrait and think how comfortably I seem to sit in my double role of wife and mother, and will never wonder if behind that quiet face burned the fire of rebellion.

I will never know. But it has already occurred to me that I might prove a disturbing wife to Mr Demarest.